A S...
To Kill

Also by Lynn Cahoon

The Tourist Trap Mysteries

A Story To Kill

WITHDRAWN

Lynn Cahoon

KENSINGTON BOOKS
http://www.kensingtonbooks.com

KENSINGTON BOOKS are published by

Kensington Publishing Corp.
119 West 40th Street
New York, NY 10018

All Kensington titles, imprints and distributed lines are available at special quantity discounts for bulk purchases for sales promotion, premiums, fund-raising, educational or institutional use. Special book excerpts or customized printings can also be created to fit specific needs. For details, write or phone the office of the Kensington Special Sales Manager: Kensington Publishing Corp., 119 West 40th Street, New York, NY, 10018. Attn. Special Sales Department. Phone: 1-800-221-2647.

Kensington and the K logo Reg. U.S. Pat. & TM Off.

ISBN-13: 978-1-4967-0435-1
ISBN-10: 1-4967-0435-5
First Kensington Mass Market Edition: September 2016

eISBN-13: 978-1-4967-0436-8
eISBN-10: 1-4967-0436-3
First Kensington Electronic Edition: September 2016

10 9 8 7 6 5 4 3 2

Printed in the United States of America

To my mother:
I wish you were here to help me celebrate.

Acknowledgments

The beginning threads of Cat Latimer's life and story started during a road trip back home to Idaho. Between Illinois and my home state, there are miles of roadway. My husband, also known as The Cowboy, doesn't like to fly, so we drive. A lot. Miles that give the writer in me time to think, plan, and bounce ideas off a captive audience. Honey, thanks for playing with me.

I'd also like to thank Amanda Sumner and Megan Kelly for taking their time for beta reads. Big thank you to Laura Bradford for her support and the occasional kick in the pants when I needed it. And, of course, thanks to the Kensington crew. Esi Sogah, you rock. Thanks for believing in Cat and the crew.

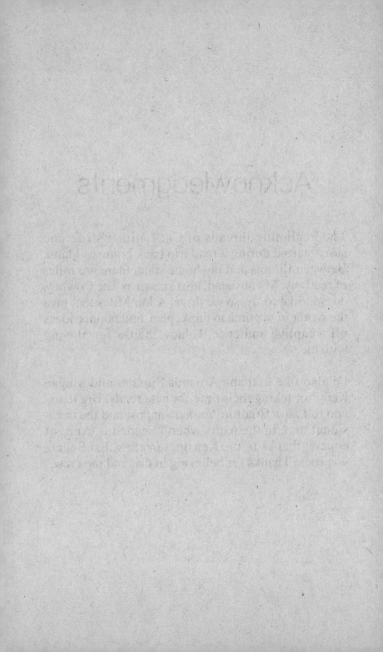

Chapter 1

When Thomas Wolfe said you can't go home again, Cat Latimer wondered if he knew he was full of crap. She stood at the turret window looking out on her backyard in Aspen Hills, Colorado. During her marriage, she'd made this circular room into her office. The wall to ceiling built-in bookshelves were now bare, waiting to be refilled with the rare and not-so-rare books she'd collected during her two years as an English professor over at Covington College. She brushed her fingers over the cool window glass, not quite believing she was back.

"So you're just standing around, staring out the window? You realize we'll have guests arriving in less than two weeks." Shauna walked into the room and put her arm around Cat. "You aren't thinking about Michael, are you?"

Shauna Mary Clodagh had been her best friend since the minute Cat met the tiny, redheaded bartender at the local pub near the apartment she'd rented in Los Angeles. It hadn't been the best job, but

Cat had jumped at the first teaching position that took her away from Aspen Hills.

Into the frying pan, her mother would have said. But she didn't regret her years in California. She'd learned how to surf, or at least how not to drown. She hoped that skill would keep her above water now.

"I love this office. I always wanted to write here. Not grade papers, not work on lesson plans, just write the stories in my head."

"Now you can. But, first, I need to talk to you about the breakfast menus. I've baked a few batches of different muffins and breads to try. Oh, and the handyman called back, and he'll be here first thing tomorrow morning." Shauna looked out the window. "You really lucked out on this deal. Good thing Michael was too busy dating all those co-eds to re-marry or change his will."

"Brutal. Good thing you're my friend." Cat picked up a notebook and a pen. "Let's go walk through the guest rooms on the second floor and make a list of what needs to be finished so the guy can get right to work."

As she shut the door to the office, she thought about Shauna's words. Why *hadn't* Michael left the house and his estate to someone in his family? She vaguely remembered him talking about a cousin somewhere in eastern Washington. She sighed. There was no use trying to figure out what Michael had been thinking, the house was hers again.

This time, *she* would make her own decisions.

Aspen Hill's largest employer and claim to fame was Covington College. The small liberal arts school was located just a few blocks away from 700 Warm Springs, her new-slash-old home. Cat made her way to the Abigail Smith building, home of the English Department and her former employer.

Behind the front desk was a large trophy case with a lighted sealed section for the Covington English Department Cup. Each year, the professors voted on the student with the most potential to make a mark in his or her career. When Cat had been a professor, she'd taken the voting seriously, nominating several of her exceptional students. One, a budding poet, got shortlisted, but mostly she noticed the final nominations looked like a popularity contest rather than true talent. She squinted to see who had won the cup this year and paused. Sara Laine. She pulled out the list Shauna had given her. Yep, it was the same. She had a cup winner attending her retreat.

A student sat at the reception desk, reading. She looked up as Cat stopped at the desk.

"You need help?" She put her finger on the line to mark her place and waited for Cat's response.

"I've got an appointment with Dean Vargas. Can I just go to his office?" Cat nodded down the hall. Some things never changed, especially the fact that the dean of the department always had the biggest office.

"Whatever." The girl went back to her reading. Work-study jobs on campus tended to be more "make work" positions, so Cat didn't blame the girl for being bored out of her skull.

Cat knocked on the door, and a muffled voice answered, "Come in, it's not locked."

She peeked around the door, making sure the man was alone. Michael wasn't the only professor with a history of enjoying time with the female students. "Dean Vargas? Do you have a minute?"

"Well, if it isn't the prodigal daughter come home. So good to see you, Catherine." Dean Vargas stood and stepped around his desk. He looked the same as he had when she'd put in her resignation letter two years ago. Hair gently graying, he stood tall and trim. She'd never been able to pinpoint his exact age and several times when she was teaching *The Picture of Dorian Gray*, Dean Vargas's image had come to mind. "So how are sales of that *Tales of a Teenage Vampire* book going?"

Cat thought about correcting him on the title, but knew he wouldn't remember anyway. "Very well, thank you for asking. The book is getting great reviews from the major players." She pulled out a list of next week's retreat guests from her tote and handed it to him. "I'm glad we could settle on the contract terms for the retreat customers. My first group is arriving next week. These are the five people who will need library passes."

Dean Vargas took the list and without looking at it, set it in a tray on his desk. "I'm happy we could be of assistance. I understand Professor Turner is doing a short presentation on the Hemingway papers as part of the retreat."

"He is. Hemingway is just such a large part of the American writer mystique; I'm sure all of my guests will enjoy his session." Cat looked around the office. On a side table, a pile of the university's latest literary journal sat on display. "I've loved the last few editions of *The Cove*. I miss working with the journal staff."

"The new professor we hired to replace you is

enjoying the task just as much as you did." He paused at the desk before returning to sit in his chair, choosing an appropriate look of concern or gravity for his facial expression. "We were shocked to hear about Michael's passing. He was a vital part of this college. The Economics Department is finding it very hard to replace him with a candidate of his stature."

Cat didn't know the etiquette regarding accepting condolences about a divorced, deceased spouse, but she decided it didn't do anyone any good to be rude or point out the obvious. "Michael will be missed by many people." She wondered if Dean Vargas had guessed her husband's extracurricular activities had been the reason behind the split, but decided to take the high road anyway. She adjusted her tote. "Anyway, lots to do. Thank you again."

Dean Vargas nodded and focused on his monitor. "You are most welcome. However, in the future, there's no need for you to bring this over in person. Just drop the list in the mail. Good day, Catherine."

Dismissed from His Excellency's presence, she hurried out of the building, hoping not to meet anyone else from her past. Dean Vargas had been a jerk to work for back then, and he was still a jerk today. Hell, he probably was born a jerk. With that thought lifting her spirits, she strolled through the commons to the street. Walking back to the house, she soaked in the warm autumn sunlight. *Indian summer*, her mother would have called the warm October day. School had been in session for a few weeks, so students were hanging around the grounds as she walked by, enjoying the summer's last hurrah of warmth.

A police car pulled up next to her; two short blasts

of the siren made her jump and brought her back to reality. The passenger window eased down and an officer leaned across toward her. "You know there's no loitering in town. I may have to arrest you."

"I'd like to see you explain that at the family reunion next summer." She squatted down by the car, her arms resting on the open window. "How are you, Uncle Pete? I was planning on stopping by the house as soon as I got settled."

"Old and crotchety, just like always. How're the house renovations going? You going to be up and ready for that group coming in next week?" He took off his baseball cap and rubbed his head with his free hand. "If you need me, I can come over and help this weekend. I'm knee-deep in paperwork from the college opening, but I could spare a few hours."

Cat shook her head. "You don't worry about it. Shauna has found a handyman who works at a reasonable rate." She checked her watch. "In fact, he should be there right now."

Her uncle frowned. "The only handyman around these parts is—" The radio in his car blared and he paused, turning his attention to the dash.

"Chief? They need you over at campus security. Some kid brought his stash of pot." The dispatcher sounded like she was in another town, on the other side of the mountain and in a well.

"Sounds like you're busy. I'll let you go." Cat tapped the car. "You stop in for coffee and a treat some morning. I'd love for you to meet Shauna."

Her uncle peered at her for a second before the radio blared again. "Chief?"

He pulled out the microphone. "I heard you."

Putting it back on the holder, he smiled. "I'll drop by soon. We might have something to talk about."

Chief Pete Edmond gunned the engine in his black Dodge Charger and pulled away from the curb.

Cat watched him as the car made its way up the road to the administration building. "The guy gets weirder every year." She loved her uncle, but sometimes—like now—he could be cryptic about the silliest things. She returned to her stroll and was walking up the stone path to her front porch when someone barreled through the front door and down the porch steps, a sheet of plywood in large rough hands.

Jumping off the sidewalk to avoid being smashed by the wood or its carrier, she waited for the guy to slap the sheet on the sawhorses set up in the middle of her front lawn. This must be the repairperson Shauna hired. Something about the guy, and his short brown hair, seemed familiar. In tighter-than-normal jeans and a faded T-shirt, at least from the back he was easy on the eyes.

"You need to watch where you're going with that," she muttered and turned toward the front door. Her day had been filled with bulldozing men, but this was the first one who actually could have run her over.

"Kitty Cat? Is that you?"

Crap. Cat stood frozen to the ground, not wanting to turn around. There was only one person who called her by that nickname. No one had dared since she beat up most of the fifth-grade class and put them straight that she was not a feline. Seth Howard had just laughed when she'd wrestled him to the ground. When he'd flipped her over, trapping her instead, he'd whispered in her ear, "You'll always be 'Kitty Cat' to me." Then he'd let her up and shrugged for the class to see.

Slowly she turned around, banishing the memory from her mind and bringing herself back to the here and now. "Seth? You're the handyman?"

He laughed that easy laugh she remembered from too many weekend trips with the gang, camping, fishing, and drinking around the campfire. He had been her first and last boyfriend before she met Michael. The two men couldn't have been more different. Seth was Colorado born and raised. He could fish, hunt, and build a small shack in the woods to live off the land. Michael preferred his fish gently poached and served with a little Riesling. Or had.

"I didn't realize you were back in town." He reached out and touched her brown hair, cut short into a pixie. "You look good; I like the new do."

She should have melted on the spot, but there was just enough ice left in her veins to cause her to nod like one of those Hawaiian dolls Uncle Pete had on his old truck's dashboard. She licked her lips, suddenly feeling her mouth dry up like the Salt Lake Desert. She should start carrying bottled water when she walked. Yeah, that was the problem, her drinking habits. She gave in, trying not to be rude. "Thanks. You look good yourself."

"You buy this?" He nodded to the weathered blue Victorian behind her.

Cat squirmed a little. Seth hadn't approved of her dating Michael. And when they got married in the little church on campus, he'd snuck in the back, standing in front of the closed doors, his hands crossed in front of him as the vows were read. Then he disappeared. A total Benjamin Braddock moment, only Seth hadn't said a word. This was the first time she'd seen him since her wedding day. "Actually, Michael left it to me." She paused. "He died earlier this year."

Seth nodded and walked closer, putting a hand on her arm. "I'm sorry to hear that. But weren't you divorced?"

So he had kept up on the gossip about her. For some reason, this made her gut tighten, just a bit. "Three years now. Believe me, I never thought he'd keep me in the will. I hadn't even talked to him since the day the papers were signed."

He searched her face, looking for something— what, she didn't know. He lowered his voice when he responded. "I am sorry."

She wondered exactly what he was sorry about, but didn't want to ask. They'd gone their separate ways and now she was back and single. That didn't mean that he was available. For all she knew, he had a wife and six kids stashed somewhere in the woods. She dropped her gaze to his hand still on her arm. His left hand with no ring. He noticed her look and dropped his arm back to his side.

"So, the house. Shauna tells me you're opening some kind of hotel?" He took a step back, increasing the distance between them.

Cat wanted to step forward, close the space back up. Hell, if she was honest with herself, she wanted to step into his arms, kiss him and drag him up to her bedroom. But no ring didn't mean no attachments. She'd learned that early in her LA dating years. Besides, how cliché was it to fall back in bed with your high school love? She banished the thoughts of what they could be doing and turned toward the house so she wouldn't have to look into those dark brown eyes.

"Actually, I'm opening a writer's retreat. People come for a week. We feed them breakfast and a few dinners and set up time for them in the college library and a couple seminars. But mostly, they are on their own to write." She regarded him; he didn't seem bored with the conversation topic yet. "I'm an author now."

Seth nodded. "Sounds about right. You always were good with stories." He nodded to the wood. "You've got some flooring that needs to be replaced in most of the second-floor bedrooms. I should be able to get that done today, and I can paint tomorrow."

She stared at him, wondering if there was something more to his comment about *stories*. "Sounds good. Let me know if you need anything."

Then she turned and ran into her house, up the three flights of stairs and into her office, shutting the door behind her. When she'd caught her breath, she stood at the end window and watched him work, willing him not to look up so she wouldn't get caught.

A knock came at the door. "Cat, you want some lunch?" Shauna rarely came into the office if the door was closed, assuming Cat was writing, unless she was dropping off coffee or food.

Which she should be doing, rather than watch the way Seth's muscles rippled in the sun, especially after he surrendered to the heat and stripped off the T-shirt to the tank underneath. "I'm not hungry right now," she called back.

Well, she was hungry, just not for the soup and sandwich Shauna had prepared.

Chapter 2

"You knew." Cat watched as her uncle stirred three teaspoons of sugar into his coffee. He reached for a fourth time, but she moved the sugar bowl out of his reach.

Uncle Pete sighed, then sipped his coffee, wincing at the bitterness that he couldn't possibly taste with all the sugar in the cup. "I'm not sure what you're talking about."

"Really, you want to play dumb?" She sipped her own coffee. "Fine. Seth Howard. You knew he was the handyman Shauna had hired."

"Guilty as charged. But in my defense, there is only one handyman in town, so it wasn't much of a leap." Uncle Pete shrugged. "So did he get you all ready for the arrivals today?"

Seth had worked long hours every day since he'd started. Luckily, Cat had been able to hole up in her office for most of that time. And she'd even got a little bit of writing done. Her deadline was fast approaching, and she wasn't nearly as close to done as she wanted to be on the latest book. However, she hadn't been able to avoid running into him in the kitchen several times. Shauna had started teasing her when she'd grab coffee and disappear, if Seth happened to be getting a drink—or worse, chatting with Shauna.

"The rooms are ready. I still want to remodel the attic into a library sitting area, but I'm sure Seth has other commitments." Or at least she hoped that was true. She needed time without worrying about running into him around the next corner all day long.

Shauna set a basket of muffins on the table and joined them. "Actually, he doesn't, so he wants to sit down with you on Monday and talk about what you want done upstairs. I said bookshelves, a couple built-in desks, and a window seat under that grand stained-glass window in front."

"Well, then there's no need for me to talk to him. You seem to have it handled." Cat hadn't meant for the words to come out as bitter as they sounded.

Shauna tore apart a banana nut muffin and buttered the insides keeping her gaze on the food. "I'm not playing in your backyard, Cat. I have no interest in the man. Although, he is fine to look at."

"I don't know what you're talking about." Cat grabbed a muffin and mirrored Shauna's actions.

Shauna turned to Uncle Pete. "Has she always been a big fat liar?"

He was busy with his own muffin. "Pretty much, especially when it came to that boy. You wouldn't believe the places I found them during their high school years. Windows in that Camaro of his were always steamed up by the time I'd see the car parked on some back road."

"You know I'm right here, listening to all of this,

right?" Cat focused on a drop of melted butter that was just about to drip off the muffin. "I'm not afraid of meeting with the man. I just have a lot of work to do, especially since we'll have guests coming in today."

This was the opening session of the writer's retreat, and she'd planned to hold one a month for the first year. Then she'd reevaluate the venture. The next three months' sessions were already starting to fill. And that was with little-to-no advertising. Writers wanted a place to get away from their daily lives and just write. But if the Warm Springs Writer's Retreat got any more popular, Cat would be the one needing a space to hide.

"You don't have to do anything except eat breakfast with the group and take them to the library to set up their passes," Shauna pointed out. "I'm handling all the guest-services stuff, like more towels and Wi-Fi access problems. That's why you hired me, right? To be the concierge so you could still put in your word count during the retreat week?"

"Well, that and your mad cooking skills." Cat took another muffin, smiling at her friend. "I give up. What time am I supposed to meet with Seth?"

"Two o'clock. I wanted you to be back from the library and have time to do your hair and makeup before he arrived." Shauna ducked as Cat threw the muffin at her. "Seriously, you have to lighten up. I haven't had this much fun teasing you since you arrived in LA and thought you were drinking at a straight bar."

"I liked that bar. Everyone was very nice." Cat smiled. "Besides, I wasn't looking to hook up. I just wanted a drink at the end of the day."

"That's why you go to a place with a good Irish name. O'Malley's was just down the street." Shauna examined the caught muffin, pulling it open for the steam to rise before she added butter. "What about you, Pete? What's your poison?"

"Beer. Draft, if possible." Uncle Pete laughed. "A small-town police chief doesn't get to sit in any kind of establishment like that for very long or very often before tongues start wagging. I kind of like my job, so I tend to only keep a six-pack in the fridge."

"Tell us your favorite brand, and we'll have a supply over here, too. That way you can say you were just visiting your niece." Cat sipped her coffee. This was nice. Quiet, peaceful Sunday morning chat with her two favorite people.

"I appreciate the offer, but I'm just as good with a glass of sun tea these days as a beer." Uncle Pete stood, adjusting the belt around his waist. He carried all the normal police gear—gun, handcuffs, nightstick, pepper spray—but Cat didn't think he'd used any of the tools for years. Aspen Hills tended to be pretty quiet. Whether that was because of the small-town atmosphere or her uncle's evenhanded reign over the enforcement of law for the last twenty years, she didn't know. However, she suspected it was the latter. Uncle Pete would be missed when he decided to retire.

"Speaking of small-town gossip, I guess I better get going. You don't want your neighbors thinking something's wrong over here." He looked at Shauna. "You mind if I take one of these for the road? They are twice as good as the ones they sell in the bakery down the street."

Shauna blushed and grabbed a to-go box. "Take

two. I'm making a couple more batches today so when the guests arrive, they can have a treat."

"Speaking of our guests, we need to make a plan for today." Cat pulled out a notebook and glanced through the arrival times of the five retreaters. "Looks like we'll have to make two airport runs."

"I told you I'd handle the runs; you just need to be hanging out in the main living room from six to nine so you can deal with any issues while I'm out." Shauna's lips curved into a grin. "You'll like it. You can talk your writer-geek stuff and actually have someone who understands what you're saying."

Uncle Pete chuckled and kissed Cat on the head. "See you later, pumpkin."

After he'd left, Cat pulled out her paper planner and went over the next week. "Still, I want to go over everything. I need the retreat to be a success. You know one of the guests is Tom Cook, a best-selling thriller author. I have no idea why he decided to come here. I read he owns an apartment in The Dakota, where he writes."

"Maybe he wanted a change of scenery from NYC. Or maybe," Shauna's eyes widened, "he's setting his new book in Colorado. This might be a research trip for him."

Cat nodded thoughtfully. "I hadn't considered that." She went back to her list. "The rest of the group is unpublished. We have two sisters writing romance, a graduate student from Covington who is working on her thesis, and a guy who just marked fiction on his questionnaire. Kind of a mixed bag, but maybe Tom will be willing to share his journey during one of the dinners. I'll have to pull him aside and ask."

Shauna picked up her cup and refilled it at the pot.

"These muffins aren't going to make themselves. I'm making a batch with pumpkin and one with cranberries." She started prepping her workstation with the ingredients for the recipes.

Cat glanced over the weekly schedule they'd printed out for the guests and made some notes in her calendar to remind her to attend at least some of the events. And Seth on Monday. No good could come of his hanging around. She realized she hadn't asked Uncle Pete if Seth was married or even dating. She'd been so busy denying her attraction, she'd missed the opportunity to be nosy. *Now* it would look like she was interested.

Even though she definitely was not.

Okay, so the word was more like *slightly*. Or even *probably*. Who was she kidding? She wanted the guy. Wanting isn't needing, she reminded herself. Her body surged in disagreement. She closed her calendar with a snap, refilled her coffee cup, and headed upstairs to work on her book. Two, maybe three, hours of glorious nothing to do but write.

And think about Seth.

She turned on her computer and pulled out the file where she kept her working notes.

A knock pulled her out of the story of Kori, and her other-worldly friends. She loved making up the High School for the Special, which could mean the kid was a shapeshifter, werewolf, or even a witch, like Kori. Since her folks had never explained her special powers, Kori saw her new world differently. A feeling Cat could relate to, especially recently.

Shauna peeked around the door. "Hey, I don't want to bother you, but you've been up here for hours. I have a potato soup on the stove with bread bowls in the oven, warming. I figured some of the guests may be hungry when they arrive."

Cat hit the save button and turned around. "Sorry, Kori's getting ready for the prom. Of course, she's not sure who she's attending with yet."

"Oh, the growing pains of high school. I still can't believe you want to write about that time. I kissed the ground on the day I graduated and never looked back." Shauna leaned against the door, her jacket on and the keys to the SUV in her hand.

"I guess I want to rewrite the ending. Although I have to admit, for the most part, I loved high school." Cat turned off the computer and stood and stretched, rubbing a spot on her left shoulder that always burned after a long writing session. "I suppose I should get ready to play the hostess. Do I have time for a shower?"

"If you promise to eat first." Shauna checked her watch. "See you in just over an hour. I checked the airline, and the romance sisters' flight is on time. Sara, the grad student, called earlier, and she will be here at seven to check in. And that leaves the two men to arrive on the six thirty flight coming out of Chicago."

Cat walked downstairs with her and stopped at the kitchen. "I'll see you soon. I'll be reading something appropriately literary in the living room when you arrive."

"As long as it's not a comic book, I think we're

good." Shauna waved and disappeared out the back door.

Pouring the warm soup into a bread bowl, Cat sat at the table and made a quick to-do list for the week. Writing the words *meet with Seth* made her think about the time they'd all jumped into his Camaro and driven to Denver to take their SATs. Five kids, all with big dreams. Everyone but her and Seth wanting to score high enough to earn scholarships to the bigger schools, farther away. Cat had always wanted to attend Covington. And Seth, he wanted to join the army, just like his dad.

Funny how memories just hit sometimes. Cat drew a (bad) version of the attic, then started making plans on how she wanted it to look. When she'd finished the soup, she closed the notebook and put it in the kitchen desk's top drawer. Then she went upstairs to her room to shower and change. Time to turn into someone else.

Rose and Daisy, the romance sisters, turned down the soup when they arrived, asking instead for a glass of wine. As they settled into the plush sofa near the fire, Rose started telling Cat about her work in progress. "I guess you would call it modern historical. I mean, really, how many dukes could there be in Regency England? I'm focused on the post–World War II years and am looking forward to working in the Hemingway papers."

"Well, I hope there's room for at least one more," her sister snapped. "My love is Regency. I adore all the gowns and parties and well-mannered men. Well,

for the most part." The gray-haired woman winked at
Cat. "I have to admit, my stories can get a bit racy."

"I'm sure you'll both love using Covington's
library. The campus is one of the oldest west of
Denver." Cat heard the bell on the front door jingle.
"Hold on, that might be another one of our group."

A young woman, her long blond hair pulled back
into a braid, stood at the reception desk. She had a
suitcase in one hand, and a laptop bag swung over her
shoulder. "You must be Sara. I can check you into
your room now, or we have some creamy loaded
potato soup in fresh baked bread bowls available for
a quick dinner if you'd rather eat something."

The girl shook her head and checked an incom-
ing text. She sat her suitcase down and keyed in a
response. "Sorry, I don't have a lot of time. I have a
meeting with my advisor tonight. Can I just get my
room key so I can drop these off?"

Cat glanced over the desk and found the envelope
with Sara's name that Shauna had prepared earlier.
"No problem. I can take you up there now. But two of
the other guests are having a glass of wine in the
living room. Would you like to meet them?"

Shaking her head, Cat could almost hear the girl's
silent sigh. "I really need to run to the campus. I'm
going to be late as it is." She grabbed the envelope
and looked at the writing. "Room 204? Up these
stairs?"

"Yep, right on your left when you get to the second
floor. Can I help with your bags?" Cat mused that
either she was bad at this check-in thing, or Sara
wasn't getting the point of a retreat.

"Nope, I'm good. What time do I have to be

back?" She paused at the foot of the stairs, waiting for Cat's answer.

"The schedule for the week is in your envelope. Breakfast is from six to nine, whenever you're hungry. Then we'll go to the library at ten, but I guess you don't need to be shown where that is." Cat smiled, hoping the girl would warm up before the end of the week.

"No, I mean tonight. What time do you lock the doors?" This time, Sara rolled her eyes in frustration at Cat's lack of understanding.

"We lock up when we go to bed, but the envelope has a security passcode that you can key into the box to the left of the front door. That will let you in. If you have any problems, push the intercom and we'll come down."

Sara turned and sprinted up the stairs. Cat returned to the living room where Rose and Daisy looked up expectantly.

"Is Mr. Cook here?" Rose poured a second glass of wine, her hand shaking a little as she waited for Cat's answer.

Cat sank into her chair. "Nope. That was Sara Laine. She's not going to be joining us this evening."

"Oh." Rose's disappointment showed on her face. "So Tom Cook *is* attending this retreat right?"

Oh no, a diehard fan. Cat knew she needed to nip this fangirl moment in the bud before the author got here or he'd be overrun with Rose's questions and attention. "He is, but remember, the purpose of the retreat is to allow the participants time to write away from their normal world. I'm sure he's going to be just as focused on his work in progress as you will be."

Daisy poked her sister. "I told you not to get your hopes up. Besides, we should see him at the group activities. I'm sure he'd sign a book for you then."

Cat smiled at the other sister. Thank God she had an ally in the discussion. "Exactly. So let's get back to your writing. What made you choose to write romance?"

Daisy took a sip of her wine, then set the glass down. "I like sex."

Chapter 3

The flight from Chicago had been delayed, so it was after eleven by the time the final two guests arrived. Cat had stayed up to wait for the group, but Rose and Daisy had retired to their room hours before. Sara still hadn't returned. Cat glanced out at the darkening night wondering where the young woman really was at this late hour. "A meeting with your thesis advisor? I don't think so."

When the lights from the SUV flashed by the window, Cat went to the front desk to get the men's envelopes ready. She'd kept the soup on low, but turned off the oven, not wanting the bread to dry out. The men followed Shauna into the lobby area and grabbed their room keys, rejecting the offer of a meal or even a drink. Tom Cook looked like he'd been sleeping on the plane, his hair doing rooster tails where he'd settled into the headrest of the seat. The other man, Billy Williams, looked the opposite. Wired, he was bouncing on the balls of his feet.

"You must get a lot of ribbing about your name." Cat smiled when she handed him the envelope.

"Why?" Billy's tone was flat, and something in his glance made the hair on the back of Cat's neck stand up. The guy was strange enough to be a character in the mystery books he claimed to write.

"Two first names? William Williams?" When the guy shook his head, she continued. "No matter. Are you sure I can't get you anything before you retire?"

"No." Tom Cook was already heading upstairs with his bags. Billy spun on his heel and followed.

Shauna waited until we heard the two doors close upstairs. "So that was weird, right?"

"A little." Cat closed the cabinet over the lobby desk and locked it. "Just wait until I tell you about Sara. These three make the romance sisters seem tame."

Cat's alarm went off at five a.m. Even though she trusted Shauna to get the breakfast buffet set out and ready for their guests, she felt a responsibility to make sure everything went smoothly. Just this first time.

Who was she kidding? Cat never slept past six even on weekends. If she wasn't needed in the kitchen, she'd spend the time in her office, working on her manuscript. She quickly showered and dressed for the day, then headed downstairs, following the smell of vanilla bean coffee.

She grabbed a cup off the sideboard in the dining room and filled it before she entered the kitchen. Shauna had been busy. Muffins, butters, and three different kinds of bread sat on the sideboard next to the three coffee pots. VANILLA, DARK, and DECAF signs were laminated and hung on each pot. If guests wandered down early, there was plenty to keep them busy until the main meal arrived.

"Good morning," she called out as she entered. Cat stopped short inside the kitchen. Shauna wasn't alone. Seth Howard sat at the table, drinking coffee. Shauna set a plate of eggs, bacon, and hash browns in front of him.

"Good morning yourself. I didn't expect you until last call for breakfast. Usually, you spend your morning in the office." Shauna grabbed a pitcher of orange juice and filled a glass, holding it out for her. "OJ?"

Cat set her coffee down. "I think I'm good. Can I talk to you?"

"Of course. I have the strata in the oven. Once I'm done slicing up the fruit bowl, I should be ready for guests." Shauna wiped her hands on her apron. "What do you want to talk about?"

"Can I talk to you in the dining room?" Cat raised her eyebrows.

"She wants to know what I'm doing here eating breakfast." Seth clarified the question. "Good morning, Cat. Nice to see you're still grumpy first thing in the morning."

"I am not grumpy." Cat sighed and sat down at the table. "Okay, so I want to know what the heck you're doing here."

Shauna set a plate in front of her, filled with the same food as Seth's. The smell of bacon made Cat's stomach growl. "It's part of the contract. On weeks we're in session, since he's on call for emergencies during the week, he gets a meal a day, just to make sure he checks in with us."

Cat decided she really needed to read better the contracts Shauna was asking her to sign. She grabbed a piece of the crunchy bacon and shrugged. "I guess that's okay."

Seth looked up from reading the morning paper. "I take it you didn't read the fine print?"

She pointed the bacon at him. "Not your concern, mister. Besides, I trust my staff."

"Well, isn't that just dandy. I'm 'staff' now, instead of your best friend." Shauna sat down at the table and sipped on her coffee. "Next, you'll be having me wear a uniform during our retreat weeks."

Not a bad idea. Cat brushed the thought away; no use getting Shauna worked up on the first day of their business adventure. "Look, I didn't mean anything."

Shauna waved away her apology. "No worries. Eat your breakfast so you'll feel more human."

They sat in silence for a while, Cat eating, Seth reading the paper and polishing off the food, and Shauna making a list of something in her notebook. Cat caved first and set her fork down. "So, Seth, we're meeting at two?"

"That's the plan." He didn't look up.

"I don't think that will work today. Can we change our meeting to Tuesday, same time?" Maybe by then she'd have her emotions under control and would be about ready to talk about the attic, not just Seth and their history.

"You're the boss." He opened the sports page of the paper.

Cat rolled her eyes and decided she'd had enough breakfast. And definitely enough of the company around the table. She took her plate to the sink and rinsed it before putting it in the dishwasher. When Seth was in a room, she could feel his presence, just like always. Heck, she could smell him. Musk, mixed with Stetson cologne and Irish Spring from his shower. Her fingers itched, wanting to touch him. She licked her dry lips before turning around.

"Okay, then, the dining room looks great. Let me know when everyone's eaten, and I'll walk them over to the library." She glanced at her watch. "Come get me at ten if I'm not down by then."

She fled out of the room, not waiting for a response. She thought she heard Seth's gentle chuckle, but maybe that was just the wind on the siding. Heading upstairs, she ran into Rose.

"Am I too early for coffee?" Rose looked down at Cat's travel mug.

Cat turned sideways on the stairs and nodded toward the dining room. "Nope, it's all set up. There's a few treats to keep you from starving before Shauna serves a full breakfast at six." She held up her mug. "And there's a travel mug for each of you so you can take the coffee with you if you want to write in your room or in the living room."

"Perfect. Daisy's still snoring, so I'll bring my laptop down here." Rose paused, before asking her question. "So are we the only ones awake?"

"So far." Cat watched the disappointment on the woman's face. She really had it bad for Tom Cook. Cat would have to watch her closely to make sure she didn't overwhelm the author during the week. Fangirl or not, the guy had paid for a quiet writing retreat, and Cat was going to honor that.

At ten, the group gathered at the foot of the stairs. Well, most of the group. Sara had left early to work at the library, and Tom wasn't down from his room yet. Cat called up to his room using the reception phone.

"Mr. Cook, we're heading over to the Covington Library to get your passes. I hate to bother you if you're writing, but I told the librarian we'd come together as a group this morning." Cat waited for an answer, holding her breath and hoping he wouldn't play the celebrity card and ask her to make an exception.

"I'm slipping on my shoes right now. Sorry, I lost track of time." Tom chuckled over the phone. "Tends to happen when I get writing. I'll be down in a flash."

When Cat hung up, she saw the anticipation in Rose's face. "We'll be ready to go in just a few minutes."

Rose leaned over to her sister and whispered. "He's coming."

Daisy slapped her arm. "I've told you to never say that to a romance writer. Now all I can think of is my next sex scene."

Cat bit her lip, trying not to laugh. When Tom arrived, she motioned them out on the porch in a group. "So, it's just a quick walk to the library from here. It's open from six in the morning until ten at night, and once you get your cards, you can work there or in the living room." She pointed to the top floor of the house. "Soon, retreaters will have the attic area to use as well. We're turning it into a cozy den with lots of desks and room to stretch out."

"It probably has mice," Billy muttered.

Well, aren't you Mister Sunshine. She tried to keep her voice neutral. "We don't have a mice problem."

Billy ignored her comment and caught up to Tom.

"So where do you get your ideas? Have you ever stolen one from a critique group member?"

"I've never stolen an idea in my life. Now, it's said there are only seven real plot lines, so I'm sure my books are like other authors' works. But it's all about the voice and how you tell the story." Tom nodded toward me. "Don't you agree, Cat? I've read your work and you have a strong unique voice, even though you're telling a story set in high school. It's not the setting or the story, it's the characters that we fall in love with as readers."

Cat nodded, glad Tom was ignoring the pointed jab and turning the question into a discussion point for the group. "*Buffy* was set in a high school, but my work isn't a rip off of that story. Or at least I try not to be the same."

"Same but different." Rose piped up. "That's what all the agents quip during the writers' conferences we attend. They want something that they can relate to and sell but isn't already out there."

"Exactly," Tom smiled at the older woman, and Cat thought Rose was going to faint. "You need to tell your story and not worry about what everyone else is doing."

Cat saw Billy staring at Tom, but when he noticed her attention, he turned his head. That one was going to be a problem, she just didn't know why. She'd pull his application and do some research to see if the guy was a real threat or just a blowhard. Maybe having Seth around this week wouldn't be such a bad idea after all.

As they crossed campus to the library building, Cat relayed the history of Covington College. Pointing out the different buildings, she focused on the places where they could write or find something to eat and, of course, the bookstore. They were meeting the head librarian, Miss Applebome, for her standard how to use the library lecture. When Cat opened the door to the library, Dean Vargas stood at the counter with Sara next to him.

"Welcome to Covington College," he boomed, in a not-so-library voice. Cat saw a staff member's head jerk up at the noise, then the woman rolled her eyes and returned to her work. "We are so happy to be working with Catherine and the writer's retreat."

"I didn't know you wound up back here, Larry." Tom stepped closer to the dean and held out a hand. "I haven't seen you in what, ten years?"

Dean Vargas shook Tom's hand and then addressed the other members of the group. "Tom and I attended Covington together back in the day. He chose popular culture and I, a more academic field."

"Tell them the real story." Tom smiled at Rose and dropped his voice to a fake whisper. "We both were in contention for the hand of the most beautiful English student ever. Linda and I have been married for fifteen years now. And of course, I also left school with the Covington Cup, all four years I might add."

"I guess the best man won." Dean Vargas smiled as he spoke, but Cat noticed the emotion didn't hit his eyes.

"You won the cup four years in a row? I thought the cup had only been retired twice?" Cat studied the man. He was a popular and successful author now; she guessed that, back in the day, his professors must have seen that drive in his early years, too. Maybe the cup hadn't always been the popularity contest it had become now.

"The rumor is true. I was the second person in history to take the cup with me at graduation. The guy who did it before me was some sort of poet and wound up teaching at Harvard. Winning the cup is good luck." Tom slapped Dean Vargas on the back. "Of course, coming in second four years in a row is quite the accomplishment as well."

"It's a beauty contest, not an academic one." The dean echoed her original thoughts when Cat had seen the award display earlier that year.

"Sara is this year's recipient." Cat had seen the girl's face fall with Dean Vargas's words. "I'm sure she worked hard to win."

"Last year's," the dean corrected. "She's a grad student this year. But yes, she's quite the accomplished writer. You're working on a coming of age story, correct?"

Sara nodded, but didn't speak.

"Congratulations!" Tom grinned at the girl. "You should come by my room later. I brought the cup along, just for giggles. It isn't every day you get to visit your past."

"I'm sure the old cup you have is just the same as the one in the display case." Dean Vargas took a step forward and positioned himself between Tom and Sara.

"Except it has my name engraved on the bottom four times," Tom countered.

Watching the men posturing, the old saying about teaching versus doing popped into Cat's head. "I didn't know you attended Covington. Small world."

With the mood broken, Dean Vargas looked at his watch. "Well, I'll let Miss Applebome take over. Enjoy your visit to Aspen Hills." He slapped Tom on the back. "Stop by my office before you leave and we'll get caught up. Maybe we can have a beer down at Bernie's to celebrate how far we've come from our old, poor student days."

"Sounds good. I'll buy." Tom said to the man's back, as he'd spun around without even waiting for a response.

Sara stepped away from the group, following the dean. "I'll be back at the house later," she called out to Cat.

"That girl doesn't know how to deal with a retreat," Daisy said. "I doubt she'll get a word written during the entire week."

Cat nodded. "Getting away from your normal life is part of the magic." She nodded to Miss Applebome. "If you think you can find your way back, I'm going to leave you here."

"No worries, I'm excellent at finding my way home. I'll take care of the group." Tom put his arms out, making waving motions. "This way, kids; we get to meet the librarian."

As Billy walked past her toward the conference room where Miss Applebome stood in the doorway, Cat heard him mutter, "What a complete ass."

She was definitely going to look up the guy's background, just to be safe.

By seven, Cat had found enough on "Billy Williams" to be relatively sure that wasn't his real name. Worse, the guy had a blog page filled with comments raging against Tom Cook. If this was the same person, he claimed Tom had stolen his idea for *One More Try*, the book that had stormed all the lists and made the author a household name. Billy claimed they were in a critique group together in 2007 when he'd read his first chapter aloud.

Cat printed off most of the comments and blog posts and put them in a folder. She planned to call Uncle Pete in the morning and have him look over the file. If she was right, she guessed she'd have to ask Mr. Williams to leave. Stalkers were one problem she'd never even considered when she'd put together the idea for the retreat business. Of course, she'd also assumed her guests wouldn't be literary superstars.

As she closed up her office for the night, she decided to take one more step. Tom needed to know about the possibility of danger. Not that she really thought the guy calling himself Billy would do anything, but she'd sleep better if she had a chat with the writer. That way he could lock his door and not agree to some late-night barhopping with the only other male in the group.

Maybe she needed to change her application-screening process. *One bad apple*, she mused as she took the stairs to the second floor and knocked on Tom's door. She'd wait until she even knew this was a problem before she changed her process. No use fixing something that wasn't broke.

Tom didn't answer the first knock. She leaned in to hear if he was in the shower, but she didn't hear running water. Voices from what she assumed was a television show via Tom's laptop murmured through the door, but nothing else. She knocked again, louder this time and called out his name.

Shauna came up the stairs as she was knocking. "What's up?"

"There's a possible problem with Tom and another guest." Cat knocked a third time. "Mr. Cook, I really need to talk to you."

"Is Rose ready to kidnap him as her personal muse?" Shauna grinned. "The woman has it bad for the guy. I sat with them tonight in the living room and after two glasses, she'll tell you anything."

"It's not Rose." Cat reached down to the doorknob and hesitated. *Please let him be dressed.* "I'm coming in, Mr. Cook."

Cat slowly opened the door but paused in the doorway. Her wish had been granted, the guy was fully clothed—laying on one of the oriental rugs she'd just purchased for all the rooms. Blood seeped out from around his head, turning the blue rug into a darker black. She turned to Shauna and blocked her from the room. "Call Uncle Pete, and have him come over now." Even though she knew it was too late, she added, "Tell him to send an ambulance."

Chapter 4

"I've finished interviewing everyone, so you're free to do whatever you had planned for today." Uncle Pete poured himself a cup of coffee from the pot and sat at the large oak table in the kitchen. "Well, everyone except this Billy Williams character. What were you thinking, not checking him out before? I can't believe he'd use such an obvious fake name."

"Honestly, it didn't hit me until he checked in. Then, when I asked him about it, he seemed not to even get the repetition." Cat refilled her own cup and grabbed a blueberry muffin. She hadn't been to bed yet. After finding Tom's body, she'd been existing on coffee and sugar. She ran her hand through her hair. "We were planning on having a free writing day, but I think we need to get everyone out of the house for a while to unwind."

Shauna took the muffin out of Cat's hand. "I'll take the crew down to the hot springs. You're going to bed."

Indian Springs was a natural hot springs that used to be just a rock formation before a local entrepreneur had bought up the land next to the national forest and put in a pool. Now the commercial spa served as a great tourist stop, the advertising complete with legends of the water's healing property. Mostly it was a great place to swim and relax. The naturally heated water kept the place open all year. Cat had loved swimming there as a kid.

"I think I'm going to take you up on that offer." Cat looked at her uncle. "Can you tell me how he died?"

"I can't release anything until Bob Jenkins gets a look at him." Cat blinked in surprise. "Yep, it's the same guy. Your classmate is now the county medical examiner. He's been in the job for three years, since Harvey passed."

Cat shook her head. She'd liked Harvey Newman. Since they were both widowers, Uncle Pete had always brought Harvey along to the family get-togethers. "No one should spend the holidays alone," he'd say when she'd first asked him why Harvey was at their Christmas dinner. She'd been ten then, and her parents had still lived in the little ranch house across town. Now they were living in a senior complex in Florida, citing their inability to take the Colorado winters. Cat had understood, but she'd missed visiting when they'd lived on opposite ends of the country. Now that she'd moved back to Aspen Hills, at least she had Uncle Pete. And Shauna. *And Seth*. She involuntarily shook her head against the idea. Seth was her past. Just like Michael. The only difference was

Seth would be here working on the house in less than an hour.

"I didn't know Harvey had died. Why didn't you tell me? I would have come back for the funeral." Cat focused her tired eyes on her uncle.

"You were still upset about the whole Michael thing. I didn't want you to have to come back and see him with whatever co-ed he'd shacked up with that week. I swear, that man went through women like some men change their shirts. I can't believe you two stayed married as long as you did." Uncle Pete stood and drained his cup. "I've got to be going. A murder is a big thing in our little town. I've got a meeting with the mayor and the president of the college in less than an hour. And the press is going to jump on this sooner or later. You need to be prepared."

"Great, my new retreat will be known as the place Thomas Cook was murdered." Cat laid her head down on the table. "I might as well give up and sell now."

Shauna pushed her shoulder. "Now don't be going all dark on me. Like they say, any press is good press. Maybe Mr. Cook's ghost will stay around and help the unpublished writers that come to the retreat after him."

"That's morbid," Cat mumbled, unnerved that she was even considering the marketing possibilities. "It seems a little callous to turn his death into a promotional ploy."

"Well, nothing is happening today except you heading off to bed." Shauna pulled Cat to her feet. "Say good-bye to your uncle and get upstairs. I'll round up the guests and take them out for the day. We might even do a picnic lunch on the college grounds."

Cat leaned into her uncle and gave him a quick

hug. "Thanks for taking care of this. I'm sorry this had to happen here."

"Nothing you did to cause this. Bad things happen everywhere, including Aspen Hills." Uncle Pete nodded to Shauna. "You take her advice and get some sleep. Things will look brighter after you wake up."

"Except for Mr. Cook," Shauna added quickly. When both Cat and Uncle Pete looked at her, she shrugged. "Someone had to say it, we were all thinking it."

Cat walked up the stairs and passed by her office. She wanted to go in and sit in front of her computer and work on her next novel. Writing calmed her in a way nothing else ever had. It made the world and all the bad things, like Michael's infidelity, disappear and she could create her own reality. One where good conquered evil and chocolate didn't make you gain weight.

Instead, she headed to her bedroom suite, closed and locked the door, and fell onto her bed, fully clothed. Exhausted by everything that had transpired, she closed her eyes and went right to sleep.

An insistent knocking pulled her out of a deep dream. She remembered running through the house, opening doors, and finding Tom Cook's body. Door after door in the dream opened onto the scene she'd etched into her memory. If she ran faster, she was sure she could stop him from being killed. So she kept opening doors. Finally, she found herself awake, sweaty, and lying on her bed in a tangle of the handmade quilt she'd bought at the local flea market.

Grabbing her bedside clock, she squinted to make

out the time. Two-thirty. The sun was still shining through her window, so it had to be in the afternoon. She sat up and swung her legs to the floor. Shauna and the gang should be arriving back from their field trip, and it was time for Cat to get back into hostess mode. One murder was not going to ruin this retreat, not if she could help it.

She followed the sound of banging up the stairs and into the attic. Seth stood there in the cleared-out space. His shirtless back glistened with sweat as he swung his hammer, finishing up a set of homemade sawhorses. Cat watched as he tucked his hammer into his tool belt and leaned back, admiring his handi-work.

"What are you doing up here?" Cat's voice echoed in the cavernous room.

He spun around, his hand on his hammer. When he saw her, he visibly relaxed and his hand dropped to his side. "What does it look like? I'm working."

Cat leaned against the doorway. "I thought you were working on the second floor rooms?"

"Well, with your uncle cordoning off the murder site, Shauna and I decided it was better for me to move to the library project rather than get in his way." He appraised her rumpled shirt and shorts. "You have a nice nap?"

She ran her hand through her hair, remembering too late she hadn't even showered that morning. "I was up all night," she said. Then she straightened her shoulders. "I don't have to explain myself to you."

He chuckled. "And yet you did."

The room got quiet for a minute, then he pointed to the wall. "You want to look at the plans?" He glanced around the room. "The place has great bones. You're going to love this when it's done."

Cat walked over to the wall, glancing at the blueprints. She pointed to a spot. "Are these window seats?"

He nodded, moving to stand next to her. She felt the heat radiating off him and took a deep breath, trying to control the tingling coursing through her. He pointed to four different spots on the diagram. "Here, here, and these other two windows. I thought it would allow people to have kind of a private spot to work on their books when they come to your retreat things."

Cat looked at him, surprised. "That's a great idea."

He shrugged. "I know my buildings. I liked the army, don't get me wrong, but remodeling old places like this? That's my passion. Did you know there was a pool in town about how long you'll stay in business?"

"What's the pool say?" She turned to look at him.

He grinned. "Most people are going less than six months." He turned back to the blueprint. "I put you at two years."

"Well at least you believe in the idea." She counted the number of built in bookshelves he'd drawn on the plans.

He bumped her with his shoulder. "I'm going long because I'm hoping I'll get to finish the remodel. Besides, I know how stubborn you can be." He pointed to a bookshelf. "I'm thinking about making a few built-in desks rather than shelves in this area."

She turned toward him. Looking at him filled her with memories. Her breath caught and she could feel the heat in her face. "Thanks, I think." She fanned herself with her hand. "We really need to get the air ducts fixed up here."

Seth shook his head. "I think you'll have to do a second unit up here. I checked out the one that cools the rest of the house and it's way too small. I know an HVAC contractor out of Denver who will give you a good deal."

"Dollar signs keep running through my head." Cat leaned against one of the sawhorses. "Now with Tom Cook's murder, who knows what could happen to the retreat. I'll be known as the place writers go to die."

"You could spread some rumors about the guy's ghost haunting the place, helping out the unpublished among the visitors." Seth walked closer to her and brushed her hair out of her eyes. "I'm sure you'll make the best of your situation. You always do."

Anger flashed through her and she bolted upright off the wooden stand. "What's that supposed to mean?"

He shrugged. "You know, you were always the one who had a few options. If plan A didn't go through, you had plans B and C ready to go. What do you think it meant?"

She narrowed her eyes. "Maybe something about my marriage to Michael?"

Seth sighed and sank onto the sawhorse, sitting almost in the same spot where Cat had just stood up. "Look, I didn't like that you were dating that old guy. I figured you were trying to make me jealous. We hadn't been broken up for long when you first started seeing him. Once you decided to get married, I realized you must have been in love with him and I left it alone."

She leaned against the wall, not able to walk away,

not yet. "I saw you at the church. I thought you might say something."

He walked over to her and lifted her chin so he could see her eyes. "It wasn't my place to say something. But if you needed a quick getaway, I wanted to be there for you."

She felt his warm breath from his words and leaned toward him. He smelled like the wintergreen mints he chewed constantly after he'd quit smoking the year they'd broken up. He dropped his hands to her arms and gently stroked her from the shoulder down to her elbow and back again. "I'm glad you're back home."

She might have purred if she'd let herself. Instead, she tilted her head, biting her bottom lip. "I'm glad to be home."

They stood looking at each other and then he pulled her close. His lips brushed hers and she felt her body melt into his. The door at the bottom of the attic stairs burst open.

"Where is everyone?" Billy Williams called up the stairs. "I thought this was supposed to be some sort of guided retreat?"

"I'll be right down." Cat called down the stairs. She whispered to Seth. "Do me a favor and call Uncle Pete and have him come over."

Seth took her arm, stopping her from moving. "Are you going to be all right? Maybe I should go down instead."

"Make the call, then come and join me. We'll be in the kitchen. I'm sure he'd appreciate a snack before he gets busy on his novel." Cat took a deep breath and took a step down. She paused, her hand on the banister, and looked at Seth. "Just hurry."

Chapter 5

Shauna filled Cat's glass with iced tea. "How long has your uncle been questioning Billy?"

Cat looked at her watch. "Since three?" She squinted at the display. "Where are the guests? Did you bring them back from the pool yet?"

"Hours ago. You were upstairs in your office." Shauna sat across from her. "Hopefully, you were writing and not just pacing."

Cat ran a hand through her hair. "I did get a few pages pounded out. Funny how stress can turn off the word faucet sometimes, and other times it makes it flow faster. You didn't answer my question, though: Where are the others? I figured they'd be huddled in here with us, trying to eavesdrop on the conversation in the living room."

"Seth took them to that buffet at the Indian casino. He said he'd stay around, let them play for a while if they want, then bring them back." Shauna raised her eyebrows. "The guy's a total hottie. And sweet. What in the world possessed you to leave him for Michael the Jerk?"

Cat took a sip of her tea. The cold flowed down her throat and took her back to the summer she'd started dating Michael. They'd met at the college. She'd been taking summer school, trying to finish her degree so she could get out into the real world. "Seth and I had broken up a few months before. He wanted me to backpack across the country that summer before he went off to the army and I'd insisted on taking classes. It hadn't seemed like a forever breakup, but by the time he got back that fall, I was head over heels for Michael. The man could be a charmer, when he wanted to be. And right then, I was what he wanted."

The front door slammed shut and Cat jumped. Uncle Pete strolled into the kitchen and nodded at Cat's glass. "You got more of that?"

Shauna jumped up and grabbed a glass out of the cupboard. "Of course. You sit down and relax."

Uncle Pete took off his baseball cap and ran his fingers through his hair. Cat wondered if that's where she'd learned the movement. "Do I look that bad?"

"You look tired." Cat tilted her head toward the front of the house. "I take it the slam was Billy leaving?"

"He said he was going to eat, but I'd bet money you could find him down at Bernie's. That's where he spent most of last night, except for the part where he followed Amy Potter home and stayed with the girl until he arrived here this afternoon."

"Amy Potter? I thought she moved somewhere back East. And didn't she get married?" Cat searched her brain for the latest news on Amy. The girl had been a few years younger than Cat, but they'd had several classes together.

"She's back, sans husband." Uncle Pete smiled. "She's been trying to work her magic on our boy Seth, but he tends to ignore her advances."

Cat felt her cheeks heat. "Doesn't matter who Seth was or is dating."

"Keep telling yourself that." Uncle Pete held up a finger when Cat tried to argue. "I saw you leaning into him when I showed up this afternoon. And he was too concerned about your safety to stay on the phone long. Basically he told me to get my butt over here. The guy's never got over losing you."

"He was so worried about you. That's why he said he'd take the others out for a dinner run." Shauna went over to the stove and, as she stirred a pot of spaghetti sauce, the smell of tomatoes and herbs filled the kitchen. She'd made the sauce from scratch as they waited for the interview to be over. "He even said he'd take half his normal rate, since all he was doing was babysitting and not repairing anything."

Cat snorted. "Of course he did. He wasn't worried about me, he wanted to pad this week's paycheck."

Shauna and Uncle Pete exchanged a look.

"If you say so." Shauna turned her attention to Uncle Pete. "So are you staying for dinner? For an Irish girl, I make a mean spaghetti."

"Actually, you can box some up and I'll take it back to the station with me." He drained his tea. "It's going to be a long night. Apparently this guy is connected to the governor somehow, and my phone's been ringing off the hook with requests for updates. I keep saying, I can't update anyone until I get a chance to investigate. It's funny how they forget about that part."

"From what I saw, the cause of death is pretty

apparent." Cat shuddered. "I don't know how I'm going to get all that blood out of the rug in that room."

"You're not. The rug's been taken in as evidence. Bob Jenkins is coming by to look around the room for something that could have been used as a weapon. Whatever it was, the thing was heavy. Bob says he died from the first strike, but the guy kept swinging. I'm surprised someone didn't hear the racket." Uncle Pete stood and adjusted his belt.

Cat wondered how the man carried all those tools around all day without his back screaming from the weight. Today, his belt was totally decked out. She guessed that he had expected to be taking Billy in for questioning or at least holding him for a while. She realized he was waiting for a response to his statement. "I was upstairs in my office all evening. Shauna had walked with most of the guests to the library for writing time, and Seth was still working on that last wing of second floor rooms we haven't opened yet. So I guess either the killer timed the attack with the construction noise, or the soundproofing Seth did in the rooms last week is really amazing."

"Even when that boy's staying out of trouble, he's smack in the middle of it." Uncle Pete chuckled. "No worries; we'll be in and out. You don't mind if we bag a few items if there's something that Bob finds suspicious?"

"Would it matter if I said yes?" Cat yawned and stretched. "Do what you have to do. I want to have the murder solved as much as you do."

A knock sounded at the front door. "Must be Bob. We'll check in when we leave and have you sign a property tag. Even though you're family, we need to do this the correct way."

"Especially since I'm family," Cat countered. "I don't want the town gossips to be thinking I killed one of my first guests."

Uncle Pete chuckled and stepped toward the door.

"Come back when you're leaving and I'll have your dinner ready. With some fresh French bread and a container filled with fresh fruit, all you'll need to add is something to drink," Shauna called after him.

He nodded to her and smiled. "I sure am glad my niece decided to bring you along when she came home to start her new adventure. I haven't ate this good since my Ginny died."

Cat stood. "I'll walk you."

Uncle Pete kissed her on the cheek. "You just sit and relax for a while. I know how to find my way to the front door."

Cat watched him leave the kitchen and waited until she heard the men making their way to the second floor. She probably should greet Bob Jenkins, but she'd wait until a more appropriate time. She turned to Shauna at the stove who was dishing up a dinner plate of spaghetti. "I don't remember him ever talking about Aunt Ginny. He paid you a huge compliment."

Shauna sat the plate in front of Cat with a bowl of parmesan and then returned to the stove to get her own dinner. "He's a sweet man. I like cooking for him."

Cat took a bite of the spaghetti and sighed. "I didn't think I'd ever be hungry again after seeing that body."

Shauna looked down at the plate she'd just set

on the table. "Well, I guess I could have been more appropriate with the dinner selection. Do you want me to make you something else?"

"Are you kidding? This is wonderful." Cat took another bite and after she swallowed, she paused, looking at her fork. "Lesson for today: Life goes on for the rest of us, even when someone leaves the playing field."

"You're acting all calm and philosophical about Tom's death." Shauna met Cat's gaze. "Do you want to tell me how you're really feeling?"

"Scared to death that the murder is going to close down the business before it ever has a chance to get going." Cat shrugged and turned her attention back to the food in front of her. "I can either give in to the fear or pretend I'm not feeling it. Either way, I'm determined to make this session a positive one for our guests, even if it's started out sucky so far."

"Rose is in shock. She adored the guy." Shauna took a sip of her tea.

Cat set her fork down and went to the fridge to get out the bottle of white zin she kept on hand. She grabbed two glasses from the cupboard and set them on the table, filling each glass with the wine. She handed one to her friend. "The session hasn't gone perfect so far, but I'm determined to fight it out. Are you with me?"

Shauna picked up the glass. "To the writing retreat, may it grow and prosper."

They clinked their glasses, but Cat paused before drinking. "And to Tom Cook, may Uncle Pete find his killer and put him away for the rest of his, or her, lifetime."

Cat and Shauna repeated the gesture, then took a

sip of the wine. They finished eating in silence, but when Cat tried to clean up after dinner, Shauna shooed her away. "I'm not done baking for tomorrow's breakfast. Let me alone so I can do my job." She took the plate out of Cat's hand. "Besides, don't you have a book deadline coming up soon?"

"You know I do." Cat glanced at the table. "But it doesn't mean I can't do my share of the chores."

"Not tonight. Go do your writing magic and leave the domestic stuff to me. Let me earn my keep here."

Cat wandered out into the foyer and glanced out the window. She wanted to go outside and sit on the swing on the front porch and polish off that bottle of wine. But Shauna was right. She was on deadline. She'd hoped she'd be able to write during the retreat, set a good example for her guests. Now two days had passed and, except for the hard-earned page or two she'd pounded out yesterday, her word count was pathetic.

She climbed the stairs to her office, started a cup of apple cider in her pod machine, and opened up her file. After a few minutes, the magic took over and she was lost in the world of a teenage witch trying to be normal.

A knock on her door brought her out of the story she was creating. She looked at the clock on the computer: already nine. Time to shut down for the night anyway. "Come on in, I'm shutting down," Cat called out. The door opened but Shauna didn't appear next to her.

"I wondered if you wanted to take a walk with me." Seth's voice gave her chills down her spine.

She spun around. "It's kind of late."

He shrugged, not looking at her. Instead, he was

thumbing through the books she'd gotten shelved last week. Boxes still littered the floor, filled with books waiting to be introduced to their new home. Or for some, their old home. Cat just hoped she'd be able to keep the house now that she'd taken out a bank loan for the renovations. "Perfect time to walk. We don't have to worry about running into those college kids avoiding their classes." He took a book off the shelf and pointed it at her. "You care if I borrow this? I'm kind of obsessed with his writing."

Cat took the book from him. It was an old H. P. Lovecraft story. She'd picked it up when she'd been teaching freshman English as a way to introduce the class to the horror genre, but had gone another way with her lesson plans. "I haven't read this yet. You'll have to tell me how you like it." She handed the book back.

"Leave it to you to have books you've never read. Don't you know most of us buy books to read them?" He nudged her toward the stairs. "We'll walk through town, and I can show you all the new stuff that's happened since you left."

"I drove through town on my way here. I think I saw most of the new stores." Cat followed him down the stairs anyway. She knew she would agree to go walking, she just wanted him to work for it.

"Fine." He took her hand at the bottom of the stairs. "I'll buy you an ice cream cone at the Big Bun."

"Now you've convinced me." She opened the door and motioned him out. "After you. And make sure you have your wallet—you're not getting out of buying that easy."

He stopped at his truck and put the book on the passenger seat. Cat glanced inside the truck, seeing he still kept his vehicles spotless. For a guy who worked construction and liked to explore the outdoors, Seth always kept his truck clean. He'd picked her up for prom in his old beat-up Ford, but when he'd opened the door to help her in, she had been surprised to see he'd power washed the inside and hand-dried the cab from top to bottom.

He noticed her watching him and shrugged. "I can't help it; I like a clean car."

They walked toward town. The air felt soft on her face, and for a spring evening, the light jacket she'd grabbed out of the hall closet before they left the house was the perfect weight. For a while, they didn't talk. Finally, Seth spoke. "Did you know Tom Cook?"

Cat sighed. "Only through his books. He signed up late and I wondered if he was *the* Tom Cook. Rose counted on him being the famous author. She's kind of an obsessed fan."

"I can't say I've read any of his work." They turned off Warm Springs and onto Main Street, walking away from the college.

"I read his breakout book. It was terrific, but I'm not into thrillers. I like my small-town settings, and Tom focused on globe-trotting heroes, saving the world from the evils that lurk in remote destinations." She cocked her head. "He really was an amazing writer, though. I looked forward to talking with him this week."

"Sounds like a book I'd like. I'll have to put it on my bookstore list." He nodded to the next storefront. "Tammy Jones took over the bookstore a couple years ago when Mrs. Henry retired. The school orders books through her, but a lot of their stuff is e-book now, so she's been struggling. I try to stop in every week or so to refill my to-be-read pile. You should talk to her; maybe you guys can do a joint promotion or something for the writers who come to your retreat."

It was a surprisingly good idea. She stopped in the middle of the sidewalk and stared at him. "When did you become so smart?"

He pulled her forward. "I got my marketing degree in college. I just don't use it much. What, you thought I was the same dumb kid you dumped that summer?"

She snuck a peek at Seth as they continued to walk through town. He had changed, and not just physically. His manner was more relaxed and, for a moment, she flashed back on their last fight. Why had she been so angry, so adamant that she was on the side of the right?

They talked about nothing and everything on the rest of the walk. When they reached the drive-in, she sat at the tables out front while he went to the walk-up window to get their ice cream. He came back with a double cone for her, strawberry cobbler on the bottom and French vanilla on the top. It had been her favorite cone since she was twelve and started walking to the drive-in by herself. He had a double chocolate cone for himself.

"You remembered." She took a bite of the vanilla, closing her eyes as the memories hit her from the rich custard taste.

"I remember a lot," he said, his voice low and husky. She opened her eyes and he kissed her. He licked his lips. "I always liked the way your vanilla mixes with my chocolate."

She watched as he took another bite of his own cone. What were they doing? Taking up where they'd

left off that summer? Like she'd never married
Michael. Like years hadn't passed since they'd sat
here together, hands entwined. Her voice sounded
shaky when she spoke. "I'm not sure what's happening here."

"Nothing you don't want. If I'm moving too fast,
I'll step back." He studied her over his ice cream. "It's
just damn good to see you, Cat. I can't believe how
much I've missed you."

The walk back to the house was quiet. Cat felt lost
in her memories. When they reached the house, she
leaned against the door. "I'm not sure I'm ready to
date again. Michael and I, well, let's just say it was a
nasty breakup."

"If the guy wasn't already dead, I'd like to kill him
for what he did to you. I wanted to punch him in his
face when I'd see him with those co-eds around town.
All he wanted was the newest version, kind of like a
guy replacing his sports car every year with the
newer model." Seth ran his finger down her cheek.
"You have nothing to be sorry about for getting out
of that marriage."

His words were true and, yet, Cat still couldn't
bring herself to hate Michael as much as she'd been
told she should. He'd been kind, easy to talk to, and
attentive, at least in the beginning. When he'd
stopped coming home for dinner, telling her he had
to work late, she'd known he was straying. And she
hadn't confronted him. Not until she'd seen the motel
receipts in his desk. And when he didn't deny the
accusation, she'd filed for divorce. And cried for a
week. When she'd moved out of the house, he'd
barely noticed and he didn't even show up for their
court date, sending his lawyer instead.

He'd been done with her and she never wanted to feel that discarded again.

She focused on Seth and felt his body heat against her own. He'd come up to her room if she gave him a speck of encouragement. And she wanted him. But not this way, not with the taste of Michael's betrayal still on her lips.

She put her hand on his chest and stopped him from coming closer. "I'm not sure what I want. I wouldn't blame you if you told me to make up my mind or walk away. I'm just not ready to do either one. Not yet."

He leaned in and kissed her, sweet and short. He tapped her nose. "Go to sleep. The world will look brighter tomorrow."

She watched him walk back to his truck, liking the view from behind as much as she liked his front view. "Get a grip, Cat. You're the one who sent him away." She waved as he got into the truck and started the engine.

He rolled down the window. "Thanks for the book." She stayed on the porch as he drove away.

When she entered the lobby, Shauna leaned against the check-in desk. "You're a complete idiot. There's no way I'd let that hunk leave, not without at least a test drive."

"You were eavesdropping." Cat pulled off her jacket and hung it on the coat rack. "That's not polite."

"Actually, I was waiting for you." Shauna pointed to the old hotel key holder they'd found on the Internet and installed behind the desk. "We have a surprise guest. I told her we'd charge her a reasonable nightly rate, but honestly, I'm not sure how to figure that out, without the retreat part of the package. We never considered opening the rooms for guests during the rest of the month."

"Someone just arrived and wanted to stay here? How did they find out about us?" Cat walked over to look at the reservation card and read the name aloud. "Linda Cook? Seriously?"

Shauna nodded. "Yep, the dead guy's wife just checked in for a week's stay."

Chapter 6

Cat leaned against the doorway Wednesday morning, listening to William Turner explain his research on Hemingway and his writing style. Rose and Daisy were busy scribbling notes, Sara appeared to be texting on her phone, and Billy was glaring at Cat. The day had started out uncomfortable when Cat had gone over the day's schedule.

Now, the tension was electric. Professor Turner looked at her and smiled. "We'll take a short break to refill our coffee and drinks and when we come back, I'll take questions about what we've discussed so far."

Billy tried to bolt through the door, but Cat grabbed his shirt and hauled him into a small sitting room near the lobby.

"What the hell are you doing?" he sputtered.

She pushed him into a chair then pulled up one to face him. "Look, I know you're angry about being questioned about Mr. Cook's death, but honestly, everyone was. And you have a reason to be mad at the guy, don't you?"

The mad seeped from Billy's demeanor and he looked beat up. "So you figured it out?" He shook his head. "I didn't want the guy dead. I just wanted him to tell everyone I'd helped with his book. I wanted him to share some of that money he made off my idea."

Cat let him vent. "You know ideas are a dime a dozen; it's how you write the story that matters. Look at me, I'm writing a teenage witch story that's not a bit like the movie version, even though they both attend high school."

Billy shrugged. "I guess. I just wanted him to take my book to his agent. Do you know how hard it is to get an agent these days? You got to know somebody." He cracked his knuckles. "The guy laughed at me. So I went to that dive bar down the street and tied one on."

"Which is why you have an alibi." Cat shrugged. "I don't really care why you came to the retreat. What I want to know is *if* you're planning on staying, will you act like a human being, or do you just want to leave?"

He shrugged. "I borrowed the money to attend from my mom. I guess I could stay and finish the book I'm working on."

"And you'll be at least civil to the rest of the group?" Cat pressed. She didn't want him ruining the experience for the other participants.

Billy smiled a million-watt smile and nodded. "I'm good at charming the ladies, just give me a chance."

Cat wanted to gag. Instead, she kept her response cordial. "I don't need you to charm them. Just be polite and involved in the conversation."

He shot her a short salute. "Ten-four." He walked over to the sideboard and filled a cup with coffee.

Cat returned to the living room where Daisy stood with Professor Turner, discussing some part of his earlier lecture. Rose sat alone and Cat decided to check in on her. She looked up when Cat paused at her chair. "Good morning, dear."

"Good morning to you. I've been meaning to check in and see how you were doing. I know you respected Mr. Cook's literary works." Cat sank down next to the woman and watched her dab her eyes.

"You mean I was a foolish old woman pretending to be a fangirl?" Rose sighed. "I just can't believe he's gone. I mean, have you read his Malone Bay series? The man was a painter with words. I wish I could be half as good as he is, I mean, was."

"I read a few of his books. He was an amazing writer. The literary world will be a sadder place without him." Cat patted Rose's hand. "Besides, you weren't out of line, I'm sure he appreciated when you told him how much you loved his work."

"I'm not sure. I snuck over to his table the other day at the library and he seemed miffed I was interrupting his work on the new novel. When I asked if it was going to be set in Malone Bay, he told me it was a whole new project for him. Kind of a kiss-and-tell book." Rose shrugged. "Then he asked me to leave him alone so he could get back to work."

"That seems kind of harsh," Cat observed, still watching Daisy and Professor Turner. If she didn't know better, she would have thought the older professor was flirting. Turner was the old maid of the English department. Cat couldn't think of a time he'd even dated. Michael used to make fun of him after faculty dinner parties, wondering about the man's non-existent sex life.

"No, it was totally appropriate. As a fellow writer, I should have respected his privacy." Rose pondered an idea, then shook her head sadly. "I guess his memoir will never be finished now. It's a great loss to all of us."

"Let's get started, shall we?" Professor Turner clapped his hands, and Cat felt Daisy standing beside her.

"I'm in your seat." Cat popped up and moved so the woman could return to her seat.

Daisy shook her head. "I'm sure there's enough room on the couch for the three of us. Professor Turner is just so fascinating; you must join us."

Cat glanced at the balding man in front of the room. *Fascinating* was not a descriptor that she would ever use for the Hemingway scholar. "Sorry, I've got things that must be done. I'll see you all after your library time this afternoon."

She wound her way to the back of the room and disappeared through the pocket door just as Turner started up. Maybe next session she should ask one of the other professors who were more interested in popular genres to speak. Maybe Hemingway was too literary for a group of writers who were more interested in finishing their manuscripts.

"Penny for your thoughts." Seth's voice interrupted her mental "what if" gymnastics.

"I think you'd be overpaying a bit." Cat laughed and nodded to the stairs. "You in the attic today? I haven't seen you before now."

"Actually, I just got here. Had an emergency house

call over at Amy's this morning." Seth leaned against the doorway, watching her.

"Amy Potter?" Cat raised her eyebrows.

He nodded. "You remember Amy? She was a couple years behind us in school. Real popular."

"Mostly because she was real easy." Cat cocked her head. "What kind of problem was she having this early in the day?"

"The pipes in that old house she inherited from her grandmother. I've told her several times it would be cheaper to tear everything out and redo the system, but she keeps piecemealing things together. I guess she likes having me around." Seth played with the hammer in his tool belt. Taking it out and twirling it like the tool was a six-shooter and Seth was playing a bit part in a cheesy spaghetti western.

"That's the rumor around town." Cat watched Seth's face for any reaction but the guy was cool as a cucumber. Or a radish. The saying didn't make sense anyway; she might as well change the vegetable to something she liked to eat.

"Jealous? Already? We've only been on one date since you got back." He slipped his hammer back into the clip on his belt. "You never were this possessive in high school."

"I'm not possessive and I'm not jealous. You can visit whoever you'd like. It's so not my business." Cat glanced at the kitchen door standing open. She'd been sure it had been closed earlier when she'd walked into the foyer. Their conversation had an audience. "Look, I've got to get busy. Thanks for taking the guys out last night. I'm sure they loved visiting the casino."

"Some of them a little more than others. I think Rose lost her entire pension check at the blackjack table. She was a little grumpy on the drive home." He walked to the stairs. "Let me know if you want to talk. I'll be upstairs in that steaming hot attic. We really need to talk about getting a second air conditioner set up for the upper floors."

Cat watched as he sauntered up the stairs, his Levi's tight on his butt. When she noticed him watching her watch him, she blew out a breath and stomped into the kitchen. She needed to get these hormones under control and fast. Seth would be in the house daily until the work was done and that seemed to be longer every day.

As she entered the kitchen, Shauna skittered to the sink.

"Eavesdropping isn't polite, you know." Cat poured herself a fresh cup of coffee and sat at the kitchen table.

"I don't know what you're talking about. I've been cleaning up the kitchen." Shauna turned toward her, wiping her hands on a dishtowel.

"I saw the kitchen door open." Cat held up her hand. "I don't want to fight; I'm here to plan out the next few days. Our stalker guy is staying so we have almost a full house, minus Tom, of course."

"Add in his wife, and we are back to being full. I sure hope Seth's able to finish up that second wing soon. Or do you have him focused on the library?" She sipped her own coffee as she joined Cat at the table.

"He's working in the library, and I think I'll have him stay there until next week when we don't have any guests. I kind of like this three-weeks-off, one-week-on schedule. If we can afford it, this will give me time to write in between the sessions." Cat opened up her retreat planner notebook and scanned the schedule for the full week.

"You're the money girl." Shauna stood and handed her a list. "This is what I need for the kitchen to get through the week. You got a problem with me using the credit card?"

Cat scanned the list, pausing when she hit the cleaning supplies. "Are you going to try to clean up Mr. Cook's room now or wait until the guests have left? We can hire someone if you feel uncomfortable with the task."

"Honey, cleaning up blood and body parts was part of my job at the bar. You realize we were in the bad part of town, right?" Shauna sipped her coffee and smiled at a memory. "Of course, you were always a Ben Franklin. You probably didn't even notice the violence around us."

"You're saying I'm naïve?" Cat added a big bag of Skittles and a can of mixed nuts to the list. She handed the list back to her friend, who raised her eyebrows as she read the additions. "What? I'm out of writing snacks."

"I'm saying you're an early to bed, early to rise person. Not naïve." Shauna put the list into her purse that was sitting on the table. "Although if the shoe fits . . ."

"Whatever. So we're good for the week? Except for the shopping trip?" Cat looked over the list of events she had planned for the next few days. Mostly it was free writing time but she'd also scheduled the group to attend the dress rehearsal for the drama club's newest production that was opening next week. She'd had to pre-purchase tickets for the next show to convince the drama professor to allow this first free event.

On the last night, the group had reservations at The Cafeteria, Aspen Hill's most elegant restaurant. Tommy Ells, the chef who opened The Cafeteria last year, thought the name was cute for a college town. Cat believed the name lost them as many reservations as it garnered them. But once someone ate at the upscale restaurant, they always came back.

She turned back to Shauna, who was watching her. "I don't know if Uncle Pete has released the room yet, so I think we should stay out of there until we hear from him." She pointed to the new guest name on the calendar. "Did Mrs. Cook say how long she would be staying? Did she ask to see his room?"

Shauna turned the page. "She paid through next Friday, so I guess we'll have a longer term guest. But no, she didn't ask to see his room. And, come to think of it, I haven't seen her today."

They looked at each other and fear grew in Cat's stomach. What would be the odds that the wife came here to follow her husband in death. "Let's go see if she's in her room."

"I don't like this," Shauna murmured as they stood at the bottom of the steps.

Cat gave her friend a quick hug then just as she raised her foot to go upstairs, the front door opened and the bell jangled, announcing a visitor.

An older woman crossed the foyer. She was dressed in what Cat would call professional-wife gear: dress pants, sandals, and a tan tank top covered with a silk shirt. A strand of pearls hung around her neck. Shauna stepped forward to greet the woman.

"Mrs. Cook, we were just wondering where you

were this morning." Shauna's voice trilled, showing her Irish roots.

"I've been down to the police station, trying to figure out when they are releasing Tom's body." She closed her eyes as she ended the sentence. "I can't believe I had to say those words. You never expect to lose your partner at any point, but murder? Tom would have loved the irony."

Cat stepped forward. "I'm Cat Latimer, owner of the writer's retreat. I am so sorry for your loss. Mr. Cook was an amazing author and a great addition to our first session." Cat held her hand out to shake.

"He was so excited when he saw your ad. Did you know we both got our undergrad degrees here at Covington? We adored the little campus." She looked behind her. "I'm planning on going out and walking the quad just to do a trip down memory lane after I take a short nap."

"I didn't know you went here too. Dean Vargas mentioned he knew Mr. Cook, but he didn't mention that fact." Cat frowned, she wondered why Dean Vargas hadn't used the famous author's attendance at Covington as a selling point for the department.

"Larry doesn't like to promote Tom's success." Linda Cook leaned forward. "I would say he's a tad bit jealous, but I wouldn't want you to think badly of the man."

Linda Cook was a sweet woman who didn't realize Cat had her own reasons for thinking badly of Dean Vargas. She snuck a peek at Shauna who was trying not to giggle. "Anyway, we're glad you decided to stay with us. I'm sure it wasn't easy finding out about your husband's death and staying at the same place where he was killed."

She patted Cat's arm. "Now don't you worry about Tom passing here. My husband was very good at making friends, but for some reason he was better at making enemies. I guess he knew what he wanted and went for it. Some people just can't understand that type of dedication." Linda Cook stepped around them and toward the staircase. "Honestly, I'm surprised someone didn't kill him sooner."

Cat and Shauna stared at the woman as she made her way up the stairway. They turned and looked at each other when they heard the door to her room open, then close. "She's taking his death pretty philosophically, don't you think?"

"I think she's weird," Sara said. The girl walked into the foyer from the small alcove between the living room and the hallway. "Who says that about their husband?"

Sara left the house through the front door, and Cat looked at Shauna who shrugged. "Maybe he's had death threats before? Maybe she's been expecting something to happen to him." *Maybe Linda had been hoping for her husband to pass on*. She decided to take a trip down to the station to talk to her uncle.

"You have any of those chocolate chip muffins left over from breakfast?" Cat aimed her friend to the kitchen.

"You're actually hungry? It's mid-day; you're never hungry after lunch." Shauna pushed the door to the kitchen open. "I could make you a sandwich or a bowl of soup."

"Just the muffins, and put several in a sack. I'm taking a treat down to Uncle Pete." Cat grabbed her keys and wallet and stuffed them into a jacket pocket. "I'll be back soon."

"Seeing if he knows Linda Cook is a little off her rocker?" Shauna held out the filled bag.

Cat nodded. "I want to make sure my guests are safe. At least the ones that aren't dead."

Chapter 7

"Sorry, the chief just left." The cheery receptionist wore an Aspen Hills official police uniform. "He was called up to the campus again. Fall semester is always a little crazy until the kids realize being away from home doesn't mean they're away from rules."

Cat held up the sack filled with muffins. "Can I leave this on his desk with a note to call me?"

The woman waved the sack closer and took it from Cat. "I can put it on his desk." She unfolded the top and peeked in. "Are those blueberry?"

"Chocolate chip. My friend made them up this morning." Cat leaned closer to read the woman's nametag. "You can have one if you want, Katie."

She pulled out the top muffin and set it on her desk. Then she peered at me. "Are you the chief's niece? Catherine, right?"

Cat held out a hand. "Everyone calls me Cat."

"Katie Bowman. Your uncle talks about you all the time. He's so happy you moved back to Aspen Hills." Katie leaned closer. "Tell me about California. Did you meet any celebrities? Any actors?"

"I thought I saw Hugh Jackman in the coffee drive-up once. The car was a sweet little roadster and the guy looked just like Hugh. I mean, it could have been someone else, but the car was way too expensive for a normal guy." Cat nodded to the muffin. "You can try the muffin. I just ate."

"I'm saving it for my three o'clock treat. Typically, I get something out of the vending machines. I need the sugar for a pick-me-up." Katie sighed. "Of course, then the sugar rush is gone by five and I'm dragging myself out of here. Hugh Jackman, that's so cool."

"I think it was him, at least." Cat leaned her arm against the high desk. "I have to tell you, meeting Tom Cook was twice as cool. Or at least it was until he was killed in one of my rooms. I mean, what's the luck that I'd have a murder the first week I'm doing this retreat thing."

"Bad business." Katie shook her head. "Sorry you had to open to that. I bet it will make the next session hard to fill."

"It might if we still don't have a murderer or theory by then." Cat peered at Katie. "You wouldn't know how the investigation is going, now would you?"

Katie leaned forward. "I'm not supposed to talk about these things, but you are family. I bet he wouldn't mind." She turned and looked both ways down the hall. When she was certain no one was around to hear her, she muttered, "They don't have a clue. I mean, the one guy seemed like a good suspect, but Amy Potter swears they were doing the nasty all night long. And you know how that girl is—she probably wasn't fibbing."

Yep, this was the same Amy inviting Seth over to

her house for early morning troubleshooting. As she turned to leave, a thought hit her. "Hey, did Mrs. Cook talk to my uncle yet?"

Katie nodded. "Poor woman, she was beside herself. The chief had to borrow a box of tissues just to get through the interview. She really loved that guy."

Overwrought hadn't been her experience with Linda Cook. "Do you know if she told Uncle Pete about knowing Dean Vargas or attending undergrad here?"

"I don't eavesdrop when your uncle is interviewing suspects. It's rude and above my pay grade here. I'm a level-one receptionist, so I greet people, answer the phone, and sometimes file." Katie squared her shoulders, her cheeks pink from the emotion Cat had instigated with the question.

"No, I just wondered if, when they were going in and making small talk, she'd said anything." Cat instinctively took a step back. "I wasn't trying to say you weren't doing your job."

Katie stared at her for a few seconds. Cat wondered if she was trying to read her sincerity from her words. "You're a lot like your uncle. You see a mystery in everything. But sometimes a death is just a death."

"Tom Cook didn't just die."

"Doesn't mean his wife had anything to do with the death." Katie paused, appearing to weigh her next words. "I know she told me about her and Tom attending school here. I have no idea if she told your uncle or not."

Cat told the police officer good-bye and left the station. She wasn't any further along in finding out who killed Tom Cook than she'd been that morning.

She stopped dead in her tracks. Wait—she was trying to solve the murder? Why? Her uncle had taken her on ride-arounds when she was in high school. Mostly, she thought at the time, to scare her away from the evils of drink and drugs. The drug part had worked. She'd never wanted to even try something that took her out of control. But she had to admit, she enjoyed a frozen drink now and then, especially on hot summer days out on the deck. That had been her and Shauna's Sunday ritual. Go to the beach, sit in the sand, and pretend they were on some exotic island where they didn't have to go back to work the next day. Or night, in Shauna's case.

She pushed away the happy memory and got back to the question at hand. Why was she "investigating" Tom Cook's murder? Uncle Pete wouldn't be happy if he found out. But maybe if she could hand him some clues to the murderer's identity, he'd forgive her.

Besides, she appeased her good side, the only reason you're interested is to save the writer's retreat. Having a death the first week in business might keep people from booking 700 Warm Springs for their next getaway. Bolstered by that thought, she headed back to the house. Time to get some words on the page.

When she reached Warm Springs, she saw the group of people walking toward her, led by Professor Turner. He waved, almost knocking off his straw fedora, and paused as they met. "Good afternoon, Miss Latimer. I'm leading the team over to the library. I promised Daisy I'd show her the college's collection of Shakespeare papers, and the rest just decided to come along as well." He grinned and looked back at the retreat guests. "I have to say, they're a determined lot. I expect to be reading all their published books next year."

Cat scanned the group: Everyone was accounted for, and it was free writing time anyway. "Sounds like a plan." She looked at Rose. "Call the house if you need Shauna or I to come walk you back later."

"You could just send that handyman who took us gambling the other night. What an alpha! I swear I'm changing the hero in my next book just to honor him." Rose poked me in the stomach. "You want to be the heroine? That way you could have your happy ending without even having to work for it."

"Thanks, but I'm kind of a do-it-yourselfer when it comes to things of the heart." Cat started to walk through the small crowd when a hand reached out and grabbed her sleeve, stopping her.

"Do you know who the other lady is that checked into your place?" Sara Laine stared at Cat with unblinking eyes.

She straightened herself and wanted to push Sara's hand off her jacket, but Cat held calm. "Linda Cook, Tom's wife? She came to collect the remains, but I guess with an ongoing investigation, she has to stay around."

"She needs to leave." Sara jerked on Cat's sleeve for emphasis.

Cat unpeeled her fingers from the cloth. The girl was beginning to act certifiable. "Look, before you go ripping up my jacket, you need to just chill. Linda's going to be around until the police release Tom's body. If you have a problem with that, you're more than welcome to leave."

Sara narrowed her eyes. "You'd like that, wouldn't

you? Then you could go into Dean Vargas's office and tell him I was unreasonable. I bet you'd even dab at fake tears to get him to look at you."

"What are you talking about?" But Sara just turned around and ran to catch up with the rest of the group. Man, this hospitality career was going to be harder than Cat had imagined. Not only had she dealt with a murder, she had not just one but two loonies sign up for the inaugural session. This didn't bode well for the rest of the sessions. She really needed to screen the next group better.

When she reached home, she hurried into the kitchen and found it empty. A note sat in the middle of the table. She picked it up and read Shauna's neat handwriting aloud. *I've gone into town to shop. I won't forget your junk food list.*

Cat grabbed a small bag of kettle chips and a soda out of the fridge. The house was empty. Even Seth's truck was missing from its normal spot out front. She was alone and itching to get some words down on the page.

She headed up to the third floor and locked herself into her office. Seth had set up a visual security system that monitored the front and back door. It only came on when someone entered the house, so she'd have plenty of time to rejoin the group when they arrived back from their library trip. But all of the crew had carried their laptops, so Cat was certain they were going to take some writing time at the majestic building. Writing by a window in the stacks had always made Cat feel like a real author, even when she was an undergraduate English major. The library had instilled a sense of calm in her as she pecked away at the keyboard and wrote her first novel.

The novel that had never been picked up, even though Michael had praised her for her lyrical prose. The next book she'd written in secret, just for her enjoyment. When that one had been finished, she'd shipped it off to several potential agents who had asked to see her next project.

She'd gotten five offers of representation. From nothing to five in less than a year. She'd been dumbfounded. She interviewed the agents, then went with her gut and hired the woman who Michael had advised against even querying. And she'd never regretted the decision. Husbands may come and go, but a good agent is in it for the long haul.

Now, writing the last book in her three-book deal, Cat felt pressure to make this book the best of the three. To wow her readers.

An hour later, with a scene complete, Cat rose and took her chip bag to the window. Finishing off the last few chips, she watched the street, wondering when she'd have to give up the solitude. She enjoyed hosting these retreats, but like most authors she was an introvert, so having this many people in her house drained her.

Thank God for Shauna, she thought. The girl loved people and talking and was a perfect ying to Cat's yang, at least in the hostess category. Most of the time, Shauna would be handling the guests, moving them from scheduled activity to free time without Cat even having to be in the area. Cat wasn't stupid. She knew people would sign up for the retreat to meet a real author. One with connections. She'd lucked out when Tom Cook had arrived. Cat's work wasn't even in the same league as this guy. But now that he was gone, she'd have to be more attentive to the group.

She saw something run across the backyard out of the corner of her eye. Coyote? Or maybe just a stray dog? She'd been hesitant to get a pet mostly because the animal might be considered food for the larger animals that stalked the area at night. They were too close to the national park for her to believe it wasn't a possibility. What if one of the guests had an allergy? There were so many things to consider for her new business.

Cat settled back down to her writing chair and dug back into the fictional world. A bang from the attic caused her to jump. "Damn, Seth, keep it down up there."

She focused back on the writing. Before long, another bang jerked her out of the story. She saved the document and pushed her chair back. She needed another soda anyway. It was time to give Seth the rules of the house, including times he could make noise in the attic. She had a deadline coming up and she had to meet her daily word goals.

Had to.

She started upstairs to the attic but paused when she heard the front door open. Stepping back down to the third floor landing she called out, "Who's that?"

"Good afternoon to you as well," Seth called back up to her, as he came up the stairs. She met him on the third-floor landing. He now stood in front of her, a bag from the local hardware store in his hand. "I ran out of finishing nails, and I wanted to finish up a sample of the window seating today. I think you're going to love it. Of course, you'll have to make decisions on the upholstery, but we can do that next week."

Cat stared at the bag. "So you were upstairs in the attic working, but then you went to the store?"

"Yep. See the evidence?" He jiggled the bag with a laugh. He started to step around her, but she grabbed his hand, stopping him. He studied her face. "What the heck's up with you? Don't tell me you're mad about last night. I thought we had fun."

"No. I mean, yes, I had fun. But this isn't about last night. When did you get back from the store?" Cat squeezed his hand, wondering if she was going to pass out.

"Are you all right? You saw me walk in with the bag, what, thirty seconds ago? A minute if you count my parking the truck?" He leaned closer. "You don't look so good. Do you need to sit down?"

She pointed to the ceiling. "I was writing and heard something in the attic." She paused. "Wait, I might have seen something in the backyard earlier. I assumed it was a dog or a coyote."

"When did you see the dog?"

Cat shrugged. "I don't know. An hour ago? I took a break from writing, stood in the window for a few minutes, then saw something cross the yard. I wasn't looking straight at it, so it could have been anything."

"And the noise? When did that happen?" Seth was calm and rubbing her upper arms.

She stepped away from the touch. "I guess about ten minutes ago. I ignored the first one. Then, when it happened again, I came out to tell you to be quiet."

His lips turned up on the ends a bit at that one.

"What? I'm a writer. I need my quiet time to get anything done. Or at least not banging." Cat looked up at the ceiling. "But it wasn't you up there."

He shook his head. "No, it wasn't. You go downstairs and take your cell with you. If I don't come back down in a few minutes, call 911. I'm sure it was just a raccoon or maybe a bird you heard, but let's not take any chances, especially with what's happened with your author friend."

"He really wasn't my friend." Cat took a deep breath.

Seth put his hands on her shoulders. "Breathe and focus. Where is your cell?"

Cat walked back into the office and took her cell off her desk. Then she waited at the top of the stairs for a second, watching Seth.

He saw her stop and waved her down. "Go," he hissed. "I'll be fine."

She took one step after another and with each movement, she felt more like a coward than a second line of defense. She tried to see up the stairwell, but there was no one there. She ran into the kitchen and stood by the table, staring at her phone. What determined a few minutes? Five, ten? No more than twenty; she was convinced of that. Hopefully, he'd be down in five.

One minute passed, then two. Then three. At four, she found the keypad on her phone and held her finger over the screen. Five, she'd call for help at five. She hadn't heard a shot or anything, but she was two stories below. Maybe she wouldn't have? She hadn't heard any noise when Tom Cook was killed, and she'd been upstairs in her office.

The kitchen door creaked open and Cat's breath caught. Shauna pushed through with an armful of plastic bags. Her face brightened when she saw Cat standing there. "Good, you're home. Come help me unload the SUV. Seth has the driveway blocked with that truck of his so I had to park on the street. And my ice cream was melting."

Cat held out the cell. Her hand shook as she held it out in front of her. "I can't leave. There's someone in the attic, and Seth went up to find out who it is."

Shauna pushed past her, dropping the bags onto the table. "Why are you in here?"

"He told me to go to the kitchen and wait for a few minutes, then call the police." Cat's heartbeat raced in her chest.

"When was that?" Shauna put her hand on Cat's arm.

She looked down at the phone. "Five minutes, thirty seconds. Should I call now?"

"Let me go upstairs and see what's going on." Shauna headed to the door.

Cat wanted to follow but her feet felt nailed to the floor. "Wait. Let me go."

Her friend turned back around. "Are you sure?"

Cat nodded and took a deep breath. "I need to see what happened." Putting a hand on the door, she felt Shauna's hand on her arm stopping her progress. She turned, meeting Shauna's gaze. "What?"

"When do *I* call the police if you don't come back?"

Chapter 8

Cat didn't have to answer because just then the door opened and Seth came into the kitchen. Cat sank into a chair. "You're all right."

He nodded and went to get a glass of water from the sink.

Cat waited for him to drink the entire glass in a few swallows before she asked the next question. "Who was in the attic?"

Seth shook his head. "No one. I went through the entire thing, twice, and there wasn't a person or animal in the place. I even checked the windows to see if that had caused the bang, but they were all locked up tight." He frowned, his gaze drifting upward toward the ceiling.

"What aren't you telling me?" Cat stepped closer and took the glass from his hand.

He dropped his gaze and considered her question. "It could be nothing." He paused, but when Cat didn't move, he shrugged. "There's just something off about the space. I didn't notice it before, but the space is off. And it appears some things have been moved around. Of course, I might just not be remembering how I left things."

"So you think someone was up there? Could someone have snuck out when we were talking?" Cat considered the third-floor layout. The attic stairway was in sight of where they'd been standing. If someone had come down those stairs, either she or Seth would have seen them. "I wasn't hearing things. I'm not crazy."

"I didn't say you were crazy." Seth looked at the bags on the table. "Crap, I'm blocking the driveway, aren't I? I was going to unload the back, then park on the street."

"No worries, you can do that as soon as you bring in the rest of the groceries. I'm going to put these away." Shauna started unpacking the thin plastic bags. She looked at Cat. "You want a glass of wine or a beer?"

"Beer and I'll get it myself." Cat waited for Seth to leave the kitchen. "I heard something, I know it."

"Sometimes you get all caught up in your stories, are you sure what you heard came from the attic? Could it have been from outside? Maybe a bird flying into the turret?" Shauna carried the box items to the cupboard and started stacking them.

Cat opened her beer and took a pull off the cool bottle. "Maybe. But I don't think so. It sounded substantial. I thought Seth had torn down a wall or something."

"Maybe until your uncle finds that murderer we shouldn't be alone in the house. Let's make a buddy system so there are always two people here. With our guests this week, that shouldn't be much of a problem."

Cat took three cartons of eggs from a sack and put them in the fridge. "Not a bad idea." She smiled at her friend. "When did you get to be so smart?"

Shauna's laugh echoed through the kitchen. "I've always been this way. You just haven't noticed, my dear."

The door to the kitchen opened and Seth walked in. "Sounds like you two are having a party in here."

"Girl talk." Shauna grabbed another bag. "Is that everything from the SUV?"

He nodded and she threw him the keys. "Make sure you park it in the driveway when you finish unloading your truck."

Seth paused, turning to Cat. "Are you sure you're okay?"

"A little shaken, but I'm fine. Shauna and I are setting up a plan to keep a few of us in the house at all times." She saw him start to say something and held up her hand. "Don't. I take it you didn't find anything?"

"Nothing. However, I think it's a great idea and make sure you put me on the schedule. Heck, with the amount of work I have here, you could be my only client for a while and the business would be fine. I do have a few odds and ends I need to finish up, but this week plan on me being here full time." Seth left the kitchen and both Cat and Shauna watched him leave.

"He's not so bad on the eyes. I guess we could do worse than having our own bodyguard." Shauna brought Cat a cup of warm apple cider she'd had simmering on the stove and took away the empty beer bottle.

Cat settled into a chair and stared at the cup. "I don't know. Seth is intense. And I'm not sure I'm ready for his kind of attention."

"You're saying you don't have feelings for the man?" Shauna sipped from her cup.

Cat set the cup on the table and faced her friend. "It's worse than that. I do have feelings for the guy. But what if I ruin it again? I was the one who moved on. I don't think I could hurt him again like that."

"Then don't." Shauna looked at the clock. "The group said they were staying in town for dinner tonight so I guess it's just the two of us, unless you want to invite Mrs. Cook to join us for dinner. And Seth, of course."

"Seth can make his own dinner." Cat stood. "I'll go see if Mrs. Cook is here. What are we having?"

"Oh, just French dip sandwiches and a pasta salad. We can add on some cheesecake if you think it would seal the deal."

Cat headed upstairs and knocked on room number five, where Mrs. Cook had been staying. No answer. She called out, knocking harder, "Mrs. Cook? Are you in there?"

A crash sounded down the hall and Cat ran to the source. Only one door was open and it was covered in crime-scene tape. She peeked around the door, staying out in the hallway, and spied Linda Cook staring back at her, holding onto a drawer from the dresser.

"What are you doing in here? The police sealed the room for evidence." Cat waved the woman closer to the door, but Linda Cook ignored her motioning.

"Seriously, you need to get out of here. Uncle Pete's going to have my hide for this."

Linda Cook's shoulders sagged, and she set the dresser drawer back into the rails and closed it. She walked over to the crime-scene tape and ducked under. Cat pulled the door closed and turned to Mrs. Cook. "What were you thinking?"

"I just wanted Tom's laptop. I'm his beta reader, so I've been reading his newest book as he finishes chapters. I just missed him tonight and wanted to escape back into his story." Tears fell down her face. "Don't call me Mrs. Cook. Just Linda please."

"I'm sure the police took it into evidence." Cat grabbed the tissue box off a hallway table and gave it to Linda, then motioned to the stairs. "Come down to the kitchen and eat dinner with Shauna and me. You'll feel better after a good meal."

Sniffing, Linda shook her head. "I know dinner isn't included in my rate. I don't want to be a bother."

"You are so not a bother. We could use the company. Things have been kind of weird around here today." Cat led Linda down the stairs to the first floor. "Hey, were you up in the attic this afternoon?"

Linda pushed through the swinging door into the brightly lit kitchen. "You have an attic? I haven't taken a tour of the place yet. I've been too busy dealing with Tom's things. His lawyer called me earlier and we met over at the coffee shop about noon. I was there until just now."

Shauna quickly poured Linda a glass of water. "Can I get you something else to drink? A cold beer or a soda? How about a cup of tea?"

"Tea would be great. I'm not sure how I'm going to get to sleep tonight without a book to read. I packed so quickly when the police called, I wasn't sure what I stuffed in my luggage." She took a long sip of the water.

"We have a great library temporarily set up in the living room. I'll take you there after we eat. And if you don't find something there, we'll check out the books I have in my office. Books are one thing we don't have a short supply of." Cat grabbed two of the already-filled plates and set one in front of Mrs. Cook and one at Shauna's chair. She went to the fridge and grabbed another beer for herself. She looked at Shauna who was just finishing the tea. "You want one?"

"Definitely." Shauna held out her hand and Cat slid a cold bottle into her friend's grip. Then she returned to the table with her own meal.

Seth entered the kitchen, but stopped just inside the door. "Oh, I see you're eating. I was just coming in to say I'm out of here and will be back tomorrow at seven sharp."

Shauna stood and grabbed a bag off the counter. "Here's your dinner. Thanks for moving my car."

He exchanged the keys for the bag and grinned. "Thanks. I'm sure this will be better than the can of chili I was planning on opening for tonight." He waved to the table and caught Cat's gaze and winked. Then he left.

When Shauna returned to the table, she shrugged. "I had an extra sandwich, so I packed Seth a meal. He did help bring in the groceries and chase down your ghost in the attic."

"Whatever." Cat took a sip off her beer. "You know if you feed strays, they never leave."

Linda Cook nodded and set her half-eaten sandwich down on the plate. "Boy, that's true. Tom was always feeding strays at the house. Now we have three indoor cats and two that are still wild but come to eat every night. I hope our housekeeper remembers to feed them. It was kind of Tom's job."

Shauna grinned, showing that she had understood Cat hadn't been talking about a stray kitten. "I'm sure she'll remember."

Linda sipped her tea. "Do you really have ghosts in the attic?"

The next morning, Cat turned off her alarm at five and pulled on jeans and a tank. Today she was determined to get her words in before the house woke up and started demanding her time. She'd scheduled a morning get-together about the writing process for after brunch and was in charge of taking the group to the library today. If words were going to get done on her own manuscript today, it needed to be now, when others weren't draining her life-force.

Shauna was already in the kitchen when she arrived. She pointed to a half-completed tray. "I was going to bring that up for you in a few minutes after the zucchini bread finishes baking. You want to take a snack up now? I've got leftover muffins from yesterday."

"Just coffee." Cat leaned against the counter as she took her first sip of the day. Heaven. Shauna ground her own beans. She'd explained that part of the draw to places like this was the food and drink choices owners made upfront. Cat signed off on the expense, knowing that even if the business went belly up, at least she'd have premium coffee. Eyeing the bunch of bananas on the counter, she ripped off a banana. "And this."

"I take it you're trying to work this morning?" Shauna kept her head down, chopping fruit for the morning spread.

"Deadlines don't wait, even if you find a dead guy." Cat chuckled. "I made a funny."

"No, you didn't." Shauna put the chopped fruit into a bowl and squeezed a fresh lemon over the top of the fruit.

Cat pointed to the other half of the lemon on the cutting board. "Won't that make the fruit sour?"

"No, it will keep it from browning on us while your writer friends sleep the day away. I swear, if I was paying these rates to finish my book, I'd get the darn thing done and start a new one." She squeezed the second lemon half over the fruit and then went to the sink to wash her hands and her knife. Cat had learned quickly not to mess with the chef knives. Shauna treated them like they were gold, and from what Cat knew, she'd probably paid enough for the knives to be made of real gold.

She watched as Shauna put the clean knife back into her carrier and put the whole thing up on a shelf. "I can't believe you don't think that was funny."

Shauna didn't even look up as she walked over and put the covered dish into the oversized fridge. "You really don't have a good sense of humor. Maybe it's a writer thing. Your guests are always saying things that they mean to be funny, but honestly, most of it just falls flat. Except for each other. That Rose used to laugh at anything Tom Cook said, funny or not."

"She was pretty besotted with the man." Cat felt her lips curve into a smile. Someday she might have rabid fans like Tom had, but not if she didn't meet the deadline on this next book. She walked to the kitchen door. "Call me if you need me to come down. I'll have my cell on the desk."

She climbed the three flights of stairs to her office. Arriving, she turned on the light and her computer, then went around the room, opening up windows for a bit of fresh air to cool down the room. Leaving the door closed when guests were in the house, the room could get a bit overheated, but Cat didn't want people coming in and assuming they could use the office.

Shauna had suggested a sign, but she knew other writers. Signs could be misinterpreted, whereas a locked door kept people out. She opened up her Word document, took a couple sips of coffee as she reread the part where she'd ended writing the story yesterday. Then she checked her notes and started creating.

An hour later, Shauna unlocked the door with her key and set the breakfast tray on the table near the window. She refilled Cat's cup and then left, without either one of them speaking. Cat's attention returned to the manuscript.

When the cell rang, she didn't look at the display before answering. "Tell them I'll be down in a few minutes. I'm just tying up this scene."

The breathing on the line got heavier and then she heard one word. "Catherine?"

She dropped the phone, staring at the display with the words call lost. This couldn't be. No one called her Catherine. Well, except for Dean Vargas no one called her Catherine. But that hadn't been the dean on the line. If she didn't know better, Cat would have sworn on a stack of bibles that she'd recognized the voice. Michael's voice. Her dead husband had called her cell.

She ignored the tray of food on the table and picked

up the phone instead. The last number received showed as private. No help there. Who would play such a horrible prank on her? She dialed Uncle Pete's private line.

"What's up, buttercup?" He'd called her by that nickname for years, even before she was old enough to know a buttercup was a flower. She assumed he'd just changed the candy bar name.

Cat paused, wondering how to ask what she was going to ask. "When Michael died, who identified the body?"

The other side of the line was quiet. "Not sure why you want to know, but it was me. I found his body in the house. The college had called when he didn't show up for his lectures and I did a wellness check."

"Are you sure it was Michael?"

"Of course it was Michael. I hadn't really talked to him much after the divorce, especially since the whole thing was his fault, but I knew your ex-husband." Uncle Pete covered the phone and Cat could hear muffled voices in the background. "Honey, what's going on? It's kind of early for digging up old bones."

"Nothing. I got a hang up and the guy, well, he just sounded like Michael. It must have been a coincidence." Cat looked at the food tray and the uneaten banana and her stomach growled. Maybe hunger was making her lightheaded and she'd just heard wrong.

"Well, I've got Bob Jenkins cooling his jets in my waiting room. I guess I better go." He paused. "Maybe I'll stop by this morning for some coffee and we can talk."

"No. Don't worry about me. I'm fine. One more thing, Mrs. Cook asked about her husband's laptop.

Do you have it over at the station?" She held her breath, hoping the answer would be yes.

"I've got the evidence list right here." Her uncle paused while he went through the list. "Nope, sorry, no laptop. We have his cell, though. Could that be what she meant?"

A writer didn't go to a retreat without a laptop. Cat mused about the last time she'd seen Tom: on the walk to the library. With his tote bag over his shoulder. Of course, that didn't mean there was anything in the tote. But Rose talked to him that day; she would know what he was writing on.

"Cat, are you really all right? I'm beginning to worry about you." Her uncle's words broke through her wandering thoughts.

She forced a small laugh. "My blood sugar must be low. I've got things to get done this morning for the retreat group, so I better get cracking."

"If you need me . . ." He let the statement go unfinished and disconnected the call.

Cat set the cell on the table and grabbed a piece of the sweet zucchini bread. She ate everything on the plate, except for the sliced kiwi Shauna had put on the tray. She was always trying to get Cat to try something new, but she'd already told her friend that she didn't like kiwi. Shauna just didn't believe her. She finished off her coffee and stared into the cup. Maybe too much caffeine had her jittery. Whatever it was, there was one thing that was certain. The call had not come from the dark beyond. She pressed her hands on the desk to try to stop the shaking. Whoever was messing with her, they were doing a pretty great job of scaring the crap out of her.

Chapter 9

When the question-and-answer session started, the four remaining retreat attendees were sitting in the living room. Sara was on her phone, texting. Rose and Daisy were busy scribbling in spiral notebooks. And Billy had his laptop on his lap, his fingers flying over the keyboard.

"Good morning." Cat smiled at the group. "I hope you all slept well and enjoyed breakfast this morning." She paused, looking at the four, and sighed. "This was where I planned on asking you how the experience had been so far, but I'm kind of afraid of your answers."

Billy looked up from his laptop. "I assume you think we'll say bad things since Tom Cook bit the big one here?" He looked around at the group. "I don't know about the rest of you, but I'm getting way more done on this manuscript than I had expected. It's funny, I assumed retreats were just for the rich playing at writing. But it's actually been helpful to be away from my normal life."

Cat smiled, but didn't add she wondered what the

guy's normal life was like if a dead body in the next room didn't cause him any stress or writer's block. She turned to the sisters, "What about you two? How has the week so far been?"

"You know I'm terribly disappointed in the way things turned out with Mr. Cook." Rose shrugged. "But with his wife here, I realized my fantasies were mostly pipe dreams anyway."

"Mostly? How about totally? You didn't have a chance with the guy mostly because you're so much older than he was." Daisy patted her sister's hand and looked up at Cat. "Sometimes reality therapy is the best idea. Anyway, I've written almost ten thousand words in the last three days. I'm so excited. It took me three months to get that much done at home."

"I'm glad the separation from your normal life is working for you." Cat looked toward Sara who must have felt everyone's attention and shoved the phone into her bag.

"What?" Her question made it clear she hadn't been paying attention.

Something about the girl felt off, but Cat couldn't pinpoint it. After Tom's death, Cat had gone back and run background checks on all the guests, not just Billy. Sara's record had been squeaky clean, but she was a graduate student at the college. "I was asking people how the retreat was working for them. Have you been able to get any work done? I'm concerned you keep going back to campus and the real world. Maybe you should try to detach while you're here for the week. You only have three days left."

"I'm getting everything I need from the retreat. I don't know why people think you have to have total silence to write. I do my best work in small diners and dive bars. At least before the drunks get too loud." Sara's phone buzzed and her attention dropped to the display. "Sorry, I've got to take this."

Then she disappeared out of the living room, taking her tote bag with her.

"Kids," Billy muttered. "They don't know what they have until they lose it. Just wait a few years, she'll be dying for a retreat away from her loser husband and the six brats."

Rose pointed a finger at him. "You stop talking bad about the girl. She's just a child. I've watched her this week. I'm sure she's missing home, especially her father. She just lights up when she talks to that dean fellow."

"Dean Vargas?" Cat focused on Rose.

"The man who knew Tom? I believe that was his name. When I left the study cube where Tom was working on his book, Sara was talking to Dean Vargas down the hallway. She must have gotten some bad news, because she looked really sad." Rose shook her head. "I walked right by and she didn't even recognize me. She almost knocked me down the stairs when she ran to the restroom."

Cat thought she knew why Sara was upset. Dean Vargas didn't keep his favorites long. He believed in a catch-and-release type of relationship. It must have been Sara's time to be released. Poor girl. No wonder she was distracted during the retreat.

"You all can play nursemaid to the kid. I'm going to my room and writing. That's what we're here for, right?" Billy stood and tucked his laptop under his arm. "I won't be attending library time today. Or maybe even tomorrow. If things go well, I might have my first draft done before I check out Sunday afternoon."

The women watched as he walked out of the room. "At least he's in a better mood now," Daisy remarked. "The man was a horror the first day we were here. All he did was throw dagger eyes at Mr. Cook."

"I'm still not convinced he didn't kill poor Tom." Rose turned her attention on Cat. "You're related to the police chief, right? What has he said about the murder?"

"Nothing to me." Cat shrugged. "Real police officers don't go blabbing their information all over before they catch a murderer. That only happens in the movies or in books."

"Not sure that's entirely accurate, my dear." Daisy set her pen down on her notebook. "I dated a cop for several years. I would have broken up with him sooner, but he would tell me the craziest stories about his job. I loved listening to him at dinner."

"Harry made up half of what he told you and the other half happened to some other cop." Rose turned a page in her notebook and started scribbling away.

Daisy narrowed her eyes at her sister, then turned back to Cat. "Okay, maybe some of that's true. But they were good stories."

Cat looked at her watch. They were due at the library in thirty minutes. The head librarian had offered to talk to the group about the research tools the school had acquired. "We better get going if we want to meet Miss Applebome on time."

Daisy tucked her notebook away in her tote. She stared at her sister. Finally Rose groaned and put her own notebook away.

"The next time we go on a retreat, I'm going to

book something in a different city than you." Rose turned toward Cat. "Let's boogie."

Daisy followed her sister out of the room. "She's just in a snit because of what I said about her and Mr. Cook."

"I can still hear you. I'm not deaf," Rose called out from the lobby area.

Daisy smiled at Cat. "Actually she is, in her right ear."

They walked out of the room to find Linda Cook standing by the front desk. Cat hurried to the area. "Mrs. Cook, I mean, Linda, can I help you with anything?"

"Looks like you're on an adventure. Where are you going?" Linda looked at the other women with interest.

"The library." Rose cocked her head. "Do you want to come with us? They're teaching us how to use their fancy machines to look at that microfilm stuff."

Linda looked at me. "Do you mind if I tag along? I'm going crazy just hanging out in my room waiting for the police chief to call me."

"No problem. You might find it a little basic since you have an advanced degree and all." Cat walked around the desk and opened the front door.

Linda strolled out first. "I'm sure I'll enjoy the lecture."

"Can't say I didn't warn you," Cat muttered as Rose and Daisy followed her out to the porch. Miss Applebome was very nice, but she could put a crackhead on a bender to sleep with her detailed descriptions of each and every step needed to properly utilize library assets. And those were her words, not Cat's.

Linda took off toward the campus and Cat had to hurry to catch up. Rose and Daisy were right behind her, bickering about whether or not they should have worn a jacket. Cat turned back. "It will stay warm until about seven, so if you want to stop to get some dinner before coming back to the inn, you should be fine."

"You should stop at The Post. It has the best pulled pork sandwiches." Linda stopped and waited for the trio to catch up with her. "The Post is still here, right?"

The place was still around, but they hadn't served food for years. It had transitioned into a bar before Cat had even been old enough to drink. She explained the current status of Linda's favorite hangout.

"Life never slows down, you know?" Linda choked on the words, but then pressed her lips together. "The diner should be open, right?"

"The diner is not only open, it's a great place to eat. They have a great new chef and the menu is fantastic."

"Well, at least something has stayed the same around here." Linda let her lips curl into a smile that seemed more sad than happy.

They walked in silence the rest of the way to the library. Cat led them in, turned them over to the librarian, and headed upstairs to see if Tom had rented a laptop storage shed when he'd been here earlier. Maybe she'd find the missing laptop there, all tucked away.

The student in charge for the afternoon, another work-study position, shrugged. "I don't have a list of who rented the slots, dude. All I do is take their money and give them a key when they pay. It's not like it's a long-term commitment." He grinned at me. "No credit check needed, just like those rent-to-own furniture ads."

"Okay, is there someone that didn't return a key in the last week?" Cat looked at the laptop storage lockers. Half appeared empty.

"You'll have to ask Miss Applebome. She does the accounting on Friday afternoon. If someone leaves their stuff longer than that, she boots them and takes their computers for ransom. I warn everyone about the Friday eviction policy." The guy leaned back in his chair and put his hands behind his head. "So are you here to rent a slot? I've got a game to get back to playing."

"I'm good. Thanks for your help." Cat walked back downstairs to tell the group she was heading back to the house. When she reached the conference room, a new member had joined their group.

Dean Vargas stood just inside the doorway, talking to Linda Cook. "You really must let me take you to dinner. I'm sure you'd feel much better if you just got away from all of this mess."

"That's very kind of you, but I've already made plans with my friends here. Thank you for your concern." Linda turned away from him and waved toward the librarian who was standing with folded arms, glaring at the two. "Sorry for the distraction. Please go ahead."

"But Linda," Dean Vargas started, but the look that she gave him stopped whatever else he had planned to say. He spun around and almost ran into Cat. "Excuse me," he hissed.

Cat wasn't sure the words were meant for her, or for Linda's benefit. But she nodded. "No problem." As she walked into the room, she saw Sara standing near the library stacks. She motioned her toward the group, but the girl pretended like she hadn't seen her and turned to go the other way.

Miss Applebome was setting up her PowerPoint presentation when Cat entered the room. "Sorry for one more distraction, but I wanted to let the group know that I was heading back to the house. Call if you have problems or need a ride back."

"Have a nice afternoon," Daisy said.

Rose raised her eyebrows. "Is that carpenter in the house? You need to seal that deal before he goes somewhere else."

Her sister poked her with an elbow.

"What?" Rose grinned at her sister, then turned back to Cat. "You're not getting any younger, you know."

Cat felt the heat run to her face and stepped back toward the door. "Anyway, I'll see you all later."

She heard the laughter as she bolted from the room, but she didn't care. This hostess thing was hard. People got to see you in your home and, because of that, people like Rose thought they knew what was best for her. She really needed to build stronger walls between her and her guests. She powerwalked home, hoping some of her energy would dissipate before she arrived.

"You look ticked." Shauna sat on the porch, a book in her hand and a glass of lemonade next to her.

Cat sank down to the porch floor and leaned against the railing, closing her eyes. "I don't know if I can do this."

"Do what?" Shauna kicked Cat's foot. "Come on, tell me. What's wrong?"

She opened her eyes and looked at her friend. "Everyone being in my business. It's bad enough I came crawling back home. Now my guests are trying to set me up for a quickie with Seth. And Rose doesn't even know we used to date."

"Rose has sex on the brain. She told you that. I think that's why she likes writing; she can daydream about things and people." Shauna's lips curved into a smile. "I think it's kind of cute. I hope I'm still in the game when I'm her age."

"She's not over, what, sixty?" Cat's heartbeat was beginning to calm. Maybe she had overreacted to the comment and the women's laughter. Seth was a sexy, good-looking man. Women noticed him.

"She told me she just turned sixty-five. Daisy's older by a few years." She set the book on the swing next to her. "I'm loving getting to know these people. Rose and Daisy would never have come into the tavern where I used to work. Well, they might have come in, but they wouldn't have stayed."

"I don't know. I like my privacy." Cat looked out on the front yard where Seth still had sawhorses set up. "I didn't see his truck. Is he here?"

"He had to run into town and unclog a kitchen sink for the Maguires. Since you left with the rest of the group, I decided to come out here until he came back."

Cat looked at the house. "Billy's actually still here. He should be in his room."

"Another good reason for me to be out here. That guy gives me the willies." She took a sip of her drink before she went on. "He's always watching me. I'd say something, but I think that's what he does with everyone. He's a creeper."

"Well, he's a paying guest this week. But I promise I'll run background checks on the people in the next session before I cash their checks." Cat grinned and held out her hands. "Pull me up and we'll go into the kitchen and I'll make lunch."

Shauna stood and held out her hands. "I'll pull you to your feet, but you are not cooking. I don't want to lose another pan."

"Hey, I forgot I had turned the heat on high. I really wasn't gone that long." She grabbed her friend's hands and pulled herself to standing. "I'm a good cook."

"Keep telling yourself that, someday someone might believe you."

Cat held the door open and then followed Shauna into the cool lobby. The grandfather clock near the stairs chimed one o'clock. "I didn't realize it was so late." She paused at the clock and opened the door, pulling the weights to reset the mechanism. Her parents had left her the clock when they moved and she had carefully moved it from Colorado to California and now back again. She closed the door and ran a hand down the smooth wood surface.

That chore done, she followed Shauna into the kitchen. "Can I at least help?"

"I'm making us chopped salad and cooking a piece of tuna to go over the top. You could get out the produce and get it washed." Shauna listed off the items as Cat pulled them from the fridge.

As she walked to the counter, she noticed a package on the table. "What's that?"

Shauna glanced toward her. "Oh, I forgot. It was

on the porch when I followed Seth out earlier. Looks like we missed a delivery."

Cat set the veggies down on the counter and walked over to the table. The package was notebook size and wrapped in brown paper. Someone had tied it up with a string along with the sealing tape to keep the paper sealed. Her full name and *700 Warm Springs, Aspen Hills* were written on the front in scrolling letters but nothing else. No postmark, no shipping stickers. This hadn't been sent through any of the normal delivery channels. Her mind went to the earlier phone call. She shook off the chill she suddenly felt in the warm kitchen.

"So what is it?" Shauna's words broke her inability to move, and Cat stepped closer and picked up the item with two hands.

"I haven't opened it yet." She turned over the package, looking for any additional clues to the sender, but there was nothing. She heard the kitchen drawer open, then Shauna set a pair of scissors next to her on the table.

"You'll have to cut off that string. I didn't think the post office allowed you to use string anymore. It tends to mess up their machines." Shauna returned to the stove where she was starting the fish. "You deal with that I'll start chopping the veggies."

Cat sat in a chair and carefully snipped the string and then cut the top of the package. She turned it upside down and a leather bound journal slipped onto her table. She immediately recognized the book and ran her hand over the soft cover. Three initials were carved in gold on the top. M E L. Michael Edward Latimer.

She'd assumed the journal had been in Michael's top lefthand side desk drawer all this time, but apparently not. Her dead husband's journal had been found and returned home.

But by who?

Chapter 10

Uncle Pete sat at the table across from Cat, looking at the journal. He used a napkin to turn the pages. Finally, he sighed and closed the book. "So this just showed up today?"

"It was out on the porch when Shauna went outside. It wasn't there when I left to take the group to campus." Cat thought back on when she'd left the house today. She was certain she would have seen a package, even though she'd been distracted by Linda's insistence on joining the group. She turned to Shauna. "Where did you find it?"

"It was right under the mail slot. I figured I must not have heard the postman knock. Now that I think of it, the mail typically comes around three. That would have been too early for him." Shauna busied herself around the kitchen, cleaning up from the salads that they'd had for lunch but neither of them had finished. "Are you sure I can't make a pot of coffee for you? Or iced tea?"

Uncle Pete shook his head. "I just had a long lunch

with the mayor about the uptick in drug use at the college. Believe me, I'm coffee'd out."

Cat tapped on the table near the book. "Are you taking it into evidence?"

"What for?" Uncle Pete appraised her with a long look. "Michael's been dead for more than six months. You know that right?"

"Of course, I know that." Cat's mind jumped to the phone call she'd gotten. It must have been from the same person that had the journal; it had just sounded so much like Michael saying her name. She involuntarily shook her head, throwing the question aside. Uncle Pete had seen Michael's body. That's all she needed to know.

"Tell me again why you asked me about Michael's death earlier." Uncle Pete waited for her answer, but Cat avoided eye contact and just shrugged. No need for him to think she was crazy and hearing things.

When it was apparent he wasn't going to leave without an answer, she broke. "Look, it was probably nothing, but someone called and said my name, then hung up."

"What does that have to do with asking about Michael's death?" Shauna sat next to her and covered Cat's hand with her own.

Now she really was going to look crazy. In for a pound, her mother always said. "It sounded like Michael. He was the only one who ever called me Catherine." She looked at both Uncle Pete and Shauna, challenging them to disagree.

"Except telemarketers who get your name off some random list." Uncle Pete nodded to Shauna. "You got a couple big Baggies I can use?"

"You're taking it in?" Cat asked again.

"Let's just say I'm interested." He tucked the wrapping paper in one bag and the journal in another. "I'll get this tested for fingerprints, then return it to you. If you want it."

The unspoken statement hung in the air. Michael's journal could be about his work or, more likely, about his conquests both during and after their marriage. Cat didn't really want to reopen that bag of pain, but something wouldn't let her throw away the journal, not since it had been returned to her. There must be a reason the anonymous gifter had wanted her to read the journal. She nodded. "Drop it off when you're done. I'm not sure I want to read it, but I might."

"Cat, there's something you need to know." Uncle Pete paused when she put up a hand.

"Not right now. It's been a little weird around here, and I just want to go upstairs and take a nap to try to get rid of this pounding headache." She forced a smile at her uncle. Then she turned to Shauna. "Wake me up if you need me."

She wandered through the house and up the stairs, memories of Michael hitting her at every turn. How he'd laughed when they were fixing the railing on the second story. How he'd complained about the boxes on boxes of books he'd carted to her office. But even Cat had known he'd been proud of her being hired at the college. For a while, their life had been perfect.

Then he'd stopped loving her.

Her head pounded and tears were building behind her eyes. She ran the back of her hand across her eyes and swore. "I will not cry for you again Michael Latimer. Never again."

She opened the door to her bedroom, and closed it after her. Falling on the bed, she kicked off her shoes and wrapped herself in the quilt she kept at the bottom of the bed. She fell asleep with memories of her ex-husband floating through her head.

When she woke, the sun had set and the room was dark. A tray sat on the table by the window with a sandwich and a glass of tea. Shauna had added two brownies to the tray and Cat took one and ate it as she stretched awake. The headache was gone and the pain from Michael's betrayal was locked back into her heart where it had laid silent for so many years.

Maybe coming back had been a bad idea. She loved the house, but it held so many memories, good and bad.

No. The only reason she was dragging down memory lane was the phone call and the journal. Someone was messing with her, and she was going to find out who and why.

She finished her dinner, then checked on her appearance in the bathroom. She ran some water over her face, brushed her hair, and decided she looked passable, even if the retreat gang was hanging out in the living room.

Carrying the tray, she maneuvered down the stairs and into the kitchen without running into anyone. Then her luck changed. Rose and Daisy sat at the table, teacups in hand and a plate of the brownies on the table in between them. They looked up as she entered.

"Well, there you are." Daisy smiled, wiping her lips with a napkin. "We were beginning to think you took off with that lovely man. But when he walked through with an arm filled with tools and wood, we figured you must just be writing."

"Or shopping." Rose added. "I like to shop when

my mind is dealing with a hard plot point. Sometimes I just don't know where the story is going, so I take off for the mall. When I come home, I've got a direction."

"And bags filled with clothes you don't need." Her sister tapped the empty chair next to her. "Come sit with us. I'd love to talk about ways you deal with writer's block."

"Give me a second, I'll be right there." Cat set the tray down on the cabinet and rinsed her plates before putting the dirty dishes into the dishwasher. Shauna would come in later tonight and run the dishwasher while everyone was asleep. She put the kettle back on the stove, turned on the gas, and got a cup and a tea bag ready for the water. Figuring she'd stalled long enough, she turned back to the sisters, now arguing over the importance of a first line.

"So what do you want to know about writer's block?" Cat snatched a brownie from the plate, took a bite of the chocolate heaven, and then, sighing, set the rest down on a napkin. "Some people say it's an excuse, not an actual problem."

Each of the sisters had her own opinion, of course, and Cat felt like a referee rather than a peer. She paused, listening to the clock in the hallway. Nine chimes; she'd been here over an hour and the two hadn't agreed on anything.

"Oh, my, is that really the time?" Rose paused after the final chime. "I need to get to bed. Tomorrow's a big day. I've got to get some words down so I can go to the dinner on Saturday. I bought a new little black dress."

Daisy smiled at Cat then shrugged her shoulders in a silent *What can you do?* gesture.

As they rose to leave, Cat remembered the question she wanted to ask Rose. "Hey, you said you talked to Tom Cook on Monday at the library?"

Rose sighed and a smile curved her lips. "I did, and I'll never forget it." She dug into her purse and pulled out a smart phone. "Look, he even took a selfie with me. I'm posting it on my Facebook, web page, and anywhere I can as soon as I get home."

She handed the phone to Cat. There in the private library carousels was Tom Cook, hugging a grinning Rose, with his laptop open to the side. She'd been right—Tom Cook had taken his laptop to the library. So where was it?

That was the million-dollar question. Something about what Linda had said poked at her memory. "Good picture. You know you can post them right from your phone, don't you?" She handed Rose back the phone and the woman stared at her image with her idol for a second before putting the phone back into her purse.

Rose didn't look up. "It's easier to do from my desktop at home. I'm still getting used to this new phone."

Cat smiled, wondering what else Rose didn't know about her phone's capabilities. She decided to move the conversation back to Tom Cook. "You said he was working on a memoir? His wife said he was writing his next thriller."

"Well, maybe she didn't know everything about him!" Rose's eyes widened and she slapped her hand over her mouth. "That came out wrong."

"Very wrong, sister." Daisy put her hand on Rose's arm. "Jealousy doesn't become you."

"I know. And I'm working on it." Rose turned her

attention to Cat. "All I can tell you is what he said. He told me he was back in Covington to research his own story, and it was going to have as much mystery and intrigue as the fiction books he wrote."

The sisters said their goodnights and Cat stayed at the table, wondering what Tom Cook had really been writing. And where his laptop had disappeared to. She knew one thing: If they found his laptop, they had his killer.

She booted up the laptop that she'd bought for Shauna when they'd moved to Colorado. The woman kept it on her desk in the kitchen, not seeing the need to keep it in her room. When Cat had asked her about it, Shauna had laughed. "I use it for the retreat work and for looking up recipes. Where else would I keep it?"

Cat had tried to explain that she could watch movies or read or research travel sites on the mini-computer, but Shauna shrugged. "I have a television and a DVR player; that's all I need. If I want to read, I'll pick up a real book. I'm not like most of my generation; I'm not going to be tied to some machine to make me happy."

So instead of the computer being Shauna's, it had become the kitchen laptop, which Cat had to admit came in very handy. She searched for Tom's web page. Scanning it, she saw he had a link to his blog. She clicked on that and scanned the last few posts to see what he was saying about writing, if anything. Linda Cook had been right; he had been in the middle of writing his next thriller, according to a blog post he posted last week. Cat went farther down the posts, but nothing verified what Rose had said, except perhaps one.

Packing up today to attend the Warm Springs
Writer's Retreat, newly opened in Aspen
Hills, Colorado. For my more recent fans, you
may or may not know I attended Covington
College in Aspen Hills and won the hand of
my fair lady on those school grounds. Of
course, I had to fight a few dragons on the
way to happiness, but what true love story
doesn't have its conflicts at the beginning?
So if you don't hear from me for a while,
I'm probably up to my old college hijinks,
attending frat parties and wearing a
lampshade or two. If you see photos, I'll be
the creepy old guy hanging out with all the
young kids. See you all soon.

That had been the last post on his blog.

Cat closed the laptop and drained her now-cold tea
into the sink and put the cup into the dishwasher.
Shauna walked into the room as she was finishing.

"Hey, I didn't expect to see you down here. I
knocked on your door, but you had already brought
the tray down. I would have dealt with that if you
wanted to sleep some more." Shauna put a dish deter-
gent pod into the machine and started up the cycle.
"I'm serving waffles with that lovely huckleberry
syrup I found at the souvenir shop last week. The
woman gave me a few bottles to display and if I sell
some, she'll keep giving us the stuff at cost."

"Sounds like you're making friends with the local
community." Cat leaned against the counter and
looked at her friend. "Are you happy here? Do you
regret moving away from home?"

"California was never my home. I followed my

last loser boyfriend out there from Ohio, so don't worry about dragging me from my roots. And no, I'm not missing Ohio. This place is amazing. I was talking to Kim, she runs the souvenir shop, and she says I can probably learn to snow ski this winter, with a few classes. Her boyfriend runs the ski school, so she's going to get me a discount." Shauna's eyes grew bright. "I'm on a pretty amazing adventure, and I don't even have to work nights at a dive bar to pay my rent."

"As long as Tom Cook's death doesn't scare away writers from attending future retreat sessions." Cat mused. "Have we had any cancelations?"

"Nothing yet, but we're still on half capacity until after January. Or whenever your boyfriend gets the other wing of guest rooms finished." Shauna picked up the booking calendar on her desk. "You can always see the reservation list here."

"He's not my boyfriend." Cat waved away the notebook. "I'm still beat. I'll see you in the morning."

A knock sounded at the back door and Seth walked in. His brown hair was still damp from a shower, he had on clean jeans and a button-down shirt, and he smelled good. Cat glared at him. "How long have you been standing out there?"

"Chill out, I only just arrived." He looked at the two women, a slow smile curving his lips. "Have you two been talking about me? Is that why Cat's so riled up?"

"No." Cat put her hands in her jeans. "Why would we be talking about you?"

Seth's gaze went to Shauna. Cat turned her head to follow his look, and caught her friend nodding like a pound puppy.

"Fine, what do you want?" Cat glared at the man in her kitchen.

He leaned against the doorway and tossed his keys. "Who said I wanted anything?"

The guy looked like a staged shot for a romance novel cover. Cat felt her body respond to his unspoken invitation. "Okay, let me change the question. Why are you here?"

He strolled over to her and put a hand on her arm. "I'm here to take you out to Bernie's for a beer. I heard about the journal showing up, and I thought you might want to get out of here for a while and talk."

"Who told you?" She turned her head and glared at Shauna.

Her hands went up in fake surrender. "I swear it wasn't me. I've been here."

Seth put a finger on her chin and turned her face back toward him. "I ran into your uncle when I was packing up for the day. He's pretty worried about you."

"Figures." Cat glanced at the clock and considered her schedule for the next day. She didn't have retreat duties, the group was on their own, but she'd planned to spend the day with her manuscript. A job better done without a hangover.

"We won't be out late." Seth seemed to read her mind. "I'll have Cinderella back in her bed before midnight."

The almost-innocent words had a touch of illicit promise to her. Not that they were there yet, but Cat felt like time had just rewound and she was with the boy she'd loved in high school.

"You should go," said Shauna. "I'll just close up

the kitchen and be off to bed. All the guests, except that Sara girl, are already in their rooms. I'll leave a light on and she should be able to find her way if she decides to sleep here." Shauna turned toward the desk to put the booking notebook away.

"You're sure you'll be okay here?" Cat didn't add the word alone, since her friend wouldn't technically be by herself; it just felt like she was skipping out on work.

"Nothing is going to happen tonight. We've already had our mandatory weird thing of the day. You can deal with tomorrow's surprise event when you get back."

Cat looked down at her jeans and T-shirt. "Should I change?"

"For Bernie's? Wearing that will look like you dressed up for a date night." He placed his hand on her back and led her toward the door. "Your chariot awaits, my dear."

"If I don't come back, tell Uncle Pete that Seth kidnapped me," Cat called over her shoulder.

Seth nuzzled his lips near her ear. "As fun as that sounds, we will have to play that game some other time. Tonight, we're only getting a couple beers." He ducked as she swung her hand upward to swat him away. Laughing, he moved around her and trotted to his truck that he'd parked in the driveway. Opening the door, he bowed low. "My lady."

"You're a dork, you know that." Cat scooted into the dark interior. She peeked inside the glove box, and found the owner's manual, the insurance card, a current registration, and a roll of wintergreen Lifesavers. She unwrapped one and popped it in her mouth. As he settled on the driver's seat, she held the roll out for him. "Want one?"

"How'd you know they'd be there?" Seth took a candy then handed the roll back to her.

She smiled at the memory. "You always kept a roll or two in your truck. When all the other kids were sneaking cigarettes, you kept the candy company in business with your purchases."

He started the engine and shrugged. "You remember Jake? Well, Jake stole a pack of Marlboros off his old man the summer before eighth grade. We went down to the creek and smoked the whole pack. I was never so sick. I think Mom knew what had happened, but she never asked. She bought me a few rolls of those. But it didn't stop me from taking up the habit as a teen."

"You never told me that." Cat turned in the seat, watching as the glow of the dashboard lights made his face stand out in the darkness of the truck.

"When I stopped again, Mom bought me one of those oversized packages that must have held fifty rolls. You know, the kind that you get at the warehouse stores. Every month for a year, she'd drop a package off at my house. Finally, I told her to stop. But it helped with the cravings." He rubbed the top of her hand with his thumb. "And I always have minty fresh breath."

"Your mom is a smart woman." She looked at their entwined hands, wondering where this evening was heading. "Look, I don't know . . ."

"Hush. I don't want to talk about the future. Or about us." He shot her a guarded look. "Tonight, I want to have a couple beers, watch you drink a few, and catch up on where we've been for the last five years. I've missed talking to you."

"All you want to do is talk?" She couldn't hide the surprise in her voice.

He turned the truck into the parking lot and after finding an empty spot near the back, turned the engine off. "You doubt my sincerity?"

"You're holding my hand." She couldn't see him in the dark of the truck now. The parking lot didn't have many lights and he'd parked away from all of them.

"I like holding your hand." He brought it toward him and kissed her fingertips. "Let's go have a few beers and pretend like we like each other."

As she waited for him to walk around and open her door, she realized she wouldn't have to pretend. No matter how long she tried to talk herself out of the emotions, she still had feelings for her high school crush.

Chapter 11

Smoke rolled out of the bar as soon as Seth opened the front door. That smell, mixed with years of spilt beer, hit Cat and instantly took her back to when this had been their Friday night hangout. Saturdays were movie night, but Fridays they'd come here to meet up with friends. The guys would play pool, and she and the girls would talk about what they were going to do with the rest of their lives. Most of her friends talked about wedding plans, but she talked about going to school and hopefully, someday, writing a book that would be sold in real, live bookstores.

She let Seth guide her to the tables in the gameroom area. As she sat, he stood over her. "Still drink Bud Light?"

She nodded and he disappeared to the bar. A female bartender came over and took his order, apparently surprised when he ordered two beers; she looked over her shoulder at Cat. The look wasn't mean or spiteful, only curious. Seth came back with the longnecks and sat one in front of her. He laid a roll of quarters on the table then sat across from her.

"We're going to need quarters?" She took a pull off the bottle.

He shrugged. "They still haven't made the pool table free, so I guess we need quarters."

"I thought we were here to talk."

"You know you want to play." He tapped the table. "I brought you here to get your mind off everything that has happened the last couple days. Besides, it will be fun. We haven't been here together since the breakup."

"Way to bring down the mood, dude." She took another sip of her beer. "This is the first time we're old enough to drink here. I don't know how Bernie used to keep the pool area open for minors."

"It was considered a billiard parlor back then." He pointed to the bar area. "That used to be the video room. The guys and I ran through our quarters pretty fast in there. Your uncle started having trouble with the place once Bernie started selling beer. So he gave him an option. Bar or billiards, but not both. I guess the bar makes more money."

"So kids aren't allowed in here anymore." Cat scanned the room. "That's kind of sad."

"Not for me. I can actually get a table now on most nights and play until the place closes or I decide to head home." He grinned a lopsided grin at her. The tiny scar on the left side of his face reminded her of his dirt bike spill and the terrifying trip to the emergency room that Saturday. She had been the one to call his mother and when his folks arrived, she'd tried to leave. But they made her welcome in the waiting room. A taste of what family meant to Seth and his clan.

"So you tell me you've gone pro with pool and

still think I want to play you?" She took out two quarters from the roll and tapped them on the table. "I guess I want to get beat."

He nodded to the quarters. "You're going to need three." He picked up the roll and shook out four more. "And we'll put up the money for next game so we're not challenged."

She looked around at the few tables that were occupied. Most of those people were deep into conversations or nursing a drink alone. "Not sure we have much competition. Besides, there's a second table."

"Try telling Marv that. He likes *this* table." Seth stood and grabbed a couple of pool cues, checking them on the green felt for warping.

She took the cue she wanted out of his hand, then chalked the tip. "So we move to the other table."

"Thing is, I like this table best, too." Seth squatted down and put the quarters into the machine and Cat heard the sound of the balls dropping. She watched as he set up the rack, rolled it a couple times to set the triangle, then took off the frame. He waved his hand. "Ladies first."

"Always a gentleman." Cat took the white ball and placed it on the table. She focused her gaze on the sweet spot, pulled back on the cue and slammed the ball into the rack. Several balls fell into pockets, and as she glanced at what was still left on the table, she called her ball. "Stripes."

Then she ran the table, calling the hole for the black eight ball before sending it rolling into the pocket.

"You've been playing, too." He said dryly as she finished the game.

"Shauna used to bartend at this little place near

my apartment. I'd go down on Saturdays when it was dead and we'd play for a couple hours." She shrugged. "I always was good. You and the boys were table hogs."

He grinned. "Point taken. So loser goes first this game?" He grabbed quarters off the table.

"I guess we'll have to play with those rules or you'll never get a turn." She returned to the table and took a drink of the beer. She had to admit, she enjoyed spending time with Seth. He'd always been easy to talk to and fun to be around. They'd spent many nights together sitting on the tailgate of his truck talking about the future. He'd wanted to play college football. She'd wanted to soak up the knowledge, read all the books in the library, and maybe take junior year abroad.

And yet, all these years later, they were right back where they'd left off. Living in Aspen Hills and hanging out at Bernie's. Seth won the next game, and ordered two more beers. When the bartender brought them over, she smiled at Cat. "Glad someone can put him in his place. I lost too many beer bets over pool with this guy."

"I'm sure my tab has covered whatever you've lost in a few beers." Seth put his hand on Cat's back. "Cat, this is Brittany. She's the best bartender in town."

Brittany held out her hand. "I'm the only one in town foolish enough to let him run a tab. You run that new bed and breakfast over at Michael's old house, right?"

Cat's stomach sank at the mention of her ex's name. Brittany was probably one of his undergrad student "friends." She fit his type: young, dark, and beautiful. She pushed the thought out of her head and put on what she hoped looked like a real smile as she shook the bartender's hand. "Cat Latimer. Michael and I were divorced."

"Oh, you're Catherine." Brittany looked from Seth back to Cat. "I didn't realize."

"Brit, are you going to talk all day or can I get another Jim and Coke?" A slurred voice called out from the bar.

"Hold your horses, Stan." Brittany turned back to the couple. "I should cut him off, but his wife will come get him in a little bit, so I don't have to worry about him driving. Glad you stopped in, and it was lovely to finally meet you."

As Brittany walked back to the bar, Cat closed her eyes. Coming home meant running into Michael memories. Hell, she lived in the house. Had she been that naïve to think she could just remodel the past away? She felt Seth walk her over to the table and gently push her into a chair.

"Are you okay? I didn't know Brit knew Michael. I mean, she's Bernie's daughter, but she grew up in Arizona with her mom. I guess she went to school here." Seth took a sip of his beer.

"I can't let Michael's indiscretions wound me every time I leave my writing desk." She took a deep breath. "I was caught off guard, that's all. And with the journal showing up this morning, the past has been on my mind more than I'd like to admit."

Seth pulled on the label on his bottle. "Did you love the guy?"

His question made her pause. "At first, I did. Or I thought I did. I was overwhelmed with the idea of being the perfect professor couple. By the end, I realized it really was just a dream."

"I'm sorry."

"I'm not. I mean, it was a learning experience. I jumped when I should have paused, and I came out at the other end alive but scarred." She put her hand over his. "I should have taken you up on your unspoken offer of a getaway car that day."

He grinned. "We would have looked like some sappy movie, you riding in your huge white dress in my old truck. I didn't have a plan other than to drive you away from that jerk."

"Sometimes plans are overrated." She glanced at Brittany who was now chatting up a couple of college-age guys at the bar. "Best thing about the fantasy that was my marriage? I got the house at 700 Warm Springs."

"Yeah, but the guy had to die before you did," Seth reminded her.

Cat took a sip from her bottle and shrugged. "I didn't kill him, so my hands are clean there."

He chuckled and looked at the table. "You ready for the tie breaker?"

She glanced at her watch: a quarter to midnight. "One more game, then you need to take me back. This Cinderella's coach may not turn into a pumpkin, but you don't want to see me in the morning with less than seven hours sleep. It's bad."

"You always were a lightweight." He went to the table and put the quarters they'd left on the felt into the machine and racked up the balls.

She watched as Seth broke the rack with the cue ball. Then a man came up in front of her and blocked her view. She could smell the whiskey radiating from his body. "What are you doing here, checking up on me?"

Cat looked up into Billy Williams's face. The red tint to his cheeks and slight slur to his words told Cat all she needed to know. "Actually, I'm playing pool with a friend."

A woman stumbled into him and pointed toward the bar. "Hey Billy, there's an empty table over there." She leaned toward Cat, spilling some of her draft beer on Cat's jeans. "I know you. You were in my art class in high school."

"Hi Amy, how have you been?" Cat took a napkin and wiped the liquid off her pants.

The woman giggled and put her arm around Billy. "Better this week than in a long time."

Seth pushed past him and came to stand next to Cat. He leaned toward her and whispered, "You okay?"

Cat nodded, not taking her eyes off Billy who was still glaring, despite Amy's warm welcome.

"Seth." Amy looked him up and down, and took a step toward him. "When you going to come over and fix my pipes?"

Billy growled and pulled her backwards. "Let's go sit down."

"I was talking to my friends," Amy whined, but the couple left for the other side of the bar.

Seth waited until they were out of earshot, then shook his head. "Interesting couple, don't you think?"

"I think Amy wants more than just Billy. She looked at you like you were dessert after a six-week diet." Cat finished her beer. "I never got that type of girl. Who needs more than one guy at a time?"

"Attention hogs." He smiled and picked up her cue. "You going to finish the game or do you want to call it a draw and go home? You look a little worn out."

"I'm beat. Home would be good." She put a hand on his arm. "Thanks for insisting I come. I did have fun."

"Except for the last ten minutes," he amended.

She shrugged and pulled on her jacket.

"Just keep your distance from that guy. I know he's one of your guests, but he gives me the creeps." Seth put his hand on the small of her back and led her out of the bar and toward his truck.

By the time they drove across town to the house, Cat wanted to close her eyes and drop into a deep sleep. Seth had taken the long way, driving past the high school, pointing out changes on Main Street, giving her a personal tour of the changes she'd missed since she'd moved away. She waited for Seth to open her door and then paused. "Thank you for the night out. I needed the break."

He pushed her hair out of her eyes. "You look beat. I could carry you upstairs and help you into some pj's. You still wear Snoopy pj's to bed?"

"I never wore Snoopy pajamas. Your mom bought those for me for Christmas one year, and I gave them away to the thrift store." She smiled at the memory.

"Well, don't ever tell her that. You're her favorite of all my ex-girlfriends. If she knew that, Caroline Bradley would move up to favorite and you'd be banished forever." He ran a finger down her cheek. "Did I tell you how glad I am that you're back?"

"Once or twice." She put a hand on his chest and raised up on her toes and gave him a kiss on the side of his face. "I'm going in now."

"You sure?" he asked. Cat could see his grin in the darkness.

She turned and walked to the house. "See you in the morning."

Shauna burst out of the kitchen door and ran toward her. "I'm so glad you're here. Come inside, quick." She waved to Seth. "You too."

"What's going on," Seth asked as he jogged toward the house, meeting up with Cat while Shauna disappeared back into the house.

Cat had a bad feeling in the pit of her stomach. "Your guess is as good as mine. I just hope there isn't another dead body."

Seth held open the door. "You always were overly dramatic, but watch your step, just in case there's a blood trail."

Cat slapped his arm as she walked by, even though, really, all she wanted was to bury her head in his chest and have him hold her. She didn't want to know what had gotten Shauna into this state. She'd been the calm one when they'd found Tom Cook's body. If it was worse than that, Cat didn't know what she'd do.

She scanned the kitchen and saw Linda Cook sitting at the table, an empty shot glass sitting in front of her. A bottle of Captain Morgan's rum sat in the middle of the table and a still-full shot sat in front of the empty chair.

The house wasn't on fire. There didn't seem to be blood anywhere. Cat caught her friend's gaze. "What's going on?"

"Linda was out tonight having a couple drinks with a friend and when she came back, I heard the scream all the way down here in the kitchen." Shauna nodded, like Cat and Seth might not believe her story.

Then she continued. "So I ran up the stairs and the room's trashed. Her clothes are all over the room and it looks horrible."

"Tell them about the mirror," Linda slurred her words. "The mirror was the thing that made me scream."

Cat winced. She'd paid a lot of money for that antique vanity in Linda's room. If it was destroyed, she'd be heartbroken. She prodded her friend. "The mirror?"

"In red lipstick—a really nice brand by the way, not cheap—someone wrote, 'Go Away.' Isn't that weird?" Shauna picked up the glass and threw back the shot. "So we're waiting for your Uncle Pete to get done at Bernie's, then he's coming here. I told Linda we'd put her up in the blue room until this gets settled."

Seth stepped closer. "Wait, what happened at Bernie's? Did he say?"

"Some couple got into a fight. I guess the girl wailed on the guy pretty hard. He's already left in an ambulance to get stitches." Shauna played with the glass in her hand, rolling it by the edge on the table. "This Bernie's sounds like that dive I worked at before we left California."

"We were just there. No one was fighting when we left." Cat looked at Seth. "You don't think it was Amy and Billy, do you?"

Seth put his hands up at his sides. "Who knows? Amy's kind of a flake. And that guy didn't like the fact she was hitting on me. Of course, she hits on everyone."

"Maybe you should convince her you're not interested," Cat muttered.

He stepped in front of her. "When are you going to get it through your head that I'm not interested in anyone besides you? Although I kind of have to be out of my head to think we can make it this time."

"Well, you don't have to stick around, we can handle this problem. Even though you think I'm an idiot," Cat shot back.

"I never said 'idiot,'" Seth responded. But before he could go any further, Linda slapped the table hard.

"Stop fighting. Life is too short. I'd give anything to have my Tom back. I'd never start another fight with him for the rest of our lives, if I could just have him back," Linda said.

The room grew quiet as they all looked at her. Cat hoped Linda wouldn't cry. She didn't know if she could keep from joining her.

The door to the kitchen opened, and Uncle Pete entered. He glanced at Cat. "You're not having a very good week, are you?"

"That's the understatement of the year." She put her purse on the bar that lined the far kitchen wall and sank onto a stool. "So was my guest the guy sent to the hospital for stitches?"

Her uncle chuckled. "Amy got in some good left hooks with the guy. He'll be fine, but I'm pretty sure the romance has soured. Especially when he told the EMTs he lived in his mother's basement and was on her health insurance. I guess Amy thought he was the next Hemingway and was going to whisk her away to his mansion back east."

"Where?" Linda asked, slurring the last word.

"Not sure, but somewhere around New York City." He stood in front of Linda. "When did you leave your room tonight?"

"I went to campus to meet with Larry about seven. We had dinner, then I came back here after." She pointed to her watch and her finger slid off the surface into the air. "Ten thirty, I checked."

He looked at Shauna. "Did you see her come in?"

Nodding, she wiped her hands on her jeans. "I was working on a marketing plan here at my desk when she came in for a drink of water before going to bed."

"I had to take my pills," Linda murmured, her eyes glassy and her head drooped over her chest.

Uncle Pete frowned at the half-gone bottle and then shook his head at Shauna. "Did you really need to relax her that much?"

"Don't judge me. My comforting skills consist of mostly opening and pouring. I am a great listener though." Shauna took the bottle away as Linda reached for it. "Let's get you some coffee and a seltzer. You're going to have a whopper hangover in the morning."

"I don't want coffee, I want another shot," Linda grumbled, sinking lower in her chair.

Uncle Pete took out his notebook and wrote a few words. "Where's her room? I'd like to get home before my morning alarm goes off."

"I'll take you." Cat stood and stretched. "I need to see the damage anyway."

Shauna dug through a drawer and pulled out a camera. "You might want to take some pictures in case we decide to file an insurance claim."

Groaning, Cat took the digital camera from her friend. "Is it really that bad?"

"I don't know. Linda screamed, I went running, and we hurried down here to call 911. I wanted to get her away from the damage." Shauna gave Cat a knowing look. Linda seemed determined to get into places she wasn't allowed. Like her dead husband's room that had been cordoned off with police tape. Cat hadn't seen a need to tell her uncle about Linda's wanderings, but she would ask about the laptop and the discrepancy in the subject of Tom Cook's final project on the way up to the room.

Seth sat down at the counter. "I'll stay."

"You really don't have to. I'll lock up as soon as Uncle Pete leaves." Cat paused, her hand on the door her uncle had just exited.

Seth shrugged. "I'm waiting for a cup of coffee, then I'll walk through the house to make sure it's clear. Then I'll leave."

His tone told Cat she wouldn't win this fight. And besides, even though she didn't want to admit it to herself, she was glad he had volunteered. Right now the house felt excessively big. He didn't need to know how scared she really felt, however. "Knock yourself out."

She caught up with her uncle on the second floor landing. He held his hand out in an *after you* gesture. "She's near the end of the hallway. We only have these six rooms open right now, so once I move her to the last one, we'll be almost full. Two rooms with crime tape, and four with people."

"I may not need to seal the room for long. What, you have the weekend with this group, then you've got a month before the next session?" Uncle Pete tried to hitch his belt up over his protruding stomach as he walked.

"If there is a next session. Shauna seems to think Tom's death will bring out the curious. I only want to run a monthly retreat where people can go to write, think about writing, and talk about writing. Is that so hard?" Cat shivered as they passed Tom's room. The yellow crime-scene tape was starting to peel off the doorframe. She hoped it wouldn't take off the varnish, then felt horrible about worrying about her décor when Tom was dead.

A door opened and Rose's head popped out. She had wrapped her hair in a cotton scarf, and it was apparent they'd woken her. "Oh, I thought I heard voices."

"Sorry ma'am. We're just checking something out." Uncle Pete nodded. "Please close the door and stay in your room."

Instead of following his instructions, she opened the door wider, revealing a pink bathrobe, and looked down the hall toward Linda's room. "Don't tell me she killed herself in grief over losing the love of her life."

"Linda's fine. She's downstairs having a nightcap before she turns in." Cat paused at the older woman's door. "You go back to sleep. You'll wake Daisy." Cat could see the other sister's form in one of the room's twin beds.

Rose laughed. "Daisy sleeps like a log. Nothing wakes her until her alarm goes off every morning at five thirty." She lowered her voice. "She denies it, but I know she takes sleeping pills. She has since before she retired. Now, it's just a habit."

"We really need for you to go back into your room and close the door," Uncle Pete reminded her.

Rose looked at Cat to see if she would counter his instructions, but when she nodded, Rose relented. "Fine. But don't plan on waking me up later to ask me questions. I'll be available tomorrow after I get

my word count in. And after breakfast, of course."
Then she shut the door, a little too hard.

"I'm winning friends all over tonight." Uncle Pete
put his hand on Cat's back. "Let's go check out
Linda's room."

He pushed open the door. Linda had left the light
on, so they could see the damage clearly. Her clothes
were strung out from one end of the room to the
other, her suitcases upended and slashed with some
sort of sharp blade. The antique mirror was still
intact, but had a message written in red lipstick. Cat
whispered the words, "Go away."

She took a step forward into the room and her
uncle pulled her back out. "I need to get my crime-
scene guys in here. Right now, all we're going to do
is close it up and lock it so no lookie lous can peek
in." He took a napkin from his pocket and nodded to
the camera. "Take your pictures now. Your insurance
company will want to know what it looked like
before the crime guys make a mess. I'm sorry about
this, but it can't be helped."

"You didn't trash Linda's room, no need to be
sorry." She powered on the camera and took several
shots of the damage. Then she nodded to her uncle.
"Go ahead and lock the door from the inside. I've got
a key downstairs."

As they made their way back to the kitchen, he
paused, looking at the front door. "Is that keyed?"

"Yep, no one can get in after nine without using
their card, or going through the kitchen door. Shauna
locks that when she turns in for the night." She looked
at her uncle. "What are you thinking?"

"I believe someone had to have access to a key
card in order to do this." He stared at the lobby area

for a minute or two. "We'll have to check the timeline, but I'm hoping we can pinpoint the vandalism between nine and ten thirty."

"Which means . . ." Cat paused, not sure she wanted to hear his conclusion.

He looked at her. "Whoever did this has a key to the house."

Chapter 12

Cat lay awake long after Uncle Pete and Seth had left. Her mind was racing, unwilling to let her body fall into the sleep she craved. While she and Uncle Pete had surveyed Linda's room, Seth had walked through the house and checked all the window locks and outside doorways. The outside entrance to the cellar had been deemed suspicious and boarded up with a 2x4 until he could get a new lock installed the next day.

She glanced at her clock. One thirty. She pulled herself up and put her robe over her pajamas. She wandered downstairs and opened the door to the one room she hadn't brought herself to enter since her return to Aspen Hills. Michael's study.

Flipping on the power, she surveyed the room. His large oak desk was cluttered with boxes and piles of books that graduate students had brought over under the economic department's chair, Professor Ngu's, watchful eye. She'd thanked Michael's colleague for his hard work, offered them drinks, and then closed the door to the office. Cat hadn't known what she'd planned to do with anything in there, but she'd hoped the memories and the door would remain closed. At least until she'd dealt with her conflicting feelings about the loss.

As she stood there, memories filled her. Better times at the beginning of their life together when he'd work at the big desk and she'd sit, curled up, in one of his wingback chairs, reading until he had finished. Then they'd go upstairs and make love. After a year, he'd moved his after-dinner work period to his campus office, claiming he needed the close access to the library. She had offered to walk with him so they could continue their time together, but he'd refused. Cat started going to bed alone, and after a few months Michael stopped even coming home for dinner.

The night she'd asked him for a divorce, she'd made up a picnic dinner of homemade chicken, coleslaw, and apple pie. She'd added a bottle of his favorite wine to the basket and driven to campus. The night should have been romantic, but instead, it had turned disasterous. Opening his office door, she'd surprised him and his latest against his desk. She'd set down the basket and stared at her husband. Her voice was unwavering when she said, "You should lock the door."

She'd found the motel receipts on his desk when she'd arrived home.

When he'd finally shown up hours later, she had listened to his apology and pleas for forgiveness. Then she'd told him she'd be seeing an attorney in the morning and she would sleep in the guest room near her office. She'd already moved some of her clothes from their room before he'd arrived.

Now, she stood in his study and wondered about

the man who had everything and kept wanting more. She opened the first box she came to, lifting out the books and stacking them near the bookshelf. She'd go through them later and set aside the ones to offer the library.

She'd finished emptying three boxes when she heard a sound. Looking up, she saw Billy Williams in the doorway, leaning against the doorjamb. He glanced at his watch. "You should be asleep. I hope you didn't stay up to wait for me to return."

Cat studied his face. He did look beat up. His left cheek sported a bandage and his right eye appeared to be on its way to a nice shiner. "Couldn't sleep. You're not having a restful retreat."

He snorted. "I've been in the back seat of your uncle's squad car too many times for my liking. But what's the saying? What doesn't kill a writer goes into his next book? I've got tons of first-hand experience with police types to make my thriller more authentic now."

She pushed her bangs out of her eyes. "Most writers do research on things like interrogations and police procedure. It's easier than really being a person of interest in a murder or a victim in an attack."

He held up his hands, a wide grin filling his face. "Totally was not on my to-do list for the week. But it's been an opportunity."

"We aim to please." Cat looked around the room. She'd only touched about half of the boxes stacked on one side of the wall. This was going to take more than just a few hours.

"What's going on in here? I thought your office was on the third floor in the castle room." He picked up a book. "*Modern Economic Theory of Emerging*

Nations? Doesn't seem like your typical bedtime read."

"My ex-husband was an economics professor at Covington. This is his study and the boxes are from his campus office." She wasn't sure why she was explaining this part of her life to the man, but now that she'd stopped organizing, she realized she was dead tired. This time when she hit the mattress, she'd go to sleep. She stood up and dusted the front of her jeans. "I'm going to turn in. Have a nice night."

Billy waited for her to walk past him. He stepped back as she reached the doorway, pulling the door shut behind her. "I'm grabbing a soda and a few cookies from the kitchen, then I'm writing for a couple hours. This story is begging to be put on paper."

She'd checked the front door before walking upstairs. Billy, true to his word, had grabbed a soda and a handful of Shauna's oatmeal chocolate chip cookies and was already on the second floor before she took her first step up to her own room. Her own manuscript would have to wait until next week when the house was clear and she could think about something besides Michael, Tom Cook, and the people who currently shared a roof with her.

Tonight, all she wanted to do was sleep. She hoped her mind would leave her alone and keep the nightmares away.

Her internal alarm went off at five Friday morning, and she groaned as she rolled out of bed. A ten-minute shower later, she almost felt awake. She stumbled into her office and booted up her computer. On the desk was a carafe of coffee and a still-warm muffin. Shauna had left a note with the tray: *Write, I've got the crew handled.*

Whispering a quick prayer of thanks, she broke open the blueberry muffin and smeared butter on it. She checked her email for any important messages, but realized she was stalling. She finished her muffin and switched over to the Word document that held her current manuscript. Within a few paragraphs, she was lost in the high-school world. She'd just helped her heroine buy a prom dress when a knock sounded at her door.

"Come in," Cat called, assuming it was Shauna. She didn't turn as she heard the door squeak open. "I'm happy you're here. I could use a refill on the coffee."

"I'll be glad to get you some more," Seth answered, causing Cat's fingers to freeze on the keyboard. She took her attention from the scene she'd been writing and slowly turned toward the door. He walked over and grabbed the carafe, filling her cup with the last few drops.

"Wait, I didn't know it was you. I can get my own coffee." She stretched her neck. "What are you doing here?"

"Working." He glanced at the screen. "That another teenage witch book?"

"Third in the series. And last one on my contract. If I miss deadline next month, it might be my last book." She rubbed her face. "And I don't have a thriving retreat business to fall back on."

"Yet." Seth added to her statement.

"What are you talking about?" Her brain was still working through the fictional scene. Talking to real people while she was in this state never turned out well.

"You said you don't have a thriving retreat business. I just added one word: You don't have one *yet*. I think this is a great idea. You'll do fine. Shauna says bookings are up this week." He leaned on the table where her tray sat.

"You and Shauna talk a lot about me and my business." Cat felt a little put out by his statement. But was it because he was getting into her business or because he spent a lot of time talking to her partner?

"Your business? I swear she thinks you two are partners." His mouth curved into a grin and he took in her ratty jean shorts and a tank top. "I like the Daisy Dukes by the way."

She reached down to her legs and tried to pull the shorts down a little. "Give me a break. It can get hot up here. Remember, you were going to get me bids on a new air system for the upper floors."

"Already in the works. Hank will be over next week to do an estimate." He cocked his head. "But if that's what you wear when you're hot, maybe I'll call him to come after the temperature drops. I'm enjoying the view."

"And I'm busy working. What do you want?" Time to get off this line of conversation before she told him how she liked the way he wore his jeans tight to show off his still-fine butt. Her gaze drifted down his body, but when she realized where her attention was going she blinked and made eye contact. Too late. Seth had noticed and the jerk was laughing.

"Working, huh?" He set a key on her desk and slid it her way. "I'll let you get back to it, but I wanted to tell you I got a new lock on the cellar door. I gave one key to Shauna and here's another. I'll keep the third until we're done with renovations, just in case."

Cat thought about the damage to Linda's room. Someone really didn't like the woman, but why? The only person who came to mind was Rose, but even she'd expressed her empathy over the woman's loss of her husband. She remembered the conversation with Sara; that had been more than odd. Something else was going on, but Cat was damned if she was going to let anything else happen in her house. Especially to rooms she'd painstakingly decorated for her guests to enjoy.

She noticed Seth watching her. "Do you think someone came through the cellar?"

He ran a hand over his hair. "There's a lot of dust on the floor down there that doesn't look like it has been disturbed in years. So, no, I don't think someone used the cellar door as access. Neither does your uncle."

"I know. He told me his theory. I just can't believe any of my guests would hate Linda that much."

"Find the answer to that question and you'll find your vandal." Seth didn't verbalize the rest, but she knew he was thinking the same thing as she was: and the murderer. He tossed the empty carafe in the air. "I'll be right back with your coffee. Then I'm heading upstairs to the attic. Those built-in bookshelves are giving me grief. Old houses are never level."

She watched him leave her office and wondered, not for the first time, what the heck she'd done moving back home. Too many memories surrounded her here. Like last night going through Michael's boxes, she'd shed tears over a marriage that had been long dead before the judge signed the divorce papers.

Now she had Seth back in her life or at least in her house causing all kinds of carnal thoughts to run through her mind. She'd had fun last night, right up to the time that Billy and Amy had confronted her. Then she'd come home to more drama.

She turned back to her monitor. Drama belonged on the pages of her story, not in her life.

Shauna brought up the coffee with a plate of still-warm shortbread cookies. "How's the writing going?"

Cat hit save before she turned around. "Good. I'm convinced that working every day is the secret to a book that holds together. I don't have to refresh myself when I come back. I might have to schedule my own writing time even on weeks we're doing the retreat."

"I can handle the group, especially around break-fast time. You just tell me when you want to write and we'll get through it." Shauna nodded to the cookies. "Tell me if you like those. I found the recipe online last night after I went to my room."

"You took the laptop with you?" Cat smiled, knowing her friend hadn't wanted to use the computer any more than she had to for work.

"Stop teasing. I'm learning." She pointed to the ceiling where hammering had started. "Seth was already here and had already started a pot of coffee when I got down to the kitchen. The boy is a hard worker, I'll give him that."

"I think he's becoming too comfortable around here. We won't be able to get rid of him once the project is done."

Shauna started walking out of the office and

paused at the door, staring at Cat. "Are you sure you want to?"

She didn't wait for an answer, but Cat wasn't sure she had one to give anyway.

When Cat turned off her computer a few hours later, happy with her progress, she ate the last cookie and grabbed her dirty dishes to take downstairs. At least with all the stair climbing, she hadn't felt the effects of Shauna's baking. Yet. There was that word again. She promised herself she would check into a local gym next week or at least schedule a hike up Sugar Hill a couple times a week. That should get her started on her way to increasing her metabolism and maybe even toning a bit. The hiking paths that wound around and up Sugar Hill had been claimed by the city a few years ago and now were marked and kept in good shape for local enthusiasts. Besides, in a few weeks, the first snow would coat the town and she'd have to resort to a gym treadmill.

A delivery guy stood at the counter with a vase full of red roses. He set them down as she maneuvered the last few stairs. "Sorry, has anyone helped you?"

"No need for a signature, we just like to know our flowers are delivered to the right place before leaving." The guy looked at his clipboard. "Is there a Linda Cook here?"

"She's one of our guests." Cat set the dishes on the sideboard and wiped her hands on her shorts. "There must be two dozen here."

"Three. The owner had to call in a loan from a

shop in the next town. No one orders three dozen red roses." The guy grinned. "I don't know what he did to get into this much trouble, but boy, he's pulling out all the stops to get out of the doghouse."

Cat watched as he left the lobby and jogged to his mini delivery van, an ASPEN HILL'S FLORAL decal on the side. She glanced around, reaching for the card as she checked for interruptions. She opened the envelope, and read aloud, "Thanks for a lovely evening. L."

Where had Linda said she'd been when her room was vandalized? Out with L, having a lovely evening with her husband not even released from the morgue to be buried? People were strange. She still had the envelope in her hand when Linda entered the front door of the lobby. Her blond hair was plastered to her head with sweat and she had on running clothes that, with the brand-name shoes, probably cost more than Cat's first car.

Linda wiped her forehead with the white towel draped over her neck and walked up to the counter. "Nothing's better for a hangover than a long run." She fingered one of the roses, petting it like a cat. "I love red roses. Tom used to send me a dozen on the first of the month. He said that if he didn't then, he'd get caught up with his writing and forget to tell me how much he loved me."

"That's sweet." Cat handed the envelope over to her. "I was checking who they were for, and guess what, it's you."

Linda frowned. "Tom couldn't have known I was coming here. And why so many? He always just sent a dozen."

"Maybe the card explains." Cat shrugged as Linda looked up at her.

Linda smiled and pulled the card out of the envelope. She read the endearment and her smile disappeared. "I knew I was making a mistake." She tore the card in half and handed Cat the pieces. "Throw that away for me and you can take the flowers. Maybe those women from your retreat would like them to brighten their room."

"You don't want them?" Cat glanced at the vase. "They are beautiful and probably cost a lot of money."

"I don't want them," Linda repeated. "I'm going upstairs to shower and then I'm going to the police station to see when I can get Tom's body released to the mortuary. I need to get out of this town."

Cat put the ripped card into the drawer in the lobby desk and grabbed the flower vase with one hand and the dirty dishes with another. If she walked slowly, she might just reach the sink before either hand gave up their treasure.

She pushed the door to the kitchen with her butt and almost ran right into Shauna. She reached out and grabbed the dishes that were wobbling with the sudden stop.

"Wow, those are gorgeous. Seth must be determined." Shauna walked over to the sink and set the dishes down.

Cat went to the table and set down the vase. "Not Seth. Some guy named 'L.'"

"You're seeing someone with an initial instead of a first name? When did this happen?" Shauna slipped into a chair and patted the table. "Sit down and fill me in. You've been keeping secrets."

"And apparently I can be in two places at the same

time," Cat added dryly. "The flowers aren't for me. They are, well were, for Linda. She wants us to put them into Rose and Daisy's room as an inn decoration. She ripped up the card."

"Well, he wasted a bunch of money then. It's never good when the recipient gives away something this lovely." Shauna pulled three of the roses out of the bundle and took them to the sink. She opened the lower cabinet and took out a crystal stem vase. Cutting the stems so the roses were at three different levels, she tucked them into the vase and added water. She set the vase on the middle of the table. "If they're for decoration, we should make good use of the beauty."

"The card said the flowers were from 'L'. I think it's Dean Vargas." Cat remembered Tom's story. Maybe they were rivals for more than just top dog in the department.

"I don't think that man has an ounce of the romantic in him. From what I hear through the grapevine, he's more interested in notches on his bed frame than wooing someone his own age. I swear those old guys give me the creeps. Who wants a guy who has to take Viagra to keep it up?"

"Eeww. I didn't need that visual." Cat grinned at her friend.

Shauna shrugged. "Seriously, I had a ton of old guys at the bar who kept offering me the moon to run away with them. I could have been a trophy wife if I'd picked the right one."

"You'd be living the life of luxury instead of working in a little town in Colorado." Cat shrugged. "I bet if you started skiing over at Vail or Breckenridge, you might find a new sugar daddy."

"Nope. When I decide to commit to someone it's going to be all about love. Of course, that means I'll probably find the ski bum who can't hold a job once the season starts and fall head over heels with him." She looked around the kitchen. "Living and working here at the retreat is sounding better and better."

"Good, because I don't know what I'd do if you decided to take off and marry Mr. Right." Cat picked the vase up. "Are the ladies writing over at the college?"

"Yep. They left just after breakfast with that Sara girl. Billy's still locked in his room. I knocked and offered him some coffee and it was like feeding lions at the zoo. I thought I was going to lose my hand."

"He's in the zone. Writers get that way when the story's talking to them." She stepped toward the door. "I'm only like that when I'm rounding the bend to the last few chapters. Those puppies always write faster for some reason."

"Don't fool yourself. I've seen that look at the beginning, middle, and end of the book. Face it, writers are nuts." Shauna booted up her laptop. "I need a new treat for this afternoon. Maybe something with apples? I bought a box over at the farmers' market this morning."

"I can feel the waistband of my jeans tightening already. I think I'll put these in the sisters' room. They should enjoy them." Cat took the steps up to the second floor landing and, using her universal key card, unlocked the door to the sisters' room. Shauna had already provided the housekeeping service they offered, including clean towels for the en suite bath, and the twin beds were made and pillows fluffed. She walked over to the window where a small table was set up with two chairs, giving the guests a place to write. She moved a laptop over and put the flowers on the table near the windows. A sound drew her attention to the sidewalk below. Seth was cutting wood in the backyard, his shirt off and his tanned skin shining with a sheen of sweat.

Her heart flipped and warmth filled her body at the sight. The guy had always been able to get to her. She really needed to get a handle on what they were together. Were they dating again? Was it a sexual attraction? Friends with benefits, maybe? Or did she have one more chance to get it right with her soul mate. He'd always laughed at the idea when they'd talk late at night under the stars. Soul mates were for romance stories and movies. Relationships took work; no one fell in love at first sight.

Except she had. Twice.

Chapter 13

Cat tied her walking shoes. She stopped at the kitchen door on her way out. "Hey, I'm taking a walk to clear my head. I'll be back in about an hour. You going to be okay alone?"

"Not alone," said Shauna. "Seth's working upstairs. Do you want me to make you some lunch before you leave? You didn't have much of a breakfast." Shauna went to the fridge and opened the door, taking out a bottle of water and handing it to Cat. "I could make up a chicken salad really fast."

"I'm not hungry. Besides, I'm stopping by the library on the way back. If I'm starving, I'll go to the diner before I come home." She took the bottle and put it in her backpack.

"Craving French fries?"

Cat nodded. "And a fish sandwich. I've been eating too clean with you doing all the cooking. I don't have any fat building up in my arteries."

"You wouldn't say that if you saw how much butter I used in those cookies you ate this morning."

Shauna waved her away. "Fine, go eat with the masses. I won't get my feelings hurt."

"Your cooking is better than anyone's in town. I'm just anxious and want to wander around a bit." Something about Rose and Daisy's room had seemed off, like one of those picture puzzles where you had to find the item that didn't belong. She'd stood in the open doorway for more than five minutes, just looking at the room. It looked perfect, but for some reason, something nagged at her. She turned and instead of exiting from the kitchen door where she might run into Seth, she headed to the front. She called back to Shauna who now stood in her place in the doorway. "See you soon."

Shauna didn't respond. Instead, she lifted her arm and pointed forward. Cat turned and ran directly into Seth's broad chest. As she tried to right herself, the smell of his shower gel filled her senses. Strong hands pulled her upright, and she found herself face to face with the man she'd been trying to avoid. "Where are you running off to?" His mouth tweaked into a crooked grin.

"For a walk." She shrugged. It wasn't his business and she really hadn't been trying to avoid him, had she? Of course, she suspected that both of them knew she had.

"Sugar Hill? They've done some work on the trails up there. It's popular with all the tourists now." Seth looked over her head at Shauna. "You should take a hike there sometime. Cat and I used to party at the parking lot with our high-school gang. Of course, they frown on that kind of behavior from the kids now."

"Sounds like lovers' lane back home." Shauna giggled. "Are you going to refresh some memories, Cat?"

"I'm going for a freaking walk, that's all." Now she knew she was going to stop and get something fried and fat-filled from the diner, just to calm her nerves. She shrugged out of Seth's grasp and stomped to the front door, knowing she was overreacting.

The October air still felt warm. The temperature was either a promise or a warning of the cold weather to come, depending on your viewpoint. She had loved the tepid temperatures year-round in California, but honestly, she missed the changing of the seasons. As she walked down the street, fallen leaves crunched under her feet, the dry oak smell somehow reminding her of being in Seth's arms just a few seconds ago. She'd have a sit down heart-to-heart with the boy sooner than later. She needed to know where they stood and make a decision on what she actually wanted. This time, she wouldn't make decisions based solely on emotion.

At the corner, Mrs. Rice waved. The neighbor was busy setting up a full-size fall extravaganza on her wide front porch. Four bales of straw sat around the area for seating and now she was binding together dried corn stalks. Pumpkins and gourds of all sizes were out on the lawn, waiting to be placed in just the perfect spot. Cat waved back and paused at the edge of the sidewalk. "Looking good."

"I love decorating for fall," Mrs. Rice called back. "I think I might have bought too many pumpkins, though. Do you want some? I got them at the farmers' market out near the high school."

"I'm sure Shauna would love some. She's been talking about trying out some new pie recipes." She nodded toward the college. "I'm running some errands, but if you want to leave a couple out on the yard, I'll grab them on my way home."

"Maybe your nice young man would come help you carry them." Mrs. Rice arranged a corn shock against the blue siding on her house. "It's so nice to see the two of you courting again."

"We're not . . ." Cat started, but just then her neighbor's cell rang. Mrs. Rice pulled her phone out of a pocket on her jacket and smiled as she read the display.

"Sorry, I've got to take this." She walked back into the house but not before Cat heard the beginning of the conversation. "Mable, you won't believe who I was just talking to. Cat Latimer. We were right about her and Seth . . ."

Cat stood rooted to the sidewalk staring at the now closed front door. Small-town gossip. If she didn't put a stop to it, she and Seth would be engaged and ready to elope even before their third date. Or their second third date. She ran her hand through her short hair and started powerwalking toward Sugar Hill.

Ten minutes later, she stood in the lower parking lot. Seth had been right; the city had done a lot of improvements on the place where they used to sit on tailgates and drink beer. The dirt lot was paved. On the lot's edge, a forest service outhouse had an asphalt walkway leading to it and a water fountain. A large sign near the trailhead marked off the official trails and distances. Pet owners were warned to keep their dogs on leashes and to clean up after them. The area had turned from a few dirt trails leading up to the mountain view overlook to this park.

Cat wasn't sure the progress made the area better. She grudgingly admitted it made the trails more accessible. She checked the trail map, reacquainting herself to her destination, taking her water from her backpack. After taking a couple of big drinks, she tightly recapped the bottle and slipped it back in her pack. Finally settled, she headed up the mountain.

It took her twenty minutes to find the place she'd remembered. As she sat on a rock, watching the eagles float above the mountain canyon, she finished her water. A sense of calm flowed through her and she closed her eyes, listening to the bird calls. Soon, she heard the whistle of wind through the trees and when that stilled, she thought she could hear the creek splashing through the narrow canyon on her left.

She took a deep breath and opened her eyes, letting her senses take in the beauty of the place. "I missed this." She hadn't meant to say it aloud, but now that she had, she realized it was true. She had loved sitting on the beach, watching the waves crash onto the sand. The beach had revived her in the same way this spot did. Then she had to drive back into town and fight the large number of people who seemed to be everywhere, enjoying the sunny California lifestyle. Here on the mountain, it was just her. And the birds. And probably a few animals. Bear, deer, and elk were hunted in this part of the forest, but she'd never run into any while hiking. She assumed they heard her and hid before she even had a clue that the animal was there.

Sated, she made a promise to come up here at least once a week before the winter weather closed down the trails or made them accessible only by snowshoe. She wondered if Michael had kept the snowshoes they'd bought their first winter together. She'd have to go digging in the basement. Now that she'd opened his study and started revisiting their life together, she might as well make herself at home.

She tucked her empty water bottle into her pack and made her way down the mountain. As she got closer, she heard loud, angry voices coming from the parking area. She stopped, wondering who else was out on a Friday afternoon. She could only tell it was a man and a woman. Or at least one couple. During high school, this area was also a great spot for breaking up since no one could overhear the fight. Especially in the middle of the day. She paused, hesitant to break into someone's personal business, but there wasn't a way off the mountain without following the trail through the parking area. The voices quieted and Cat decided that the major part of the fight must be over. She heard a car leave and she walked toward the lot.

Her stomach growled, reminding her of her missed lunch. She turned the corner and heard the engine of another car start up. As she broke through the tree line into the clearing, she got a glimpse of the driver as he pulled out of the lot.

The little red convertible MGB was familiar on campus, as was the driver, Dean Vargas.

By the time she'd walked back into town, she'd had a lot of time to think about who could have been the woman fighting with Dean Vargas. She'd been too far away to distinguish much about the voice, except she knew the other party had been female and clearly not happy with the discussion.

Walking into the restaurant, she had her choice of tables as she'd missed the lunch rush and it was way too early for even the older, early-bird diners. The older crowd, like Mrs. Rice and her best friend, Mable, liked to visit over their evening meals and apparently were spreading the latest gossip about her and Seth's possible relationship.

A woman in her early twenties took her order, and Cat wondered if the piercing-studded waitress was a townie or if she was a student, working her way to her bachelor's degree. The town kids tended to leave after high school, some for Denver to attend a cheaper, state facility, some to work either in the national parks or in the local factories. Many of the guys in her class had signed up for the military, believing the television ad copy about seeing the world. After moving away and now back, Cat realized that maybe Aspen Hills was all the world she really wanted to see.

Her food came quickly, and she opened her journal and started writing about her day. She'd kept a journal since she'd been a kid. Of course, back then it had been a diary and had been filled with her hopes and dreams about her future. As she grew, the entries became a study of her and Seth and the happy couple they would be, once they were married. She'd read the journals while researching for her current series, wanting to get back into her high-school mindset, and had been shocked at the amount of happiness she'd poured into the pages.

Angst had not been part of her personal high school experience, and she had to use her own experience as that of a secondary character in the book, a best friend for her heroine to want to model, even though her life as a teenage witch had been filled with conflict and heartbreak.

She wrote about her writing time, making notes on what she wanted to accomplish with her next writing session. When she started writing about today's outing, her mind kept returning to Seth and his easy smile. But she avoided waxing poetically about the man and, instead, wrote about the nature she'd found during her walk. She was just about to record the fight scene when a voice interrupted her thoughts.

"Why are you here eating when you could be having one of those lovely sandwiches your chef makes? I swear, I'm going to try to steal her away from you when I leave to return to New York." Linda Cook stood to her right, reading over her shoulder. "You were out at Sugar Hill today?"

When Cat nodded and closed her journal, Linda didn't seem to notice. "I loved that place. Tom used to take me out there every Friday after classes were over. We'd drink a six-pack, talk about our future together, and, well, you know."

The smile on her face didn't match the sadness in her eyes or in her voice. The woman had loved her husband, that was certain. Linda sank into the chair across from Cat. After ordering a cup of tea from the waitress, she took in the room. "We had such wonderful times here. Larry, Tom, and I were inseparable until senior year. Then we all just grew apart."

"Because you and Tom were serious?" The question popped out before Cat could soften it.

"Maybe." Linda shrugged and took her tea from the waitress. "Honestly, I don't think we were serious until after graduation. We were all so focused on our future and the writing, it kind of consumed us."

"I studied at Covington, too. After I completed my master's, they offered me a teaching spot. Of course, that could have been because they didn't want to lose my ex-husband from the faculty." Cat tapped the cover of her journal with a pen. "I'd like to think it was my outstanding thesis on the romance of Edgar Allan Poe and the rise of the dark, angsty hero."

Linda laughed, a clear, happy sound. "Mine was worse. I did a summary of the role of supporting female characters in thrillers and the effect of women's liberation over the years."

"So what was the effect?" Cat loved philosophical discussions, which was why she had enjoyed teaching. The rest of the job had drained her.

"There was none. I had one of the stats students run the numbers through a program, and women didn't make any gains in the literary world, at least as a sidekick in that particular genre." She stood and put a five-dollar bill on the table. "You were writing. I don't want to bother you with my ramblings. Besides, I was on the way to the police station. They want an official report on what happened to my room. Seriously, I'm spending way too much time in the company of your uncle. People are going to start to talk."

"I'm sure they understand it's about the investigation."

Linda put her hand on Cat's shoulder. "My dear, the moment I became a widow, I became the highlight of any scandal. Everything I do is under some nosy biddy's watchful eye."

Cat watched Linda stroll out of the diner. Hadn't she felt the same way when she and Michael divorced? Even living in another state hadn't alleviated the unease she'd felt eating alone that first year. And walking into a bar? She'd felt like she wore a sign declaring she was looking for a good time, when actually what she really wanted was adult conversation about something besides literature or grades.

Something Linda had said was nagging at her. What had happened between junior and senior year to cause the trio to break up? She tucked her journal away into her pack and finished her lunch. Determined, she paid her check and started walking toward campus. She knew just where she might find her answers.

The fifth floor of the library housed campus history. Old literary journals from the campus press lined the first few shelves, but Cat didn't stop there. Instead, she weaved her way through the dusty stacks until the light from the windows dimmed. Turning a corner, she found what she'd been looking for: old yearbooks. During her own undergrad experience, the yearbook had been more a photo list of her classmates with staged shots of the on-campus clubs and award winners. The teachers had their own section, and Michael always loved what he'd called picture day. He'd dress up in a powder blue shirt, get his hair cut the week before, and once, she'd caught him whitening his teeth with a home preparation. When she teased him about being worse than a teenage girl, he'd pulled her close and whispered in her ear. "I'll only be this age once. But in the yearbooks, I can be young forever."

She passed by the more recent editions, running her hand over the bound volumes. She could almost feel Michael's arms around her as she moved into the earlier years. When had Linda and Tom graduated? 1969?

She took all of the '60s and the first five years of the '70s and set them on a library table on a window-less side wall. A yellowing overhead lamp made the area too dim to see much, but on the table was a read-ing lamp. She pulled the chain and the lamp cast a bright circle of light on the surface. Opening the first book, she searched for Tom Cook and Larry Vargas in the class pictures. She'd gone through seven books before she found Tom's freshman photo. He'd been a looker, even then, but the most arresting feature had been those piercing eyes. Even in this old photo, you could feel his intensity. She quickly found the next four yearbooks and opened them to the class picture and set the other books on the table out of the way next to her.

She opened her journal and put a pen between the covers to mark her place on the blank page. Then she scanned through all the female photos, stopping at each Linda before she found the right one. Linda's hair was all puffed up in one of those bumps at the back, and cat eye glasses framed her eyes. Linda White. She wrote the three names in her book and under each one, the clubs they were members of. There were three listed under each name. The Liter-ary Journal, the Poetry Club, and Campus Demo-crats. The men also had listed Wild Adventures. Cat found the pages for all the clubs, then looked for the trio. The first picture she found was a foursome. A petite blond was also in the photo, her hand on Larry's chest in most of the poses. Linda hadn't mentioned another girl.

Cat went back to the class photos to try to identify

the newcomer. It didn't take long. Gloria Jenson was her name, but she didn't have any of the same clubs. Her activities seemed to focus on cheerleading and being part of any royalty court for campus formals. Her first year she'd been a princess in no less than five courts, including homecoming. The next two years, she'd moved on to taking the queen slot. And senior year there was no picture.

She searched both the junior and senior yearbooks for any clue, but she was there, then she wasn't.

"Curious," Cat said aloud. Her cell phone buzzed, causing her to jump. She unlocked the screen saver and answered, "Yep?"

"Cat?" Shauna's voice sounded worried. "Is that you?"

Cat focused on the junior picture of Gloria. *What happened to you?* She focused on the phone call. "It's me. What's going on?"

"I was just worried when you didn't come home. You're not still out on the trail are you?"

Now Cat could hear the reproof in her friend's words. "No, I'm on campus." She glanced at the display and whistled, "Boy, I didn't realize it was that late. I'll be home in a few."

"I didn't mean to check up on you, I was just worried." Shauna continued to explain away her actions. "And the sisters have some writing questions that I told them you would be the expert to ask. I'm useless when it comes to the book stuff."

"You're not useless. Remember when I tried to make pancakes? We both have our own strengths and weaknesses." Cat looked at the books. On the front page, where there was usually a barcode, these all had the following note stamped in red. *Reference only. Do not remove from this floor.* Well, that ruined her plans to take them home. Instead, she stacked three of them neatly on the table and tucked the junior yearbook into her bag along with her notebook. If she went out the professor exit where the security system had been turned off, even if the book was tagged, she shouldn't set off an alarm when she left the building. "I'll be home in ten."

"Sounds good," Shauna answered.

Cat paused. "Hey, is Linda there?"

"She just came in and went right up to her room, why?"

Weaving her way through the stacks, Cat tucked her tote under her arm and started toward the stairs that would lead her to the back exit. "I need to find out what else she isn't telling me."

Chapter 14

Rose caught her as soon as Cat walked in the front door. "Thank God you're here." The older woman took Cat's arm and pulled her toward the living room.

"Has something happened?" Cat dropped her tote on the table in the foyer as she was half-dragged to the living room. Daisy sat at the small table near the window, her attention focused on the laptop open in front of her.

"Would you please tell Daisy that writing in third person is old school? No one writes that way anymore." Rose pushed Cat closer to the table.

Daisy didn't even look up. "She's on a first-person crusade. Saving the world of readers one aspiring author at a time."

Cat turned back toward Rose. "Actually, point of view is a writer's personal choice. A lot of books are written in both viewpoints. One isn't more modern or valid than the other."

"Told you," Daisy muttered under her breath.

Rose glared at her sister. "I'm sure I read that

in Tom Cook's writing book. Why would he say something like that if it wasn't true?"

Maybe to preach to his fan base? Cat shook off the uncharitable thought and patted Rose's hand. "I'm sure for him, there wasn't any other choice. But it doesn't mean his style of writing is any more valid than Daisy's or yours, or even mine."

Rose sank into an overstuffed chair, shaking her head. "I just don't get how a rule could just be a suggestion. Why isn't there a rulebook for people to follow? That would be so much easier."

"Easier, but not as much fun." Cat glanced upward like she could see through the flooring to Linda's room. "Look, I've got to go handle something, but I'll be back and we can talk more over hot chocolate. Would you like that?"

"Sure." Rose slunk deeper into her chair and didn't meet Cat's gaze.

"What my sister means to say is that would be very nice, thank you." Daisy's tone held an echo of humor and Cat smiled at the gentle rebuke toward Rose.

Cat started toward the foyer. "I'll be back as soon as possible." Sighing, she paused at the bottom of the staircase. Grabbing the yearbook from her tote, she marched up the stairs, wondering how she was going to ask about Gloria.

She knocked on Linda's door and it swung open after one hard knock. Linda Cook sat on the bed, looking at a framed picture of her late husband. Tears flowed down her cheeks. She must have heard the knock as she set the picture down on the bed and wiped the tears away with both hands.

A small smile curved her lips, but Cat sensed the

woman's insincerity in the greeting. Linda wanted to be alone. "Sorry to interrupt."

Linda waved her in. "Come sit by me. I'm so tired of being alone right now. It's not all fun and games as the merry widow."

Cat sat and put the yearbook on her lap so Linda could see it.

The woman took the bait. She snatched it off Cat's lap and opened it to the class pictures. "Oh my, where did you find this? I've got all our old yearbooks at home, but I haven't seen any of these here. Do they even still do yearbooks?"

Linda wasn't waiting for Cat's answers to her shot-gun questions. Cat pointed to the smiling photo of Gloria. "Do you know her?"

The look Linda gave her basically called Cat an idiot. "Of course I do. Gloria dated Larry off and on through college. Then before senior year she moved away. Or maybe just dropped out. I always wondered if Larry was just too serious for her. He was always talking about their future." Linda touched the picture. "She was so beautiful. Inside and out."

"She just disappeared?" An uncomfortable pit formed in the bottom of Cat's stomach.

Linda turned the page, lost in the memories of the past. "Her room was cleaned out and someone else was assigned to that bed. People left all the time. Covington isn't cheap. I don't believe her parents were wealthy, so maybe she lost her scholarship funding."

"Were you friends?" Something about Linda's story didn't feel right.

A cry of joy interrupted whatever answer Linda was going to give. She pointed to a group picture of four laughing students, sitting on a plaid blanket spread over the ground in the middle of the campus quad. "There we are. I can't believe I was ever that young."

Cat stared at the picture and the four people with their lives in front of them. Linda, Tom, Gloria, and Larry, just a bunch of kids on an impromptu picnic.

A noise at the door caused Cat to look up just in time to see Sara barrel through the room, her hands outstretched in claws. "I told you to leave. Now everything is ruined." The girl wailed as she put her hands around Linda's neck. "He told me we were over. I don't know if I can live without him."

Linda gurgled as Cat put her arms around Sara's waist and pulled her off into a corner of the room. She braced herself and yelled over Sara's shoulder. "Get out of here. Tell Shauna to call my uncle."

Linda rubbed her neck as she followed Cat's instructions. As she left the room, Sara began to cry.

"It's not fair. We were happy. He would have married me, just as soon as I graduated. We would have been married. Just like you and Michael were." The tension fell out of Sara's muscles as she stopped fighting and sagged against Cat.

Was that really how people saw her marriage? Yes, Michael had been a professor when they'd met, but she'd only taken one class from him. "Michael was never my professor," she said defensively to the crying pile of what had been a girl just a few hours ago. *Okay, so that wasn't quite true.* But they hadn't started dating until the next semester.

"It's just not fair," Sara curled up in a ball and continued sobbing. The smell of fruity wine filled the room. The woman must have stopped by the bar before deciding to come back to the house and confront Linda.

Cat sank down to the floor, her knees to her chest and her back against the wall as she watched Sara. There was no fight left in her. If she hadn't just tried to strangle another guest, Cat would be pouring the girl into her bed and letting her sleep off the drunk.

Footsteps sounded on the steps and a few seconds later, her uncle strode into the room. He stopped short and appraised the scene. He nodded to Sara whose sobs had started to subside. "This the trouble-maker?"

Cat pushed herself to her feet and walked over to stand near her uncle. She leaned into him for support. "That's the one. Be gentle with her; she has a broken heart."

"The end of a relationship doesn't give people carte blanche to assault others. Especially someone who's not the other party." He shrugged. "But we'll take care of her. She needs a quiet night in the drunk tank. In the morning, she'll probably have to be reminded of her misdeeds. Mrs. Cook said she didn't want to press charges, but after seeing the marks on the woman's neck, I'm not sure that's the best idea."

"He doesn't want me anymore," Sara sniffed and collapsed on the floor, a new round of sobs starting in earnest. "Why can't he love me? I'm pretty. I'm young. I'm smart."

"This is all because of a boy?" He pulled up his belt over his paunchy middle.

Sara narrowed her eyes, and if she could have she would have shot razor-sharp lasers at him. "He's not a boy." Her eyes widened a bit as she tilted her head to consider him. "Are you dating someone? I'm a great catch."

Uncle Pete shrugged. "Okay, maybe she isn't in her right mind this minute. I'll make a decision whether or not to charge her when I get her sober and talking in the morning." He walked over and pulled the girl to her feet. Putting his arm around her, he walked her out of the room. As they left, Shauna came in to the room and handed Cat a chilled bottle of beer.

"You okay?" Shauna picked up a rug and straightened it back under the end of the bed. "Linda's downstairs in the living room with the sisters and a double whiskey sour."

Cat gratefully sipped the cold liquid. It was almost half-gone before she leaned against the dresser and answered Shauna's question. "Maybe this writer retreat thing was a bad idea. All we've had this week is chaos."

"I don't think you planned to have a murder in the house your first week out." She led Cat over to the bed and lowered her down to the edge. "And then this thing with Sara. That one you have to blame on the school. They paid for her retreat. Didn't they know she was a kook?"

"I think she's a mixed-up kid who got tied up with the wrong guy." Cat finished off her bottle. She thought about the angry scene out on Sugar Hill. Had that been Sara and Dean Vargas breaking up? Uncle Pete should get that information out of Sara tomorrow once she sobered up, but Cat felt in her gut she was correct. Especially after that crack about her and Michael. She turned to her friend. "Do you think I was stupid for marrying Michael?"

Shauna shrugged. "I didn't know the guy, but I don't believe you could have done anything else at the time. Why beat yourself up over old decisions? Besides, if you hadn't married him," she raised her hands in an inclusive gesture and pointed around the room, "we wouldn't be here."

"That might just be a good thing after this week." Cat put her forearms on her knees and leaned forward. "A murder, a vandalized room, and now an attack on one of our guests. What else can go wrong this week?"

Billy stuck his head into the room. "Hey, I don't mean to intrude, but there's something burning in the kitchen."

"Oh, no. My pasta . . ." Shauna leaped up and ran out of the room.

Cat stood to follow, but Billy blocked the door. "What's going on? I heard your uncle was here again last night? And just now? Man, you've got issues here."

"Nothing important." *Nothing that I want to tell you about*, Cat said internally.

"I think you're holding out on me. I know trouble when I smell it." He tilted his head and studied her face. "Maybe you all found out who killed Tom already? In the movies, it's always the wife or her new lover."

"Nothing as exciting as that, I'm afraid." Cat pushed her hand against his shoulder and not expecting him to move out of her way, she tumbled out into the hallway. Her foot caught on the carpet and she went flying. A pair of arms caught her before she hit the hallway floor and pulled her to her feet.

"You okay?" Seth held her tightly but adrenaline

had pumped through Cat's body from the almost-fall and she could feel herself shaking.

"I wish people would stop asking me that." She took a deep breath and watched Billy leave the hallway and re-enter his room. After the door closed, she muttered, "Jerk."

"Me or him?" Now she could see humor in Seth's eyes.

"Definitely him. I don't know, I just don't like the guy." Cat shook off his hands. "I better get downstairs. Linda's drinking after the attack and Shauna's burning food. It's been a crappy Friday."

He fell in step beside her. "I don't have good news either so I better say it now so tomorrow can start fresh. There's a fake wall in the attic. I thought my initial measurements were way off so I went with the outer measurements of the house when I drew up my plans for the room. Now that I've begun destruction I can tell the measurements were spot on, but there's a wall where there shouldn't be."

Cat stopped at the stairwell and glanced upward, even though she couldn't see the attic entrance from where she stood. Her mind was racing with thoughts of Michael. "What are you saying?"

"I'm saying the project is going to take longer than I'd planned." He ran a hand through his hair. "Hell, I'm not even sure I can take the wall down. Maybe it's a retaining wall they added to bolster the structure. I need to think about this some more."

"Do you think there's a room behind the wall?" Cat was surprised how calm she sounded, even with the alarm bells going off in her head.

"There's definitely space there. Now, it might just be unfinished area, planks and rafters. Maybe the original owners only needed part of the attic, so they blocked off the other section so they wouldn't have to heat the space. This is a big house you know." Seth now looked upward too, like he could imagine the secret area. "I need to go to the courthouse and see if I can find the original building permit. It should be there."

"Or at the college. This house was built for the college as the first president's home when it opened in 1920. They sold it to a private party to keep the college open after the stock market crashed." Cat recited the information from memory. It was part of the charm when she and Michael had purchased the house.

"Either way, I'm not comfortable just swinging a sledgehammer into the wall before I figure out its purpose. So I'll be checking it out on Monday, but until then I'm kind of at a standstill with the attic project. You want me to work on something else this weekend?" Seth leaned against the wall, his smile widening. "Or we could take off and spend a day in the woods. The fall fishing is pretty amazing, but we'll have to keep our orange vests on so some novice deer hunter doesn't see us as prey."

"As charming as that sounds, especially the un-spoken part about no running water or bathrooms for the weekend, I have guests. I can't just leave in the middle of a retreat." Cat started down the stairs.

"We would have a good time." Seth lifted his body off the wall where he'd been leaning and they made their way down to the first floor. The smell of burned tomato sauce became more pungent as they came closer to the kitchen door.

Seth kissed her quickly on the lips as they reached the bottom of the stairs. "If you're sure, I'm taking off. There's a game tonight over at the high school that I said I'd attend. If I don't hurry, I'll miss the last quarter. You want to come?"

"Again," she held out her arms in the same gesture Shauna had used to indicate the house, "writer's retreat happening. I need to be here for my guests."

"A guy's got to try." He looked at the kitchen door, then walked the other way. "I'm going out the front. Whatever she killed in there smells awful."

Cat watched Seth leave. A smile came unbidden to her lips. There really could be something there after all these years. More mature, but the spark was still there between them. Not for the first time that day, she questioned her first marriage. "Water under the bridge," she muttered as she took a deep breath and plunged into the smoky kitchen.

Chapter 15

It took over an hour to get the smoke cleared out of the kitchen. While Cat and Shauna positioned another fan to blow the air out the screen door, Linda stepped into the room.

"Whoa, This reminds me of when I used to cook for Tom when we were first married. He swore I could burn boiling water. After a few months, he took over the cooking duties. His mom was Italian, so he knew how to make spaghetti. When his book took off, the first thing we did was hire a full-time chef and housekeeper. Now Helga and I will be lost in that big old house." Linda sank into a chair, watching the others use towels to move the remaining smoke out of the room.

Cat opened the fridge and grabbed another beer. She held a bottle toward Linda and Shauna, who both nodded. They joined Linda at the table and twisted off the caps.

Shauna was the first one to speak. "I'm not a counselor, but when I was bartending, I talked to a lot of people who were grieving the loss of a loved one.

All of them were told the same thing by their real counselors. You're not supposed to make any decisions for a year."

"I'm not running home, selling the house, and giving my money away to a charity, girls." Linda took a sip of the beer. "This is good. I don't think I've had a beer for years."

"Keep hanging with us and you'll be a beer connoisseur in no time." Cat took a sip of her own beer considering how to bring up the subject. "What a crazy night. Any idea why Sara would attack you?"

Linda shrugged and squirmed in her seat. She cast her gaze down at the bottle of beer and cast a sideways glace at Cat.

"You know why, don't you?" Cat sat straighter in her seat, leaning toward the other woman. "Come on, spill the beans."

"It's stupid." Linda waited for a minute but when neither Cat or Shauna spoke, she filled the silence. "Larry told me he'd been dating the girl. He claimed it had started out platonic, but one night she tempted him and he fell."

Cat snorted and Shauna laughed out loud. "Oh, the horror. I've heard this story from so many married men. They were walking down the street, fell, and their manhood accidentally entered some poor, insanely beautiful, and young girl."

Linda held up her hand. "Look, I didn't say I believed him. Larry always did have a thing for young, beautiful blondes."

"Like Gloria," Cat prompted.

Linda shook her head. "He was madly in love with that girl. When she took off that semester, he wouldn't even talk about her. He said they'd broken up that summer and he didn't care to look back."

Shauna looked perplexed between the two of them. "I thought we were talking about Sara. Who's Gloria?"

Cat explained about the fourth member of the group's college crew and that she'd disappeared. When she finished, Shauna stood up and picked up her laptop from the desk. "What's her full name?"

Linda answered and watched as Shauna keyed the name into a search engine. "Too many hits on name alone. What was her major? Maybe we can find where she is now by her profession."

"She was going into business management, if I remember right. It's been a long time," Linda mused.

"Hold on, I've got an idea." Cat left the room, and when she returned she had the yearbook. Opening the book, she flipped through the pages until she found the right one. "Here. She listed her future goal as international tax accountant."

"I didn't remember that. That's weird." Linda rubbed the bridge of her nose. "Gloria was a party girl. I never even heard her talk about her classes or being interesting in tax stuff. She did like to travel, though. She kept talking about us going to Europe the summer after senior year. In fact, when she disappeared I figured she hadn't waited to graduate and had gone without us."

Shauna stared at her screen. "Still nothing."

"Where did she grow up? Maybe we'll find something in her local newspaper, like a hometown-girl-does-good story." Cat peeled the label off her beer and took another sip.

"A small town in Iowa. Near Davenport, maybe?"

Linda rubbed her face. "Look, it's been a long day. I'm going up to my room to take a long soak." She held up the empty beer bottle. "You have another one of these I can steal?"

Cat stood and got her a fresh bottle from the fridge. "You need anything else?"

Linda rolled her shoulders. "Maybe the name of a good masseuse?" She took the bottle. "For tonight, the hot bath and this beer should do the trick. See you girls tomorrow morning."

Cat took two more bottles out of the fridge and set one in front of Shauna who was still staring at her laptop. "Dead end?"

"Not really." Shauna turned the screen around so Cat could read what was on the screen.

Cat peered at the screen, then whistled and read the front-page headline aloud: LOCAL GIRL MISSING AT COLLEGE. PARENTS PUT UP $10,000 REWARD FOR LEADS. Under the headline was the same picture of Gloria that Cat had found in the yearbook.

Neither woman spoke for a minute, then Cat said the obvious. "This isn't good at all."

A quiet knock sounded at the door and Daisy peeked her head into the room. "Oh, I'm sorry, but have you seen my sister?"

"Not since we were all three talking earlier." Cat motioned the woman into the room. "What's going on? Do you need a drink? Or a snack?"

Daisy shook her head. "I went up early to bed after we spoke. Rose said she was following as soon as she finished her chapter. When I woke a few minutes ago, she still hadn't come up."

"Did you look in the living room?" Cat stood and

took a couple steps to the door but Daisy stopped her with a hand on her arm.

"First place I looked. I figured she'd fallen asleep in one of those chairs of yours. She's always doing that. You wouldn't believe the places I catch her sleeping at home." Daisy sank into a chair. "I guess I would like a cup of tea, if it's not too much trouble."

Shauna turned the laptop screen away from Daisy and stood. "I'll just put the kettle on then. Something herbal to help you get back to sleep or full-on Earl Gray to keep you up?"

"I'd love more of that apple cinnamon we had this evening." Daisy smiled up at Shauna and for a second, Cat forgot all the bad things that had happened in the last few days. It was moments like this that she'd imagined when she decided to put together a writer's retreat. Not all the drama. Just writers, sitting around talking about life and the craft.

But that wasn't why Daisy was in her kitchen at— Cat peered at the clock—eleven-thirty. Where had the evening gone? "I'm sure Rose just went for a walk or something. Do you want me to go out and look for her?"

Daisy shook her head. "She's a grown woman. I just worry sometimes. I guess it's my curse." She peeked at the computer screen. "You researching a new book? I didn't think mysteries were your genre."

Cat looked up at Shauna who was putting a tea bag into a cup at the stove. "We were just checking out some local history."

"I always feel so sad when young girls go missing. We had a classmate who disappeared the summer after senior year. Rose always thought she took off for New York City or Las Vegas. The girl did yearn

for the big city. Thank you." Daisy accepted the cup
that Shauna brought over and started dunking her tea
bag. "I thought the worst. Tina's stepdad was a drunk
and he liked to beat up her mom."

"So you figured he decided to start beating on
Tina, too?" Cat guessed the end of the story.

"I think Tina was finally getting out of that crazy
house and he didn't want to lose her." Daisy lowered
her voice. "She told me once he would visit her bedroom at night. I told her to tell the cops, but she said
no one would believe a kid."

Everyone around the table was silent. Cat stood
and dumped out the rest of her beer in the sink and
got a soda out of the fridge.

"Get me a Coke, too." Shauna pushed her own
beer away.

When she returned to her chair, Daisy continued
with her story. "A few years after Rose and I had
graduated college and moved away, Mom told us
they'd found the girl's body in the cornfield behind
the old house. I guess the stepdad had died of a
heart attack and the mom had sold the place to a
subdivision developer."

The hum of the refrigerator was the only sound in
the room for several minutes. Daisy stood. "Well, I
can see I totally ruined the mood here. When my
sister gets back from wandering, I'll be in our room.
I bet she went down to that little convenience store
for a treat. She likes to sneak a Payday every once in
a while. Especially when she's writing."

After Daisy left the room, Shauna tapped the
laptop. "If that's what happened to Gloria, that's a
secret worth killing over."

Cat didn't answer at first, thinking over what

they'd learned. "All we know is the girl didn't come back to school and she didn't go home. Maybe she ran off to Paris or Europe like Linda suggested. I'll see if there's anything else in the library about her." Cat paused. "Maybe Uncle Pete keeps missing person's files. She could have been found since that article."

As Cat went up the stairs to her room, she couldn't help but think about the missing girl and where she might have disappeared to. She said a quick prayer for Gloria's safety, but in her heart she felt like she knew the answer to the mystery surrounding the girl's long-ago disappearance.

The next morning, Cat arrived in the breakfast room around nine, after spending three hours in her office finishing a chapter. The book was still on her mind and if the house hadn't been filled with writing retreat guests on their last full day of the session, she would have stayed locked up in her room until the characters stopped talking to her. As it was, she itched to get back to the writing, so she'd written a quick must-do list and headed downstairs to make an appearance.

The breakfast room was empty. Cat went over to the sideboard and poured coffee into her travel mug she carried around most of the morning. Then she poured a glass of orange juice and chose a banana and one of Shauna's chocolate-chocolate chip muffins.

As she sat at the table to eat, Shauna floated into the room with an empty tray. "Good morning. I was just about to bring you something. How's the writing going?"

"Great. If I stay on this path, I might just make that deadline." Cat waved a hand around the empty table. "Did everyone else sleep in?"

"Heavens, no." Shauna laughed. "Rose and Daisy left just a few minutes ago to head to the library. Billy is back in his room with a carafe of coffee and a dozen muffins. He said not to bother him for anything until he comes up for air. He's deep into his story."

"And Sara? Did you hear from Uncle Pete yet?" Cat had hoped the girl would be back in her room this morning feeling embarrassed about yesterday's outburst.

"Nothing." Shauna loaded the tray with the baskets of muffins and set it on the table next to Cat. "Linda took off early, saying she was doing a day of sight-seeing, trying to remember the good times. I worry about her. She seems to be missing her husband terribly."

"I think reality is finally setting in." Cat finished off her orange juice and took a banana nut muffin from the basket. "He traveled a lot; maybe she's used to being alone. Now, she has to deal with the fact he's never, ever coming home."

Shauna poured herself a cup of coffee and sat down next to Cat. "She told me she's heading home mid next week, if that's okay. We've never dealt with a real guest outside of the retreat schedule. I'm okay providing her breakfast, if it's okay with you for her to stay on."

Cat wiped crumbs off her mouth with a napkin.

"I think it's the least we can do. I won't be available a lot next week as I'm coming to the end of the book. I don't like stepping away from it when I'm that close."

"I'll handle the guest relations." Shauna smiled. "You just be the reclusive author. It adds to your mystique."

"Yep, that's me, the mysterious author." Cat laughed, enjoying the sweep of positive emotions that filled her. She enjoyed spending time with her friend, which was a bonus since they went into business together as well as lived in the same house.

Shauna sipped her coffee. "You going back up to work today?"

Shaking her head, Cat answered. "Not this morning. I'm walking over to talk to Uncle Pete about Sara and what happened to Gloria. Then I'm heading to the library. I want to talk to the librarian about the laptop storage. Linda still doesn't know where Tom's computer is, and I'd like to find it before she leaves next week."

"Well, don't forget you have dinner reservations at The Cafeteria with the retreat gang this evening. Seth's driving you all to the restaurant and staying around for dinner, too." Shauna stood and picked up the tray. "I figured he could take my spot since I'm busy tonight."

"What are you doing?" Cat asked Shauna's retreating figure before she got to the connecting door with the kitchen.

Shauna turned and pushed the swinging door open with her back. "Washing my hair."

Cat stepped out onto the porch to see if she needed a jacket. With the long-sleeve shirt she'd chosen to

wear that morning, she'd be fine, if not a little hot
due to the walk to the station then to the library. She
decided to take the chance and not stuff a jacket into
her backpack next to the yearbook she would sneak
back onto the shelves without anyone noticing. At
least, she hoped.

Mrs. Rice was out watering her hydrangeas and
Cat waved as she quickly walked by, hoping to escape
before her neighbor waved her down to chat. As she
passed by, Mrs. Rice pulled her cell out of her apron
with her free hand. Probably time to report to the
Aspen Hill's gossip chain on Cat's activities.

Even Shauna was playing matchmaker. Cat slowed
her pace as she examined her feelings for Seth. She'd
loved him as a kid, but did that emotion carry over as
an adult? Or had their paths taken them farther away
from each other, not closer? He had always been the
complete opposite of Michael. Where her ex had
loved talking books and walking through antique
stores with her, Seth was more at home at a sporting
event or even a hike up Sugar Hill. Feeling the tight-
ness in her calves from the hike yesterday, Cat made
a promise to herself to be more active, especially
while the weather held.

Just as soon as this retreat was over and she had
the house and her time to herself again.

She walked down the tree-lined street, enjoying
the morning air, and cleared her mind of all things
Seth and retreat business. When she was in California, she'd taken a few months of yoga classes. Even
though she never loved the poses, she enjoyed the
focus on breathing and clearing your mind during
the hour-long session. At the beginning of the class,
the teacher would ask each student to dedicate their

practice to something or someone. The first week, she focused on not hating Michael. Then as she began to heal from the process, she focused on her own development.

Today she reverted back to that practice and dedicated the walk to being clearheaded and focused. She just hoped the magic would kick in before she reached the police station.

It took two blocks of consciously thinking about nothing before she was able to focus enough on the beautiful surroundings and not on the thoughts racing through her head. As she turned down White Street, away from the college and toward town, she felt her spirits lift. Most of the tenured professors lived in this area of modest homes. But the one on the corner was huge. It was owned by the college and served as the home of the dean of the English department. And a red convertible MGB sat in front of the house in a curved driveway, parked next to a black BMW sedan. The MGB was the same car she'd seen up on Sugar Hill yesterday. As she considered what would happen if she walked up to the front door, knocked, and bluntly asked if he'd been having an affair with Sara, the door opened.

Cat hid behind a large oak growing between the road and the sidewalk. The trunk was just wide enough to hide her from the dean's sight. For a second, she felt silly. But then she heard a woman's laugh. She peeked around the tree and saw Linda Cook being helped into the car by Dean Vargas. She kept watching as he eased out onto White Street. As the car turned away from Cat, Linda caught her eye and winked some sort of silent communication.

Linda hadn't seemed upset that Cat had seen her; in fact, she had acknowledged Cat's presence.

Even her yoga training hadn't kept her thoughts from going back to when Tom, Linda, Dean Vargas, and the missing Gloria were all students at this campus. She had to find out what happened that summer between junior and senior year. That was the clue everyone was missing. And she had a bad feeling that Linda had realized the same thing and that was why the recently widowed Linda was visiting with the dean.

Hoping the woman wouldn't do anything stupid, Cat opened the door to the police station to find the reception area filled with students and officers. As she made her way to the reception desk, the smell of day-old beer and a sweet smell of marijuana filled the crowded room.

The woman at the desk was the same one who she'd met before. "Katie, you're busy today. You have a two-for-one sale on arrests?"

The woman fish-eyed the room. "Frat party hazing gone bad. We've got one freshmen in the hospital and the other puking his guts out in the drunk tank."

Cat followed her gaze. "Are all of these kids under arrest?"

"Nope, here for questioning. Your uncle hopes to put the fear of God or at least the local cops in a few of them and to find out who bought the beer and the pot for the party. That guy's in big trouble." Katie shook her head and returned her gaze to Cat. "But you are probably here to see your uncle. I'm afraid he's in the interrogation room with a suspect."

"Actually, I came by to see if I could walk Sara

back to the house. I'd like to talk to her about what happened yesterday."

"Sara Laine?"

Cat nodded. "Yeah, there was a brush-up between two of our guests, and since Sara was a little drunk and a lot in the wrong, Uncle Pete brought her in to sober up."

Katie leaned forward and checked who was standing in earshot. Then she whispered, "You didn't hear this from me, but she's being questioned about Tom Cook's murder."

Chapter 16

Cat left a message for Uncle Pete to call her. According to Katie, some of Tom's belongings had been found in Sara's dorm room, and as she left Cat had to wonder if the missing laptop had been recovered.

She paused at the corner of White and Warm Springs, staring at the dean's house for a few minutes. No way could Sara have killed Tom. Unless . . . Tom was the older man the girl had been dating and not Dean Vargas. Cat had assumed when Sara had compared her marriage to her own situation that Sara had been seeing a professor. But maybe it was just the difference in her and Michael's ages. She *had* hit on Uncle Pete as he dragged her out of the house.

Cat had been surprised when Tom Cook had signed up for her writer's retreat. Maybe he'd been seeing Sara for a while and they'd used the retreat as an excuse to get together. Not liking the idea, but admitting the possibility, Cat left her spot leaning against the large oak in front of the Vargas home before someone called the station and reported her as a stalker.

"I might as well go talk to the librarian, just in case Uncle Pete didn't find the laptop," she muttered to herself, looking at her watch. It was only eleven and she had time to get one chore off her list and still be back at the keyboard long before she needed to start getting ready for the group dinner. Of course, the guests were dropping out one by one. With that morbid thought, she headed for campus.

When she checked at the front desk, she was told that Miss Applebome was up at the laptop storage area. Cat took the stairs and thought about heading straight to the college history stacks to get rid of the book, but the girl at the desk had warned her that the head librarian only had ten more minutes on her shift. "And she never works late on Saturday," the girl whispered.

As Cat approached the desk, the librarian looked up from a large ledger where she'd been making notes. "Can I help you, Miss Latimer?"

Cat sat in the chair next to the desk and took out a notebook and a pen from her backpack. She tucked the tote under the chair and opened her pad. "I wanted to ask you a few questions about Monday. Do you remember Tom Cook coming into the study area?"

The woman's gray eyebrows raised and she peered over a pair of silver glasses at Cat without answering. Leaning back, she slipped the glasses off her face, letting them dangle from a silver chain around her neck. "I'm old, Miss Latimer, not senile. Of course I remember Mr. Cook arriving. He's one of our most famous alumni. He's always sending signed copies of his books for the library."

"I didn't mean to imply," Cat started, but the woman waved her off.

"Just ask me what you want to know. I'm trying to close the books for the week and I don't want to work overtime. I have a show that comes on at one." Miss Applebome set her pen down on the desk surface with a sigh.

"Did he have his laptop when he came in?" Cat thought it didn't hurt to double-check Rose's story; besides, the woman was so enamored with the now-deceased author, who knew what she really remembered, except talking to her idol.

"Most writers do." The librarian eyed Cat thoughtfully. "Don't tell me you write longhand. I wouldn't think you could plot as tightly as you do without using some type of word processing program."

"You're right, I draft on a computer." She leaned forward, trying to process the fact the librarian had even read her book. "Tom's laptop is gone, and I'm trying to find out where it was last seen."

Again the woman paused before speaking. "Isn't that your uncle's job? Or someone on his police force? Why are you asking these questions when the police haven't?"

Cat decided to go with the most obvious answer: a lie. "The insurance company will raise my rates if I get a claim filed stating we lost Tom's computer. I'm already worried about the vandalism Sara caused at the house. I can't take any higher costs."

Miss Applebome must have found the answer plausible because this time she answered the question. "Yes, he came in with a laptop. A Mac, I believe.

I don't own one; lord knows with my salary I can't afford much of a machine. Then after Dean Vargas showed up, Mr. Cook rented a locker before he left with the dean."

"Wait, he left the library with Dean Vargas?" Cat stopped taking notes and stared at the woman.

Miss Applebome shrugged. "Those two were thick as thieves when they attended classes here. I always wondered what broke their friendship."

"You were working here when they were in college?" Cat knew the woman had been at the library forever, but she hadn't considered she might have been working when the trio was going to school here.

She looked thoughtful as she responded to Cat's question. "I was hired after graduation the year before. Mostly I restacked and set up books with a checkout cardholder and put them in the card catalog. Library work wasn't computerized back then. I think I touched every book that we brought into the library for over ten years."

"Did you hear what they were talking about?" Cat had to get the librarian off the trip down memory lane and back on Tom Cook and Dean Vargas.

The faraway look disappeared and the woman picked up her pen and wrote something in the journal.

"Miss Applebome? Did you hear what they were saying?" Cat pressed.

"It would have been hard not to. They were yelling. I didn't interrupt because they were the only people in the area, but the names they called each other. I swear, you wouldn't know they'd ever liked each other." Miss Applebome twisted the chain above her glasses, causing them to spin. "Especially when Mr. Cook said he was writing the"—she paused, leaned forward then lowered her voice—"damn book, and Dean Vargas could go screw himself if he didn't like it."

"Did he say what the book was about?" Cat wondered who had been right about the subject of the work, Rose or Linda.

"Nope. I think I must have dropped something because they realized I was over at the desk. Mr. Cook apologized for his language and then gave me his laptop and a five-dollar bill. Then without even signing the contract, he took Dean Vargas's arm and led him toward the stairs. I tried to give him his change back when he came for the laptop later that afternoon, but he told me to put it into the library fund and buy his next book."

Cat had a lot to think about, but she wanted to ask one more question while she had the woman's attention. "Did anyone mention Gloria?"

"Oh, my, that's a name I haven't heard for years. You are talking about Gloria Jenson, right?" When Cat nodded, the woman continued. "She was such a beautiful girl. Everyone thought she'd be in the movies, sooner or later. When she just left campus, it was a sad thing."

"But Tom and Dean Vargas didn't mention her when they were fighting?"

Miss Applebome checked her watch. "Not on Monday. I heard them talking years ago, but I'm not sure I can remember what they'd said. All I knew was Larry was heartbroken. Then they all graduated, and I didn't see Tom again until this week."

Cat watched as the woman returned her glasses to her face and picked up her pen. Apparently the question-and-answer period was over. Unfortunately, it had only built more questions in Cat's mind, not fewer. She stood and put her notebook and pen in the backpack. "I'll be going now. I've got some more research to do."

"Ex-professors really aren't supposed to borrow books without checking them out, you do realize that." The woman didn't look up from her journal.

"Excuse me?" Cat's stomach twisted. How had she been found out?

With a quick jerk, the librarian took the backpack away from her. Miss Applebome pulled out the yearbook and started paging through it. "Well, it looks like it's not damaged, so I guess this can be our little secret. But from now on, please do your research in the library when you're working with priceless manuscripts like these. There's a reason we mark these as non-circulating, you know." She handed the book back to Cat. "Check out page 101, the picture on that page had always bothered me."

Then she sat back down and started writing in her journal. Cat had been dismissed.

Cat made her way up to the university history section and sat down at a table next to the yearbook rack. She opened it up to the page the librarian had mentioned, and she knew exactly the picture Miss Applebome had meant. The boy was smiling down on the girl, his hand cupped on her face, and it appeared they'd just kissed. His other hand was wrapped around the girl's waist. And in the back of the shot, standing near the bleachers, Cat saw an unsmiling Linda glaring at her boyfriend and Gloria.

* * *

On the way back to the house, Cat thought about that picture and how casual Linda had been when she'd been asked about Gloria. Did old hurts still pain her? Or was that kiss a silly flirtation? Linda had married the man after all. But, Cat amended, they were married *after* Gloria disappeared.

Cat's cell rang and she answered as she walked. "Hello?"

"Hey, kiddo. I hear I missed you at the station today. Did you want something?" Uncle Pete sounded tired.

"I was coming over to help Sara find her way back to the retreat. I wanted to make sure she was done being a WWE Diva before I let her back into the house." Cat adjusted the almost empty backpack over her shoulder. "Did you charge her?"

"Yep."

Cat's heart started pounding. Had the girl actually killed Tom Cook? "I can't believe it."

"You saw the damage. I had to charge her, or the insurance company wouldn't think you were serious. You are going to testify during the trial, right?"

"Wait, you're talking about the vandalism? What about Tom's murder?" Cat waved to Mrs. Rice as she walked by and lowered her voice to at least slow the gossip train. "Are you charging her with murder?"

"I swear I'm going to put Katie on solitary duty where she can't run her mouth. Did she tell you that Sara had been charged?" Cat heard papers shuffled on her uncle's desk. "Hold on a minute."

She heard a door slam shut and then her uncle was back on the phone. "We found some books and what appears to be notes about his first book in her room.

Talking to the library staff, we learned they were part of his personal collection in the alumni room and had been missing for weeks. She figured out some way to get them out without the alarm sounding when she left the building."

Cat pressed her lips together. She probably could tell Uncle Pete just how Sara got the papers out of the library, but she wanted to know more before she incriminated herself. "So what are you charging her with?"

"Vandalism and destruction of property. And assault, if I can get Linda to testify. That woman seemed hell-bent on giving the kid another chance."

Cat let loose a breath she'd been holding. "So Sara didn't kill Tom?"

"Let's say she has a good alibi. Apparently, she was having dinner with her mother at the diner from four to six, and then they drove out to their house near Denver so Sara could grab some books she needed. Her mom even has a list of people Sara talked to while they were at the house, to back up her story."

She sat on the front porch steps. "I'm glad she didn't. I would hate to see her have to deal with something like that the rest of her life."

"Now we just have to figure out why she's got it in for Linda. Boy, the girl hates her and I'm pretty sure they just met this week." Her uncle paused. "I dropped Michael's journal off at the house with Shauna a little while ago. I was hoping to see you there."

"You don't need it for evidence or anything?" Didn't the police typically keep things like that until the investigation was over? Then she got it; the investigation *was* over. "You didn't find anything."

"Just a few of Michael's fingerprints and a couple of yours. You both were easy to match, since the college fingerprints their employees. The weird thing was there was a big section of the book cover that had been wiped clean." Uncle Pete cleared his throat. "I don't know who's playing games with you but, sweetheart, I'll find out."

Cat felt chilled to the bone. "You don't think I'm in danger, do you?"

"Of course not." Uncle Pete's answer was too quick. "But if you're concerned, make sure you lock up good and tight and keep a close eye on those extra keys when your guests leave."

"I'll be careful. And besides," Cat smiled as she kicked a leaf off the deck, "I have you to come save the day."

"I may be the police chief, but I'm sure not your prince charming," Uncle Pete teased. "I think someone else is auditioning for that part."

"He can keep auditioning for all I care." Cat hoped her voice sounded casual.

"Keep telling yourself that. I'm sure someday you might believe it." He chuckled. Cat heard a phone ring in the background. "Look, I'm expecting a call from the DA. I need to take this."

"We'll talk later," Cat said, but then she realized she was speaking to dead air. Her uncle had already ended his side of the conversation.

"I figured you'd be up writing since your houseguests are all entertaining themselves." Seth eased down next to her and handed her a large glass filled with iced tea. "You looked thirsty."

"Thanks, I am." Cat took a long sip from the drink, letting the chill flow down her throat and cool her body. "I thought you were off researching the house."

"It's Saturday, remember? I can't get into the county records until Monday. And·there's not much in the open section of the university's history section, although I've got Miss Applebome looking for the original plans."

"She must love you. I had to beg her to answer a few questions this afternoon." Cat pressed the cold glass on her forehead to cool herself. She'd been right about one thing; she hadn't needed a jacket.

"You don't have the Howard touch." He pushed a lock of hair out of her eyes and behind her ear. He bent down close to whisper, "Women will do anything I ask."

"Some, poor pathetic women, maybe. And even then, I'd doubt it." She felt her body lean into his and she bolted upright. "Got to go write."

She heard his laugh all the way up to the second floor. Pausing on the second floor landing she glanced down the hall.

The door to the sisters' room was wide open. Cat checked her watch. If she went right up to her office, she could get another two hours of writing in before they left for dinner. Or, if she went to check on her guests, Rose and Daisy could talk her ear off and eat up all her time. "One week a month," she muttered as she headed to check out the sisters' room. "All I have to do is get through one week a month."

Bolstered by her new mantra, she paused at the open doorway. Neither of the sisters were in their room. Their laptops sat on the little writing table she'd provided for each room. Cat turned to leave and put her hand on the door to shut it after her when she froze.

Turning back around, she counted the laptops again. There was Daisy's with a crown pasted on the front with scotch tape. And Rose's had been covered with a collage of couples in various stages of undress and playfulness. Next to the window was a third, a thin black Mac. The laptop she'd seen pulled out of a leather case when its owner had shown up to write with the group.

She'd found Tom Cook's laptop. She reached into her pocket and pulled out her phone, dialing a number she knew by heart. "Uncle Pete? You need to come over here quickly."

Chapter 17

The sisters were still nowhere to be found, but Uncle Pete had the laptop on the desk in the living room and had powered it up. "It's got password protection."

Linda Cook crossed the room. "I know it." She hit a few keystrokes and the screen opened up to a picture of the couple on a yacht in the middle of some deep blue ocean. "That picture was taken last year on our trip to Fiji. Tom loved our time on that boat."

"Can you show us his latest manuscript?" Cat leaned closer. This computer could hold the secret to what really happened to Gloria. Or, as Linda surmised, it could just be Tom's last work. A story that would never be finished or read by the fans who adored his books.

Linda sat down in the desk chair and opened a few folders. After a few minutes, she shrugged. "Sorry it's taking so long. Tom liked to hide his work so I couldn't get in when he was drafting and influence the story. I only got to read when he said so."

Uncle Pete and I watched as she clicked and

double-clicked on several folders. Finally, she looked up at us and grinned. "Found it. He'd moved it from where I last read, but he used the same five folders, so it was easy to uncover." She turned the laptop so that Cat and Uncle Pete could read the screen. "White Water Regrets."

"That's what he titled the book?" Cat leaned closer, thinking about the missing Gloria. "Did you read it?"

Linda shrugged. "Just the first half. It wasn't like most of Tom's work, a coming of age theme rather than the thrillers he was known for. I'm not sure how well it would have been taken if he had finished the manuscript."

"Hey, you can't be in that. It's mine." Rose rushed into the living room and slammed down the screen, closing the laptop. She went to pick it up when Uncle Pete pulled her aside.

He sat her in a chair and stood in front of her. "What do you mean it's yours?"

"Tom gave it to me. It's mine." Rose strained to see where the laptop was. "You don't understand. He wanted me to have it."

"He didn't even know you. Why would he give you his laptop?" Linda put her hands on her hips. "I can't believe you've had it all this time, just down the hall from me."

"You don't think this was the reason Mrs. Cook's room was trashed, do you?" Cat walked around the desk so she could see her uncle's face while he talked. The man might be able to lie, but not to her face.

He blew out a breath. "I can't see how they're related. Besides, Sara all but confessed to the vandalism and attacking Linda for one reason. She thought

Linda was standing in the way of her happy-ever-after with her lover."

"What's going on here?" Daisy came into the room, a cookie in her hand.

Rose tried to stand up, but Uncle Pete gently moved her back into her chair. "I think we should take this conversation down to the station. Do you mind?" He pointed to the laptop from the desk in front of Linda. "May I have this? I'll return this at the end of the investigation."

Linda held her hand up. "Let me send a copy of the manuscript to my email account. I'd like to read what my husband was working on." With a few keystrokes, she finished and closed the laptop, handing it to Uncle Pete.

"Thank you." He turned toward Rose and held out a hand. "Ready to go?"

"I suppose if I say no, you'll just cuff me and take me anyway." Rose shrugged. "I have nothing to hide, so I'll go willingly."

She stood and walked with Uncle Pete toward the door. Daisy followed along. "I can't believe you're in trouble again. I'm always bailing you out for something. You need to start acting your age."

"I didn't do anything." Rose mumbled again, but Daisy's response was muffled by the house walls.

When Cat turned back toward Linda, she'd been reading on her phone. She looked up when she noticed Cat staring. "You think Tom's story holds the answers to why he was killed, right?"

Cat ignored the question and asked one of her own. "Why were you with Dean Vargas this morning?"

"I knew that was you hiding behind the tree." Linda closed the laptop again. "Larry knows more than he's saying about what happened to Tom. I tried to sweet talk the information out of him, but he kept changing the subject. That man can talk about nothing forever."

"You think Dean Vargas killed Tom?" Cat watched the other woman's face as she responded.

"No way. Larry is a pain in the butt, but he's too docile to actually do anything to anyone." But something about her tone made Cat wonder if Linda really believed her words.

Linda stood. "I'm heading upstairs to spend some time with what's left of my husband. If I come across a name written in blood, I'll let you know."

Cat glanced around the empty room and then checked her watch again. If she could focus after all this, she might just have time to finish her chapter.

An hour later, she saved her manuscript and turned off the computer. The story wasn't flowing. Writing sessions like this made every sentence feel like it was squeezed from a stone. She disappeared into her room. Time for a long hot bath and maybe an hour of reading before she had to get ready for the dinner.

Returning to her private suite, Cat turned the water on in the bath, pouring in a couple capfuls of her favorite bubble bath. Then she went back into her room, and after undressing grabbed the mystery she'd been reading. She loved the way the amateur sleuth in the series had a few quirks. It made her more human in her eyes. Besides, the girl was funny. Settling in the bathtub, she put a rolled up towel behind her head and closed her eyes. This retreat had been a total disaster. The only writer who seemed to be progressing on his book was the guy she'd thought was a stalker at the beginning of the week.

Hopefully, Uncle Pete would finish his interview with Rose and the two sisters could come to the dinner and have at least a little relaxation time. Rose had worshiped Tom Cook. She couldn't have killed him, any more than she could have killed anyone. Cat shook the thought away like it was a summer fly buzzing around her head. She opened the book, moved her book mark, and settled in to read more about the little Californian tourist town.

A loud rapping sounded at her bedroom door. "Cat? Are you in there?"

Cat put the book down and stood, regretfully letting the warm water flow off her body. Wrapping herself in a large sheet towel, she rushed to the door. "Daisy? What's wrong?"

The woman burst into the room and sat on Cat's bed. "It's awful. I can't believe this is happening to Rose. I feel sick when I think about her in that dank holding cell. You really have to talk to your uncle."

Cat sat next to her and adjusted her towel a little closer. "What's going on? Is the interview over?"

"They came and searched our room while we were down at the station." Daisy put her hand over her heart. "I swear to God, it isn't mine or Rose's."

"Slow down. So the cops came and searched your room and found what?" Cat wasn't following the woman's frantic story. She couldn't blame Uncle Pete, but to accuse Rose of murder just because she had possession of Tom's laptop? That was crazy talk.

Daisy took two long breaths, then licked her lips. "Sorry, I'm a little flustered." She took another breath, then answered Cat's question. "I came back with the officer to make sure they didn't dig through our underwear. And when he opened Rose's suitcase, there was a large trophy wrapped in one of your lovely soft towels. I told that young man that some-one must have planted it, but he didn't look like he believed me."

"The Covington English Cup?" Cat held up her hand. "Don't answer that. I don't want to know. Poor Rose, she must be beside herself."

Daisy's laugh was low and short. "She's fine. My sister asked for a notebook and a pen to take notes about the station and what it's like to be interrogated. She's acting more like she's on a ride-along rather than being questioned for murder. I only convinced her to hire a lawyer because I told her she needed to experience the whole package."

"Not the type of experience I had in mind for my guests when I designed the retreat." Cat thought about the way Tom had looked when she found his body. Could Rose have swung the cup that high to ac-tually land the killing shot? And was she strong enough? From what she could see, Rose was more likely to walk for exercise than pump iron. "Do you still want to go to the retreat dinner tonight? Right now it's you, Billy, and me. I thought I'd invite Linda Cook too since the restaurant is expecting six."

"I'm hoping Rose will be able to attend, but you should invite that young man who's always working around the house as well. He's very charming and tells the most interesting stories. I've been writing down everything he says. I'm trying to work on my dialogue." Daisy blushed. "I know it's eavesdropping, but I don't get around men his age much anymore."

Cat smiled. The woman was a true writer, a word

magpie, stealing from what she heard to make her story more believable.

"Seth's driving us to the restaurant. So you'll get plenty of time to chat." Cat wondered how he'd feel about being Daisy's hero in development.

The older woman stood. "Thanks for talking me down. I can't believe what a roller coaster of a trip this has been. I'm going to go down to the station one last time and see if they are holding Rose or not." Her thin lips curved into a smile. "At least it's not boring."

As Cat watched the woman walk out of the room she nodded to herself. That was one thing she could agree with Daisy on, the week hadn't been the least bit boring. Honestly, she could do with a little boring in her life right now.

Cat returned to the bathroom, but her water had gone cold. Instead of refilling and trying again, she pulled the stopper to drain the tub and returned to lie on her bed. Looking around, she realized she'd left her book in the bathroom. Michael's journal sat near the bed. Sighing, she opened it and started reading, trying to find out what her ex-husband had been thinking, but not wanting to really know.

April 16th
   I met the most amazing girl in class today. I know, I'd sworn off even considering dating a co-ed, especially after the last fiasco, but this girl, woman, is different. Besides, next year she'll be in grad school and my moral code won't be offended by ravaging her. Okay, so maybe part of the charm is her innocence, but she's wicked smart and has a laugh that

comes too easily at times. Lord help me, my journal is turning into the diary of a sixteen-year-old schoolgirl.

September 8th
I met her again. This time, she was at the dive bar most of the students spend way too much time at rather than studying. I guess I can't judge since I was there with a few other professors in my department. We were celebrating Chad's journal acceptance, and the next thing I knew, she was sitting next to me. We talked for hours, long after the others had left to go home to their wives. She gets me. And she just broke it off with a local boy who apparently left her to join the military. If she'd been mine, I wouldn't have left her alone for an instant. I'm taking her for coffee and a ride up into the mountains on Saturday. Need to take it slow so I don't scare her off. She might be the one.

After slipping a piece of paper to keep her place, Cat set the journal down and stared at the worn leather. This was the Michael she'd fallen in love with. The man who she'd promised her life to. A man who had promised her trips to Paris and Greece after they'd saved up for a few years. Cat had believed her new husband had just been dreaming. What had happened to cause Michael to fall out of love with her?

There was a brief knock before the door opened to reveal Shauna. Cat wiped the back of her hand over her eyes. Shauna was in a little black dress that hugged her curves and showed off her red hair she wore loose over her shoulders. "I changed my mind about going. We're gathering everyone downstairs in five minutes." She tilted her head and studied Cat. "You're not even dressed?"

Cat jumped off the bed and ran to her closet. "I'll be ready before you get everyone in the car."

"We don't have to do this, you know." Shauna followed her to the closet and put a hand on Cat's shoulder, turning her. "No one would think less of you. It's been a crazy week."

Cat closed her eyes and then shook her head. When she looked at Shauna again, she felt even stronger. "Nope. It's in the plan, we're going to do it. Daisy and Rose—well, Daisy—deserves to get the full retreat experience. I take it Rose hasn't come back from the station?"

Shauna shook her head. "I talked to Pete and he said he was keeping her for a while, mostly because he doesn't have any other prospects. And the DA wants to charge her. Can you believe it?"

"You don't think Rose could have just snapped, do you?" Cat took a dress out of her closet and laid it on her bed.

"I don't, and you don't either. Rose needs at least a few of us in her corner. Now get ready." She walked over to the open doorway and left the room.

Cat knew having a celebration dinner was probably not in the best of taste, but she wanted to start a tradition for the rest of the retreats. And who knew what might happen next month? Even with Tom's death, Sara's arrest, and now Rose being held for questioning, there had to be something for the group to celebrate. Even if it was only living through the week.

She slipped on the red fit and flare dress with a

keyhole neckline, adding dressy sandals. Since the dress was sleeveless, she put on a black crocheted jacket to give her some cover if the night turned cold. Running a brush through her hair, she put on makeup and, as promised, made it downstairs before the last guest. The group was still waiting on Linda when Cat arrived.

"You look beautiful," Seth whispered in her ear as he pulled her close. She saw Daisy watching and memorizing the moment.

She tilted her head toward his. "Be careful or you're going to wind up as the hero for Daisy's latest romance novel."

He chuckled. "There are worse ways to be memorialized. I remember you telling me you were going to kill me off if you ever wrote a mystery."

"I was mad." Cat remembered the fight. She'd just told him she'd been accepted into Covington's master's program, and he wanted her to relocate to Fort Hood, Washington, and move in with him. Not only was it a heated argument, it had been their last real fight. She'd stayed in town, met Michael, and gotten married. Seth had done his tour with the army, then come home to work for his dad on the farm. By that time, she'd already divorced Michael and moved to California. They were like ships passing in the night. After high school was over, neither had been in the same town for more than a week, until now. "Besides, you were pretty safe. I'm writing new adult paranormal stories, not mysteries."

"I'm pretty sure you can do whatever you want, so I'll just stay on your good side from now on. I'd hate to be killed off in a particularly gruesome manner." He nodded to the stairway. "Here's our latecomer."

Linda heard his comment and smiled. She looked rumpled, like she'd just woken from a nap, her hair flat on one side. "A gentleman never mentions the delay caused by a lady. Didn't your mama ever teach you that?"

Seth walked up and offered his arm. "I apologize for the slight, Mrs. Cook. May I escort you to the chariot?"

"Seriously, you all take yourselves too seriously. Just because her old man made her rich, doesn't mean we should have to kiss her feet." Billy grumbled and exited the door first, letting the screen slam right in front of Shauna.

"Looks like you're the only gentleman in our company tonight, Seth." Shauna held the door open for the rest of the group.

"Too bad Rose can't be here to enjoy the dinner and the company," Daisy said as she climbed into the back of the SUV and sat on the other bench seat away from Billy. By the time Cat got there, the seat next to the less-than-positive man was the only one available. She climbed in and shut the door. She was the hostess. If anyone had to sit by the grump of the group, it should be her.

"How's your writing going this week?" Billy asked her. Then before she could answer, he continued. "I can't believe how much I've gotten done. It's like a dam burst and the words are just flowing out of my fingertips. Maybe I'm being possessed by Tom Cook's spirit. Could be the guy feels bad for stealing my idea, and now he's paying me back from beyond the grave."

Cat heard Linda's snort and saw her turn her attention toward them.

Before Linda could go off on the man, Cat jumped in with her canned "why retreats are helpful" speech. "My writing is going great. I'm a big believer in writing every day to keep the story alive. I'm sure that's what you're feeling. And being away from the stress of everyday life makes it even more powerful. I'm so glad everyone could take time out of their busy schedule to come to the retreat. I'm sure you'll all agree it was time well spent."

"Except for Tom Cook, of course," Billy added.

Daisy turned around. "And Rose. I'm sure she'll wake up soon and realize this was the worst week ever."

The rest of the ride to the restaurant was quiet with each of the group seemingly lost in their own thoughts.

Cat just couldn't wait for the week to be over.

Chapter 18

Seth waved the waiter over to the table. "Let's do another pitcher of margaritas." He looked at Cat and shrugged. He, as the designated driver, had a large Coke in front of him. The rest of the party had drained the first pitcher before the appetizers had arrived and had gone through four baskets of chips and salsa already.

"The quesadillas are coming right out," the waiter said quickly. Cat figured he wanted to stave off a request for more chips because he took the empty pitcher and disappeared back into the kitchen area. The next time she called for a reservation, the host might just tell her that the place was full, just to keep them from eating all the food in the place.

"So, Daisy, did you get any research done for your work in progress?" Cat turned toward the woman sitting next to her. Since Cat was paying for the dinner, she wanted to get something out of the group before they left, maybe even some quotes she could put up on the website to bring other writers in. Something other than "My husband died here" or "My sister was charged with murder."

Who was she kidding? The week had been a total disaster.

Daisy set her margarita down and licked her lips. Cat could see the glaze starting to come over the woman's eyes. "Actually, before all this craziness with Rose happened, I did a lot of great research in the stacks. The library has an amazing collection of Regency-related material, including some that was actually written in the times. Of course, that Hemingway professor wasn't too bad to listen too, either." She burped and covered her mouth. "His butt looked amazing in those tight jeans. I wish he liked older women."

Billy laughed, the sound hard and cruel. "Why do you think these old guys teach at a no-name college like this? Fresh meat every semester. I can see why that Vargas character stays around."

"I don't believe all professors are here to be lecherous old fools." Linda sipped her margarita. "Besides, that type of behavior happens in all types of industries, not just academia. Men just think they rule the world, so they act like idiots."

Billy grabbed the fresh pitcher of margaritas from the waiter, nodding toward Cat. "I think you're wrong. Even our hostess had a husband that couldn't resist the jailbait, right Cat?"

The hair on the back of her neck bristled as she leaned forward, meeting his challenging gaze. "I don't believe that's any of your business."

Billy shrugged, hiding a grin, obviously happy he'd scored a point in some game only he was playing. "That's the rumor down at Bernie's."

"Let's change the subject," Seth growled. "She's already said it wasn't your business so stop harassing her." An unspoken threat hung in the air between the two men.

Finally, Billy flung up his hands and stood. "I'm going to the bar for a real drink. Have them send my food there. You all can have the woman's liberation party without me."

The group at the table was silent until Billy left the room and entered the closed-off bar area.

Shauna was the first to speak. "It's guys like him that make me glad I'm not bartending anymore." She turned to Cat. "I want to say thank you again for rescuing me from that life and those people."

"And yet we got one in the first retreat group." Cat looked around the table and addressed the rest of the company. "Sorry for that. I hope you can still enjoy your dinner."

"Honey, if you think that little snot is going to ruin my evening, you don't know me well enough." Linda held up a glass. "To the Warm Springs Writer's Retreat. May you survive, thrive, and prosper."

The rest of the table held up their glasses and joined Linda in the toast. Just then, the quesadillas arrived and people started eating. Cat just hoped this wouldn't be the opening and closing act on the retreat that was supposed to be her supplemental income until she could live on the book royalties.

As they drove back to the house, Billy sprawled out and fell asleep—or, rather, passed out—in the back seat, and Cat was forced to sit with Daisy and Linda. They hadn't gone too far when Daisy, sitting near the window, had her head leaned back and was snoring.

"I really appreciate what you said about the retreat. I know this hasn't been an easy week for you." Cat watched the woman's reflection in the darkened window.

Linda shrugged. "This wasn't your fault. Unfortunately, you and your retreat got caught up in the middle of something that's been festering for way too long."

"I don't understand." Cat frowned. "You don't think Dean Vargas had anything to do with Tom's death, do you? I mean, I know the men were rivals over that cup thing, but is that enough to kill over?"

"What cup thing? You mean the Covington Cup? Larry was never in the running for that; I took second place every year I attended school here. Back then, they'd never let a woman win, it just wasn't done. Everyone thought the only reason I was in school was to nab a husband. And of course, what did I do?"

"You have a career, right?" Cat realized she'd never talked about what Linda did, at least before her husband started making enough to keep them well-off all by himself.

"No. I'm the society wife. I run the household, oversee the financials, and look pretty when Tom takes me to industry parties. Of course, I tell everyone I'm working on my own book, but honestly, I haven't written a word for years." Linda stared straight ahead, not looking at Cat when she talked. "I can't believe I've let myself just vegetate for so many years. What am I going to do now?"

"What do you want to do? Tom must have left you

financially set. I bet you could do anything you wanted, including go back to school."

Linda turned toward her and put on a smile that, even in the dark car, Cat could tell she didn't feel. "I guess you're right. Why am I being such a Debbie Downer? I probably have more money than most people earn in their lifetimes, and it's all because my husband was unlucky enough to wind up dead before he could spend it."

"Look, I didn't mean that you were better off without him." Cat paused. She could tell she was just digging herself in deeper trouble. "I just think you need to consider your options now and find your passion. Work's a whole lot more fun when you're doing something you love."

"I know you meant well, my dear. I'm just a little tired from all the craziness this week. I still can't believe Tom is gone." Linda dug into her purse and pulled out a tissue, dabbing it at her eyes.

"Did you read his manuscript? Does it talk about what happened that summer?" Cat realized Linda hadn't said a word about Tom's story since last night.

"I was too beat to read last night, and today I just couldn't bring myself to." Linda sighed. "I really just want to close my eyes for a few minutes, if you don't mind."

Cat stared out to the front of the SUV. In the driver's seat, Seth leaned back with one arm out the window. Shauna reached up to change the radio station as they left the reach of the classic rock station they'd found on their way to dinner. Now, she searched for a new station with a stronger signal. "93.5," she said at the same time as Seth.

"Wow, stereo," Shauna teased as she tuned the radio.

"It's been the rock station here since we were kids." Seth caught Cat's gaze in the rearview mirror. "Cat spent a summer interning there back when she wanted to be a radio DJ."

"Seriously?" Shauna turned in her seat and faced Cat. "You never told me that."

"It was just something I explored in high school. I decided to go to college instead." She turned to Seth when he snorted. "What?"

Seth looked at Shauna. "She was damn good. The station offered her full time as soon as she graduated from high school. Then once she went to college, she dropped them without a second thought."

"I didn't drop them. I gave two weeks. Having a job and trying to keep up with my classwork just didn't work for me. I needed time to study." Cat defended her long-ago decision, but in her heart she knew she had screwed up as soon as she'd turned in her notice. She had loved working at the station and the manager would have worked around her schedule, but she'd wanted to be like the other kids in her dorm, free of responsibilities besides school. She leaned back in her seat. "Okay, I kind of dropped them."

"Sometimes you don't realize what you want until it slips through your fingers." Seth's voice was soft and for a second, their gaze met in the reflection in the mirror. Then a new song came on and a little squeal came out of Shauna. She turned up the volume on the speakers.

"I love this song," she declared, and started singing along full blast.

Cat closed her eyes and thought about Seth's words. Did he mean she should look at what she gave up? Or was it more basic than that? Did *he* regret letting her go so many years ago? The last fight wasn't any different than the ones they'd had in the past. But that time, she'd started dating Michael, and before she knew it, she was married.

Cat's phone buzzed, waking her the next morning. She'd gone straight to bed last night after they'd arrived home, the margaritas she'd consumed making her maudlin rather than provide her the typical happy buzz. Without glancing at the display, she croaked out an answer. "Hello?"

"Don't tell me I woke you." Uncle Pete's voice sounded amused. "Late night with someone I know? Don't tell me he's sleeping next to you."

Cat glanced at the other side of the bed making sure it was empty, then mentally kicked herself for looking. "I'm alone. What do you want? I'm sure you didn't call to see if my love life had improved overnight."

He responded with a real chuckle this time. "Actually, you're right. I did have a reason to call. One, we're holding your guest for murder. The DA's not sure he can make the charges stick so he's getting a grand jury involved. I think he's just concerned about all the phone calls he's getting, demanding he find Tom's murderer."

"Poor Rose, I hate that she has to go through this just to please the angry mob." Cat pulled her quilt up around her and scooted up to a seated position.

"Well, there is the matter that the laptop and the

murder weapon were found in her room," Uncle Pete said. "But I don't want to talk about that. I wanted to tell you I found your missing person."

Cat slid her knees to her chest and felt her heart try to beat out of her chest. "You found Gloria?"

"Actually, I found the missing person's report. Sorry I wasn't clear. Her parents filed it in September of that year when they hadn't heard from her."

Now, her heart stopped racing and her stomach dropped. "And it was never closed?"

"I'd love to say it's dormant, but I talked to the original investigating officer, and he gets a call every year on Gloria's birthday. He said it breaks his heart when he sees the display on his cell. But he still answers. Ed's a good man."

"Linda said she thought Gloria moved to Europe." Cat had really hoped the woman had surfaced by now.

"Unlikely. She didn't take anything from her dorm room. One day she was there, the next she was never heard from again. So Linda Cook knew this girl?" Uncle Pete had his cop voice on. "I sure would like to get her into the interrogation room and talk about a few things. But that twit of a district attorney I'm working with told me to leave her alone. I guess the Cook name still has some pull, even way out here in Colorado."

Cat bit her bottom lip. She had suspicions about what happened to Gloria, and it involved the dean of the English department of Covington College, but saying it aloud without anything to back it up would make her look like a conspiracy theorist. She decided to tell her uncle the facts she knew and keep her opinions private. At least until she knew more. "They were all friends in college. Linda says Larry and

Gloria dated, but there was a picture in the yearbook showing Gloria kissing Tom. But maybe it was just a kiss, who knows. Or it could have been staged for the photograph. You know how it goes."

"Do you think they did something to Gloria?" His question was blunt but not unexpected.

Cat shrugged uncomfortably. "I don't have anything to prove it."

"But you think there was something there."

Her head nodded, even though her uncle couldn't see her. "Maybe. Let me dig through some of the old journals. Maybe there's something more that we don't know." She hesitated. "Can you give me the mom's phone number? I'd like to talk to her."

"Won't do any good; the one in the file has been disconnected. I am a detective, you know." His voice dropped. "Don't push this—and be careful. I don't want you to wind up missing like this poor girl."

Cat ran her hand through her hair. "You know better than that. No one would want to keep me."

"I'm serious, Cat. If you think you're in too deep, back off and tell me. I'm the guy with the badge. I'm paid to take the risks." Uncle Pete's warning chilled her bones.

As they said their good-byes, she noticed he hadn't told her not to look into the journals. Maybe he thought keeping her in the library would be the safest place for her. She glanced at her watch. Six in the morning. So much for sleeping in on a Sunday.

She pushed off the quilt and headed to the bathroom to shower. Time to write, then she'd head downstairs to talk to Daisy and the rest of her guests before they left. The library didn't open until after noon on Sundays. By mid-week, she and Shauna would be alone in the house again. And the world could go back to normal.

Before she opened her word processing program, she ran a search on Gloria's mother just to see if there was a number listed. When she found one that matched the city and state where Shauna had found the missing persons article, she wrote it down on a slip of paper.

Staring at the number, she grabbed her cell and dialed. Reaching voice mail, she left a message asking someone to call her, leaving her number, but not any details. Maybe the mom would think she was from the college.

Cat would play that role, if—she stopped and corrected herself—when Gloria's mother returned her call. Positive thinking made the path easier. She grinned at her mental gymnastics and dove into her writing.

Two hours later, she was on the first floor and heading into the dining room when she heard a noise that sounded like it was coming from Michael's study. Frowning, she turned left and went down the hallway to his door. The large walnut door was shut tight. Cat leaned in, her ear on the cool wood. Nothing.

She turned the doorknob and slowly swung the door open. There, sitting at Michael's desk was Linda Cook, a laptop open in front of her and tears streaming down her face.

"Linda? What's wrong?" Cat didn't ask what she was doing in the office. It was partially her fault. No one had told Linda where she could go and what was off limits. Before the next retreat, she needed to get some PRIVATE signs to mark out the personal space.

And until she had Michael's study cleaned out, this had to be kept private.

The woman didn't even look up. "This is probably the best thing Tom ever wrote. I can't believe he won't be here to finish the story."

"Is it about what happened to Gloria?" Cat crossed the room and stood in front of Michael's oversized desk.

"Don't worry about that. You really need to leave Gloria alone. The girl never hurt anyone." The other woman slammed shut the laptop and stood. "All I meant was the man was a genius wordsmith."

Cat doubted Linda's explanation, but she didn't press the issue. She decided to change the subject. "Are you coming to breakfast? I'm sure some of the guests will be leaving today, if you want to say good-bye."

"I've got to make some calls, but I'll try to get downstairs before anyone leaves." Linda breezed past her, a laptop tucked under her arm. Cat really wanted to get a peek at Tom's last manuscript, but asking the woman for the manuscript seemed forward. Cat straightened the books on Michael's bookshelf, then stopped as her hand touched a book on third-world countries and their economic building power. He'd never been interested in economics of anything but what he'd called the privileged countries. In fact, Michael had bragged how Dean Ngu had promised he'd never have to teach the one session on third-world economics that Covington offered.

Maybe he'd lost his pull with the dean after their divorce. Glancing around the bookcase, she found several other books on the subject. Just another thing about Michael she wouldn't ever understand.

Her phone buzzed and checking the display, she realized it was the return call she'd been waiting for. "This is Cat Latimer. Thanks for returning my call."

A pause at the other end made Cat wonder if the woman would hang up on her. "I'm sorry, but how can I help you?"

"I was wondering if you could tell me about the circumstances around your daughter's disappearance." Cat thought about how to play the request. "I'm a writer and I'm looking into the problem of women disappearing from college campuses. I understand your daughter was never found?"

"No, Gloria was never found." The woman cleared her throat. "I'm really not comfortable talking about this."

"Maybe I could drop by and explain my project a bit." Cat bit her lip as she waited for the woman to respond.

"I'm sure you'll do really well with your studies, but I'm not interested in dragging up the past. Please don't call me again." The line disconnected.

Cat put the phone in her purse and wondered what mother wouldn't want a spotlight that could bring out new information about where her daughter was or how she was killed. It was almost like Gloria's mother knew exactly what had happened to her daughter.

Chapter 19

"You're lost in thought." Shauna refilled Cat's coffee cup before sitting down next to her at the table. "Is Seth on your mind?"

Cat hid her smile by taking a sip of her coffee. "Seriously, I don't live and breathe for that man. I do have other thoughts in my head."

"Child, if he looked at me the way he looks at you, all I'd be able to think about is taking that fine specimen to bed." Shauna pulled out her calendar. "So Billy's flight leaves at noon, which gives me thirty minutes before I have to leave. Is Daisy staying over since Rose has been detained with your uncle?"

"Let's hope detained is all that happens." Cat popped the last bit of banana nut muffin into her mouth and brushed her hands off over her plate. "I'll talk to her right now before I go up to write. I have to visit the library at noon, so if I'm not here when you get back, come get me. I still don't like the thought of you here alone."

"Not alone, remember? Seth is here finishing the cleanup on Tom's room since your uncle released the scene last night. I guess with the pictures and the rest, they have everything they might need for trial." Shauna's voice dropped off as the door to the kitchen opened. Daisy stood there, a cup of coffee in one hand and a plate of fruit in the other.

"Is there something wrong with the food?" Shauna stood and rushed over to the woman, holding the door open.

Daisy shook her head. She looked on the verge of tears. "I was just wondering, if, you didn't mind, could I eat in here with you? The dining room is so empty without Rose."

"Of course," Cat stood and pulled out a chair. "I should have invited you. We were wondering if you've made any plans for today?"

"Am I leaving on my five p.m. flight, you mean?" Daisy shrugged. "I hate to leave Rose all alone here, but I can't afford to stay. Besides, they're expecting me back at my job at the hotel. I'm their bookkeeper, and I bet they haven't even made a deposit since I've been gone."

Cat looked at Shauna who nodded. This needed to be both of their decision, since what she was about to say would affect the bottom line. Sometimes, everything wasn't about money. "Daisy, if you want to stay, we won't charge you a room fee. You'll have to pay for your own food, but you wouldn't have to worry about the room."

Daisy shook her head. "That's very kind of you, but I'm heading home. We have responsibilities there, and I need to take care of things until Rose can make her way home. My sister is a survivor. I'm sure she's filling a notebook right now with a story she's sure will sell millions." Cat watched as Daisy's lips curved into a smile making her look younger than her years.

"If you decide to come back, the door's always open." Cat stood and gave the woman a hug. "I'm heading up to my office to work. If you want, you can come with me to the library. I'll be walking over about eleven forty-five."

"I'd like that." Daisy nodded. "There are several citations I'd like to get in case I can't find any of the same research books at home."

Cat filled up a travel mug with coffee and left Daisy and Shauna talking about muffin recipes. She would miss the women when they left. Of course, she could and would visit Rose in jail until they figured out she couldn't be the murderer. She had taken the first step on the riser when she stopped and came back down.

Something had looked off, and when she scanned the hallway again, she saw it. The door to Michael's study was ajar. She was going to find a key and lock it up so people couldn't just wander in.

She walked down the hall and pushed the door open. "Look, I hate to be rude, but this room is off limits."

No one responded to her. The room was completely empty. Feeling foolish, she walked the edges of the room, and even checked under the desk and in the closet. No one. She went back to the door and pulled it shut behind her, checking the catch to make sure it held. Maybe she hadn't closed it when she'd found Linda in the room earlier. That was the only explanation that made any sense at all. But she knew she was fooling herself—she had closed the door solidly behind her the last time she'd left the room. And yet the door had been open a few minutes later.

Shaking off the eerie feeling that she was being watched, Cat climbed the stairs to her office, closing the door soundly behind her and, feeling silly, turning the lock in the knob. At least no one could sneak up behind her today.

Turning on her computer, she opened the word-processing program and got lost for a few hours. When she looked down at her computer screen, she realized Daisy was probably already waiting for her downstairs. Reluctantly, she saved the document, then made a couple of notes to settle her back into the story when she sat down tomorrow. With the retreat winding down, she'd soon be able to settle in for several hours a day, which would ensure she met deadline.

Humming to herself, she pulled open her office door and stopped short. There, on the floor in front of her, was a single white carnation, her favorite flower. Michael used to tease her that she had the sophistication of a schoolgirl, but he'd stopped bringing her roses after she declared her love for the simple, cheaper flower. It was hard for her to believe that Seth would have remembered after all these years, but logically, it was the only explanation.

Then why did her hand shake when she reached down to grab the stem?

When she reached the bottom of the stairs, Daisy was sitting on the lobby couch reading her notebook. She looked up and smiled when she saw Cat, but something made her smile dim. The woman stood and walked over to Cat. "Are you okay, my dear?"

Nodding, Cat laid the flower on the reception

desk. "I'm just a little distracted, that's all. Let me grab my tote, and we can get going."

Daisy waited nearby, but Cat could feel the woman's watchful gaze on her. *Fake it until you make it.* Cat repeated the mantra silently three times, then pasted on a fake smile as she stuffed her notebook into her bag. She turned around and faced Daisy. "Let's go."

As they walked past Mrs. Rice's yard, Daisy touched the white picket fence. "It must be nice to live here. It feels a little like a village in a fairy tale."

She'd never thought of it that way. "You're right; it was a great place to grow up. We had the great outdoors for our backyard, and if we wanted something more cultural, we had the college for plays and stuff. I remember attending the community sing-along every Christmas and learning 'Hallelujah' standing in between my mom and dad. I know it sounds corny, but that is one of my favorite memories of my childhood."

"It's sweet, not corny. You're very lucky to have good parents. Do they still live in town?" The pace was a little slower than Cat's normal stride, but it allowed them to carry on a conversation without any trouble.

"The folks turned into snow birds and are already down in Florida setting up their winter life. I don't think they spend more than two months here in Colorado now. My dad complains if it's too cold."

"I totally understand. When we signed up for the retreat I prayed it would be a warm fall. My arthritis gets pretty bad during the winter." Daisy absently rubbed the joints in her hands. "Rose still loves making snow angels. I'll leave that to the younger group."

Campus was empty when they arrived. The library could open at two in the afternoon on Sundays and no one would notice. Either the students were catching up on some needed sleep, or they were sleeping off too much fun on Saturday night. The only people Cat typically saw on Sundays were the professors who were either working on their pet project or, more likely, looking for the next career move to get them tenure. She held the glass door to the library open for Daisy. "You ready to come inside?"

Daisy ducked inside to the cool foyer and walked through the double doors. Miss Applebome was sitting at the front desk, watching them enter. "I need to talk to the librarian," Cat said. "Do you want me to find you when I'm ready to leave?"

Daisy smiled and patted Cat's shoulder. "Don't worry about me. I'll head home in time to get my bags packed and ready for Shauna to drive me to the airport. I am a grown woman, you realize."

Cat must have blushed because she felt the heat on her cheeks. "I didn't mean you couldn't walk home alone, I just wanted to offer you a walking companion. If you wanted it."

"Oh, dear, and I just bit the hand that feeds me. So, so sorry. My only excuse is I'm not sleeping well." Daisy nodded toward the librarian. "You go do your thing. I'll be fine.

Cat watched her walk to the bank of elevators and push the button. She turned toward Miss Applebome. "No time like the present," she mumbled to herself.

The woman pretended to be busy as Cat approached the checkout desk. "Are you lost? I don't think I've seen you this much since you were building your lesson plans that first year."

"I wanted to know if you knew anything more about Tom, Linda, Larry, and Gloria." She watched the woman's face closely.

"If I'd known something, I would have told you." She pushed a stack of books away, then leaned into her chair. "What are you thinking I might know?"

"I'm trying to figure out what happened to Gloria. Did she just leave? And if so, why? And what did the other three know about her disappearance?" Cat slipped into a seat next to the desk. "What do you think happened?"

At first, Cat didn't think Miss Applebome was going to say anything besides "get out of my chair." But then she started talking about the old days. "You have to understand. We didn't know we had any power back then. Oh, some girls knew they had power over men, but if you didn't use your sexuality to increase your position, you were just here biding time until your marriage."

"And Gloria knew how to play the game?" Cat asked. "I saw the picture of her and Tom. From the look on Linda's face, she wasn't too happy about what was happening."

"There were rumors that Gloria and Larry were fighting. Several times she missed school, and when she did come back, she wore long sleeve sweaters for a while." The librarian studied me. "Back then, you didn't get involved unless you knew for certain. And we didn't."

"So what do you think happened to Gloria?" Cat pressed the question.

"I hope that she's safe somewhere, living a new life." Miss Applebome sighed. "But if I had to guess, I figure she was a victim of foul play."

Cat stood and paused at the desk. "I'm going upstairs to see if I can find any clues. Thank you for your time and honesty."

"I hope you find her." She turned away and started working on her computer. Cat knew she'd gotten everything she could from the discussion.

As she climbed the stairs, she thought about the picture and Linda's glare. Could she have taken out her rival? And what did this whole thing have to do with Tom's death, if anything?

Cat pulled everything published in the four years the Cooks had attended Covington: yearbooks, student handbooks, even the worn editions of *The Cove*, the department's literary magazine. On a whim, she grabbed the two years after the Cooks left as well.

Two hours later, she closed the last yearbook. Except for a few candid photos and snide comments written in faded ink about the cheerleaders' outfits, she hadn't learned anything new. The only thing she had left was to review *The Cove*.

She flipped through the first two years quickly, but in the third year she noticed that Linda was listed as one of the editors. Slowing her scanning down, she was impressed with the opening essays that Linda had penned. The woman had a nice voice, especially when she was opining about who she felt was oppressed in the world.

Like women.

It was in the last *Cove* she opened that she found the clue. The journal had been dedicated to all women fighting for their lives and their dignity. The last words of the paragraph chilled Cat's bones. She read aloud: "Especially those who can't fight for themselves anymore."

By the time she made it back to the house, the SUV was back in the driveway. One guest gone, and two to go. Well, three, if you counted Rose, but she was technically staying in Uncle Pete's own version of a bed and breakfast: a cot and three hots. Sara had been released after her parents posted bail, and they had whisked her away to their home. Shauna had gotten a call telling her where to send the few belongings Sara had left in her room.

All in all, if you didn't count the murder, the vandalism, or the attack, the retreat had been a success. She sank into one of the white rockers on the front porch. Who was she kidding? The retreat had been a disaster. Why had she thought this would be a good idea? Cat put her feet up on the seat and hugged her knees in tightly.

"Uh, oh. I know that look. What are you obsessing over now?" Seth's deep baritone caused her to look up into his eyes. "And you're crying. Why are you crying, Kitty Cat?"

She waved her arm wildly at him. "Don't call me that, and I'm not crying."

"You think I don't know tears when they fall on your cheeks?" He sat on the porch rail and looked at her. "Tell me what's wrong?"

She wiped away the evidence and put on an amusement-park soda-jerk smile. "I'm just worn out and worried about my new venture. I probably should have thought about the negative things that could happen during a writer's retreat, rather than just all the fun when I was planning."

"You couldn't plan for what happened this week." He ran his fingers through his hair. "Seriously, Cat, I'm not sure how you got through finding Tom, much less all the other crap that's gone on. You're a strong woman."

She studied him, waiting for the zinger at the end. But when a clarifier never came, she squared her shoulders and took the compliment. "Thanks. I just wanted a place where people could go write without all the drama."

"Where there are people, there's drama. I figured that out during my years in the service. You wouldn't believe what people can complain about. My motto is to be grateful for what you have now, not worried about what you might not have tomorrow." He took in the front yard of the house, covered with brown dried oak leaves. "Not to change the subject, but are you going to hire a landscaper? Or do you want me to rake up your yard? The city picks up the leaves off the curb until the end of the month. After that, the chances of snow are pretty high."

Cat nodded. "One more thing on my to-do list. Although I assumed Shauna had already thought about this."

"She's a city girl," he laughed. "I don't think she's ever had to mow a yard or deal with six inches of snow in the morning. Her first winter here is going to be an eye-opener for her."

"If you have time, I'll pay you for the cleanup."

She leaned back and took in the smell of the fallen oak leaves. Sometimes it felt like the trees were also mourning the passing of summer. This warm weather wouldn't last much longer, and Cat wanted to sink it all into her memory file before the season changed.

The front door banged closed. Cat looked over and saw Daisy with her suitcases standing on the porch.

"Hey, I didn't know you were already back from the library." Cat stood and stretched. "Did you get what you needed?"

"I think so," the older woman looked around. "Even with the craziness, this has been a wonderful week. Thank you for sharing your lovely home with us."

Cat could see the emotion Daisy was trying to hide. "I'm serious about that offer. If you decide to stay to support Rose, I'll give you a room."

She came up and gave Cat a quick hug. "I know you are, but I really feel like I should go home."

The screen door banged again and Shauna joined them on the porch, tossing the set of keys to the vehicles up and down. "I guess we're ready then?"

Daisy nodded and reached down to get her suitcases.

"Let me." Seth grabbed the handles and took the luggage to the SUV, where he put them in the back.

Daisy paused before she followed Shauna off the porch. "Just tell me you'll check on Rose every once in a while. She'd love to see you."

Cat linked her arm with the other woman and walked with her to the driveway. She opened the passenger door and waited for her to climb in before she spoke. "Of course I will. You and I both know Rose couldn't have killed Tom. We just need to find out who did before this goes too far."

Daisy lowered her voice. "That's the thing." She paused as she clicked her seat belt locked, staring straight forward and not meeting Cat's gaze. "I'm not sure she didn't."

Chapter 20

"I'm going to get the front yard done this afternoon," Seth said as he stood next to Cat on the sidewalk, watching the car disappear down the road. "You okay alone in the house?"

"Shauna needs to keep her mouth shut about some things." Cat shook her head. "I've been alone before. I'm sure I can manage a couple hours all by myself."

"Unless you really want some company." He stepped closer and whispered in her ear. "I could put off the chores for a little afternoon delight."

Cat ached to lean back into his arms and take his lips in her own in a deep kiss. One that Mrs. Rice could report back to her gossip girls. Instead, she shook her head. "As tempting as that sounds, I'm going up to write for a while."

He called after her, "You don't know what you're missing."

Of course, she did know. And she regretted every step away from the man, but she wasn't quite ready to go there again. Her lips curved into a smile. She was close, very close to seeing if the high-school sweethearts could manage a very adult relationship now. She stepped into the cool of the foyer and headed upstairs. The quiet of the house seemed strange after having so many people in it just a day ago. Even when they were all doing their own thing, the hum of laptops, or the clacking of keystrokes, had made the house feel lived in.

She paused on the steps and took in the bottom floor. No matter what happened, she'd made a decision. She was going to continue the monthly retreats just like she'd planned. At the end of the year, she'd sit down with the numbers and make a business decision on what the next year would hold. But for today, she wasn't going to worry about it.

With her mood lighter, she climbed the rest of the way to the third floor and, after locking her door, sat down at her desk.

But instead of turning on her computer, she opened a notebook and listed all the things that didn't make sense about Rose killing Tom. After she finished that, she made a list of what she knew about Gloria and her disappearance. The second list was longer.

Even though she didn't know how or why, she knew the two incidents were linked somehow. She just needed to find the link. Hopefully, before Rose was convicted of her favorite author's murder.

She closed the notebook and looked out the front window. True to his word, Seth had most of the yard cleared, with bags of leaves sitting out at the curb. The brown paper bags seemed to blend in with the entire look. One day, once the outside was refreshed, maybe in spring, she'd hire a photographer to take some promotional shots of the place.

A knock on her door broke her thoughts, but before she turned from the window she looked at the driveway: empty.

She swung the door open. "Hey Linda." The woman was all decked out in a soft peach pantsuit. Dark circles under her eyes hadn't been completely hidden with the woman's makeup.

Linda lowered her hand, which had been raised to knock again. "I guess I am the only guest left. I need to talk to you."

"Come on in." Cat pointed to the floral sofa she'd bought to go under the tower's windows. She loved sitting and reading in the spot, although that had been a pleasure she'd had to put off while they prepped for the retreat. "What's going on? Are you leaving, too?"

Linda sat perched on the edge of the sofa, clearly uncomfortable. "I overheard you talking to the librarian today. You need to leave this Gloria thing alone."

"I don't understand—why are you so worried about me asking about a decades-old disappearance?" Cat sat next to Linda, but turned so she could watch her responses.

"Can't you just leave it alone?" Linda patted her hair like it had gone rogue in the last few minutes.

"Not until you tell me what you know. Did Gloria go after Tom? Is that what this is about?" Noticing Linda's shocked look, Cat pressed on. "Don't try to deny it. I saw the photo in the yearbook."

"It wasn't what you think. I mean, yes, she did try to get Tom to intervene, but I believe she was just looking for a way out, and using her sex appeal was the only tool she had at the time." Linda relaxed into the sofa. "It was a different world and Gloria was beautiful. She knew how to use that to her favor.

But I'm getting ahead of myself. I guess it's time to tell the whole story, then you can make your own decision."

"I'm listening." Cat put her arm over the back of the couch and tried to look relaxed.

Linda paused, clearly thinking about her words. "Gloria fell hard for Larry. By the time sophomore year was over, she was already talking wedding plans and picking out a church. But junior year, things changed. I noticed them fighting more. Gloria told me Larry wanted her to quit cheerleading, even though she loved it."

"He was jealous," Cat guessed. She could see the dean not wanting his prize possession outside his control.

"Extremely. By the end of the year, Gloria had tried to call it off, but Larry wasn't listening. He told her that they would be married at the end of senior year and she needed to get on board." Linda shook her head. "That poor girl. Larry had visited her folks with her on Christmas break and sold them the line of goods, too. Everyone was so happy for Gloria; she'd found the one. The only problem was she wasn't happy."

Cat tried to process what Linda was saying. "So why didn't she just break up with Larry?"

"No one listened to her. No one saw the bruises. She was helpless. And there wasn't a lot of support for domestic violence victims, not like there is today. Besides, she wasn't his wife. They didn't realize what kind of power he held over her." Linda pressed her lips together like she was considering her next words. "So I convinced Tom to take Larry on a week-long white water rafting trip. The girls would stay home and go shopping."

"And by the time they got back, Gloria had disappeared."

Linda twisted the wedding ring on her hand. "Yes. I'd gotten hold of a group of women from the college who ran a type of underground railroad system for battered women. We bought her a few clothes, gave her as much money as I could scrape up, and she escaped into another life."

Cat wasn't sure she believed the story. "What about her folks? She just left them to wonder about where she was all these years?"

Linda smiled. "Actually, her mom comes to New York annually, and I get Gloria a room under my name. It's probably overkill, but she's still scared of Larry."

"But her mom calls the detective on the missing person case every year on Gloria's birthday."

"Gloria thinks it's the best way to keep Larry in check for future women. If the police still have him on their short list for potentially killing her, she knows he'll think twice about giving them cause by hurting someone else. And for the most part, it's worked. I do feel sorry for that Sara girl. She thought the man would marry her. He's such an ass."

"It's a good story, but what proof do you have that Gloria's even alive?" Cat decided to lay the cards on the table. "Maybe you killed Gloria because you were jealous. Tom and Larry were out of town; you could have gotten rid of her easily."

Linda picked up her phone and dialed a number. When the call was answered, she spoke into the phone. "Yeah, you need to speak to the woman. She's not convinced."

Cat took the phone as Linda passed it to her. "Who is this?"

"I think you know, but I'll go through the motions for you. I'm Gloria Jenson, or I used to be. Now I'm Brandi Moore." The woman formerly known as Gloria went through the story again, filling in bits and pieces that Linda had left out. As the conversation ended, she made one last plea to Cat. "Now that you know this, I need you to keep it to yourself. Please don't come looking for me. I promise I'm happier than I ever dreamed I'd be."

Cat assured the woman that what they'd discussed would be kept between them. As she hung up, she handed the phone back to Linda. "Well, there's one mystery solved, but I know Rose didn't kill your husband."

"I don't think she did either, but I know what you're thinking. I didn't kill Tom. I loved him. Good or bad times, he was there for me." Linda stood and walked to the door. "Thank you for listening."

Cat turned back and opened her notebook to the page where she'd written down all the information about Gloria. She tore out the page and dumped out her trash can on the desk. Grabbing the matches she used to light her scented candles, she scratched one and put the flame to the page.

As it started to consume the paper, she let the flaming ball fall into the aluminum trash container. As it burned out, she whispered, "I hope your life is all you wanted it to be."

She closed up her office and headed downstairs.

As soon as she reached the lobby, the front door opened and Shauna entered.

"Hey, thanks for driving today. I appreciate you getting the guests all back to the airport."

"Well, about that," Shauna started but then Daisy burst in and started talking over her.

"I just couldn't leave knowing poor Rose was in that jail cell. I won't be a burden, and I can help clean the place to get ready for your next session. I swear I'll leave as soon as I know what's happening with my sister."

After they got Daisy set back up in her room, Cat and Shauna met in the kitchen. "What a day."

Cat laughed. "I didn't realize the hard part of a retreat was going to be how to get the customers to leave."

"I know. I felt so bad for her on the drive to the airport. I could tell she was fighting with herself over leaving. We got her suitcase out of the car and she just froze." Shauna held up the bottle of white zin. "Wine or beer?"

"Seems like we're asking that a lot lately." Cat nodded. "Beer. Maybe it will help me sleep tonight. I had a long talk with Linda earlier."

"Linda? Don't tell me she's planning on moving in temporarily while she gets her life figured out." Shauna set a bottle of beer in front of Cat along with a bag of salt-and-vinegar potato chips. When Cat looked at her, she shrugged. "If we're doing the late-night thing, we're going to do it right."

Cat ripped open the bag and took a handful of chips, placing them on a CELEBRATE COLORADO napkin that Shauna had bought on sale from the souvenir shop. She pushed the bag toward her friend. "I feel so bad for Daisy. We all know that Rose wouldn't have killed Tom. She adored the guy. Kidnapped him and made him write only for her, that I could believe. But not murder."

Shauna choked on her beer. "Seriously, that *would* be an option." She ate a few chips, puckering at the sour taste. "So what did Linda want?"

"She told me what happened to Gloria." Cat let the words settle, hoping it wouldn't cause Shauna to choke again.

"Wait, you've solved the mystery? What happened to her? Did Tom kill the girl or was it Larry?" Shauna held up her hand, "Wait, don't tell me. It was Linda. She killed her in a jealous rage and hid the body out at Sugar Hill."

Cat smiled at the smug look on her friend's face. "So you're saying Colonel Mustard in the drawing room with the lead pipe?"

"Am I wrong?"

"It does feel like we're living a game of Clue lately, doesn't it?" Cat took a draw off her beer. "Actually, Gloria isn't dead. Well, Gloria is, but the woman formerly known as Gloria is alive and well. But you have to keep this to yourself."

"You can't just leave it at that. Tell me the story, and I'll swear myself to secrecy." Shauna held her hand up in a Girl Scout salute. "Don't look at me that way. I was a Scout from Brownie to junior high, when I reached the gold level. Just ask my mother; she'll verify."

"I trust you." Cat looked around the empty kitchen. "So, Linda helped Gloria disappear because Larry was abusing her."

"Dean Vargas. *That* Larry?" Shauna slumped back into her chair. "Shut the front door."

"Exactly. That's why this needs to stay between us." Cat shook her head. "Now it makes sense why he goes through women so fast. He has to catch and release before he becomes a total jerk. I can't believe no one has reported problems with him before."

"Maybe they have, and the college has swept it under the rug. Or maybe he changed his treatment of women after Gloria left?" Shauna shook her head even as the words left her mouth. "Men don't change like that, do they?"

"Statistically, no." Cat sipped on her beer. "But maybe Gloria's disappearance scared him straight. It could happen. I'd like to give him the benefit of the doubt."

"I'm just glad I decided to give him a wide berth when I met him over at Bernie's last month when I was there." Shauna finished off her beer. "You want another one?"

"I'm good. I'm going upstairs. I'm beat." Cat took one more chip out of the bag and threw her napkin away.

"Now that we know about Gloria, there's only one more thing we need to figure out." Shauna pulled the bag closer to her and took out more chips.

"What's that?" Cat paused at the door.

She took a beer out of the fridge, opening the bottle and taking a swig before she sat down. "Who killed Tom Cook?"

Cat grabbed the clock next to her bedstead and read the display: three thirty. Groaning, she climbed out of bed where she'd been lying for the last two hours, trying to get back to sleep. Finally giving up, she pulled a robe on and padded downstairs to Michael's study. A few more sleepless nights and she'd have all the boxes cleaned out and the books up on the shelves. Eventually she'd cull through what was there and probably donate a lot of the materials to the college library. But for now, just having them out of boxes and sitting on the shelves made her feel better.

She stopped in the kitchen to make a cup of tea before she started on the boxes. While she was waiting for the tea kettle, she thumbed through the registration book Shauna had set up. November, December, and January retreats were full at six people per session. Or were full for now. Once Seth finished that last wing, the retreat size could be doubled with no problem. Which would allow her to pay off the remodeling loan long before the ten-year term she'd originally agreed to with the bank.

Armed with a steaming cup of Dozy Do tea that she hoped would help her calm down and eventually return to sleep, she headed into the office and started pulling books out of boxes and putting them on the empty shelves. In less than an hour, the teacup was empty, and Cat had only one more box to empty. She'd take the empty boxes to the recycling pile tomorrow. She opened the last box and pulled out the last of the economic textbooks she knew she'd never read. At the bottom of the box was an envelope.

She shelved the books then threw the box into the pile with the rest. She sat on the chaise she'd bought for Michael's study where she used to read while he worked and looked at the sealed envelope.

One word was written on the front. "Catherine."

With a shaky hand she opened the seal. A slip of paper fell out onto her lap along with a small key.

She read the note. Then she set it down and stared at the key. She would need to call Seth first thing in the morning. She knew why the attic space didn't match his plan. Michael had one more secret he'd been keeping from her.

Dearest Catherine. Please forgive me for all the pain and heartache I've caused in your life. If I could take one thing back, it would be hurting you. If you're reading this, I'm no longer able to fix the mess I've found myself in. Take care of yourself and know you were the one love of my life.

> *Forever yours,*
> *Michael*

Chapter 21

"Did you get any sleep?" Shauna refilled Cat's coffee cup and then filled her own. She had a pile of muffins she'd taken out of the freezer last night for their impromptu breakfast guests.

"Not much. After I found Michael's note, I walked through the attic a few times, looking for a keyhole, but it's hidden pretty well. I'm hoping Seth can help me." Cat leaned her head into her hands. "I'm afraid of what might be up there. Michael's secret life is crashing down on me now that he's dead. Maybe it's his BDSM cave he wanted me to clean out before I sold the house?"

Shauna stopped arranging the muffins and sat at the table next to Cat. "I didn't know the man, but you'd think he wouldn't be that cruel."

"I'm sure he didn't expect to die this young. Everyone has secrets they don't want exposed. Michael has already proven that." Cat stared at the key sitting next to the note on the table. "I guess it's like ripping off a Band-Aid. Better to do it quick than let it fester, right?"

Shauna looked at the clock. "Seth should be here

any minute for his breakfast. This can wait until he's here to help. Besides, what if there's some animal holed up in there. That could be the noises you heard last week."

"So you want me to wait for the big strong man to help save me?" Cat laughed. "I have shooed away wild animals before. I'm not totally incompetent."

"Now, I didn't say that . . ." Shauna's words were interrupted by the slam of the screen door. Seth strolled up to the coffee pot and refilled his travel cup with the Writer's Retreat logo Cat had designed. Cat side-eyed Shauna, who ignored her pointed look.

"Who needs a big strong man to save them?" he asked as he took a chair across the table from the women.

"No one," Cat shot back, and she pinched Shauna for opening up the subject. "Did you leave a flower outside my office the other day?"

Seth took a sip of coffee before he answered. "No. Although if you want, I could order you some. Why?"

She thought about the flower and the phone call. Someone was messing with her, and now, with the letter and the key, she wondered if it had anything to do with her being the one who inherited the house. Even Brit at the bar had known things about Cat and Michael. How much had he told the women who'd followed her?

"You didn't tell me someone left you a flower." Shauna's voice brought Cat back from her mental wanderings.

Cat shrugged. "I kind of forgot about it."

Seth focused his gaze on Cat. "You need to tell me everything that's going on. I'm starting to worry about you."

Cat shook her head. "Let's handle one problem at a time. I need to talk to you about the attic."

Cat told him about the note and the key. After she got the story out, he whistled. "I knew there was something funky about the space, but a hidden room? Wow. Your ex was amazing at this secret-life thing."

"I still don't know what he meant when he wrote in his journal about putting me in danger." She looked at the note again. "You don't think maybe he had a brain tumor too? That might cause delusions, right? I know he died of a heart attack, but maybe there was more."

"Maybe. I've heard of old people getting senile, but then they find out they just have a medicine mix-up. Was Michael on any drugs?" Shauna sipped her coffee but set it down when Cat stared at her. "What? It's a logical question."

Cat leaned back into her chair and sighed. "You're right. The problem is, I don't know what got into his head. I mean, we were only married for a few years before he, well, we divorced. I was shocked he left me the house. I kind of thought he had family, some-where."

Seth picked up the note. "This doesn't sound like a guy who wanted the divorce. Are you sure he cheated?"

A memory of Michael and the co-ed in a clinch worthy of an old romance-novel cover flashed through her mind. "I caught him in the act. Or at least the opening scenes. And I found the motel receipts on his desk to confirm the affair."

"On his desk? Like on top of the desk?" Seth leaned against the counter.

Cat ran a hand through her hair. "Yep, right there

where I could see them." The room was silent as she digested what she had just said. "Where I could see them."

"No guy who wants to hide an affair from his wife keeps the motel receipts. So he wanted you to find out about his extra-curricular activities."

"But why? Was he already tired of playing house?" Cat didn't want to open up to the idea that Michael had staged the whole affair. Had she been so easy to manipulate into a divorce? She remembered how she'd dropped the receipts twice, her hands shook so bad. She'd pulled herself together for the fight, but that entire day a noise like a freight train had been running through her head, dulling the emotions she let show.

Shauna touched Cat's hand. "Maybe you need to read the journal. It could tell you what you want to know."

"That's just it: I'm not sure I want to know anything. I was happy with what I thought I knew about how my marriage exploded." Cat finished her coffee and picked up the key, turning it over in her hand. "So, Hardy Boy, you want to go sleuthing with me?"

"Am I the cute brother or the smart one?" Seth followed her out of the room.

Cat paused and turned to look at him at the bottom of the stairs. "I guess we'll find out if we find Michael's secret lair."

They met Linda on the stairway, coming down. "Am I too late for coffee?"

Cat appraised the woman. Instead of the well-put-together author's wife Linda had appeared when she'd first arrived, now she looked drawn and rumpled. Cat wasn't sure the woman hadn't slept in the same clothes she'd worn yesterday. The smell of whiskey hung around her. The grief of being a widow had started to take its toll. Cat wondered if she'd looked this downtrodden when she'd moved out to California after the divorce. She remembered sitting on the beach trying to clear her head of anything related to Michael. It had taken months before her first thoughts were of the life he'd thrown away.

"Of course not. Shauna's in the kitchen with a pile of muffins, but if you wanted something else she could whip it up in a flash." Cat leaned against the stair rail. "Did you not sleep well? Sorry if I'm being rude."

"Actually I've been reading Tom's last manuscript. It's not what I expected. I think he'd been keeping it from me, giving me an old manuscript to read while he wrote this one." Linda shrugged. "Of course, he got the mystery wrong. I should have told him the truth years ago." Linda turned and headed down the stairs.

When they reached the third floor landing and paused at the entrance to the attic, Seth put a hand on her arm. "Do I want to know?"

"Too many secrets floating around. Let's focus on Michael's riddle." She stilled her mind and marched up the last flight of stairs.

In the attic, she turned around a couple times, orienting herself to the floor plan in reference to the rest of the house. The warning in the letter echoed in her ears. What had Michael been hiding? And why hadn't she been able to see that something was going on with him? Cat struggled with that question the most. Shouldn't she have seen a problem in the man she'd vowed to love for better and worse?

Shaking off the questions that kept running through her mind, she focused on the attic room. Finally, she stopped and stared at the wall to her left. "There. That's the wall that doesn't belong, right?"

"Exactly." Seth walked over to the wall and ran his hand over the surface. "I thought this was just old wallpaper the prior owner had painted over, but feel how this area is different than the rest." He motioned her to come and touch the wall as well. "How tall was Michael? Six two?"

"Six three, just a tad shorter than you. He always joked that I'd gone down a size when I started dating him." Cat felt her lips twitch at the memory.

"I didn't realize he even knew who I was." Seth stood so close to her, she wanted to lean on him for support through this, but no way would she let him see how much she was affected by the day's events.

"We talked about our pasts a lot that first month we started dating. Of course, my list was a hell of a lot shorter than his." Cat shook her head and ran her hand over the wall. Changing the subject, she reached up on her tiptoes to see if she could find anything that felt different.

"Not that high; go about hand height." He reached for her hand as she moved it downward. "Not your arm's reach, his."

And then she found it. A place where the wall seemed to dip into itself. She felt around the edges of the dip and found a loose edge of what appeared to be wallpaper. Lifting the edge, she peered into the hole and saw the keyhole set deep into the wall. She took the key out of her jeans pocket and put it into the keyhole. Pausing, she looked up at Seth. "You ready?"

He smiled and put a hand on her back. "I should be asking you that. You don't have to do this, you know. You can leave all this stuff with Michael packed away in whatever box you put the guy into when you divorced. No one would think anything less of you."

"Except for me." She faced him. "I know it may change the way I see the guy. Or it may not. Either way, he's still dead. I'd rather put this chapter of my life behind me today than let it fester for years. I'm living in the house we bought together. There's too many ghosts already here; I don't want to add one more."

Seth put his hand out to stop her from turning. "Right now, he's just the guy who broke your heart."

"I don't know. All I know is, if I don't figure out what Michael was about, I won't be able to make any sort of decision." She smiled. "I think it's the writer in me. If there's a void in information, I'll fill it and my fictional answer may be more hurtful than the truth."

"Then let's go all Indiana Jones on this attic hide-out and get this behind us. I've got a perfect place for dinner on Saturday night." He leaned down and kissed her lips. Slow, sweet, and promising more.

Cat opened her eyes after he leaned back and smiled. "Did Indiana Jones have a sidekick?"

"Of course—some woman who was always getting him into trouble." Seth ran a hand up the wall next to where she'd entered the key. "I think it will open inwards, away from us."

"We need better fictional counterparts. I want to be the main character, not you." She took a deep breath, knowing she was stalling.

"You're always the main character in your own life, didn't you tell me that once?" Seth nodded to the wall turned into a doorway. "Quit stalling and open the door to the past."

"I think you saw that in a movie. I never said that." When Seth didn't answer, she turned back to the door. "Fine, here we go."

She turned the key and besides a small click, nothing happened. She turned to Seth, who put his hands on the wall above the keyhole and pushed. The wall moved inward. Windows lined the other side of the attic, filling the area with morning light. She realized this part of the attic was directly over her office and this is where the noises she'd heard had come from. In the middle of the space was a large oak desk. And next to that, a table filled with piles of papers. A large mobile white board like the ones in the classrooms at Covington. Michael's lair looked more like a second office than anything needing to be hidden in a secret room.

Seth walked around the room. "No foot prints, no wild animals, nothing but this desk set up. Do you know what he was working on?"

"Economics stuff? I didn't really understand when he talked about his work because you know how I am with math. Believe me, I tried to follow, but the guy was a freaking genius when it came to that stuff. Did you know the president's staff called him once to ask his opinion on a proposed policy change?" Cat sat at the desk and powered up the computer. A password-protected sign-in box leaped onto the screen. "That's funny." She keyed in a password and a box telling her the sign on was incorrect covered the screen. She tried a second one. Same result.

Seth was watching over her shoulder. "No luck?"

"Michael didn't like passwords. He kept forgetting them, so he always used the same two. Both of those failed." Cat frowned. "He didn't even set one up on his personal computer downstairs in his office."

"And yet this one is locked down?" Seth flipped through some pages on the desk. "These all look like graphs and Excel spreadsheets. No smoking gun here."

"Maybe the brain tumor explanation is more and more logical." She stood and glanced around the room. "I guess we box this stuff up and move it down to his study until I can figure out what we have here. Maybe one of his colleagues could help me figure out what he was working on."

Seth examined the wall. "This is all temporary. I can have it down in a day if that's what you want."

Cat nodded. "Let's clear out the secrets. Shauna and I will box the papers up, and we can keep the desk and table up here for the new library." Smiling, she took Seth's hand. "I feel a ton lighter knowing that Michael's secret was probably just a new economics theory. Important to people in the field, but really just academic."

"Then I'll get working on taking down the wall. What's your plan for the day?" He picked a bit of cobweb off her hair and showed it to her, which made her shudder.

"Looks like a quick shower to rinse the bugs off, and then I'm locking myself into the office and writing. I'm still on deadline, and I didn't get half the word count done I'd planned last week with the retreat. I may have to lower my expectations on what I can get done on retreat weeks."

As they walked into the other part of the attic, he paused at the top of the stairs. "I think your next retreat should be a bit less complicated."

"You mean sans murder and mayhem?" Cat laughed as she took the stairs to her own room. "One can only hope."

Chapter 22

Three hours later, Cat emerged from her writing cave satisfied with the day's work. She loved this part of the process, where the words just flew on the page. All she had to do now was finalize the final chapter, and she could set the book aside for a week or two while she brainstormed a proposal for a renewal for her agent. The day had been cool enough that Cat had even had to shut her office windows and slip on the sweater she kept by her desk. Winter wasn't far away.

The noise from Seth's hammering had stopped, and she wondered if he'd taken a break for lunch. That probably was why the house seemed so quiet. The group of them were probably all in the kitchen with Shauna laughing and talking about little to nothing. Her social-butterfly skill was one of the reasons Cat had offered the partnership to her friend when she'd come up with the idea for the retreat. She knew even though she could be pleasant enough, people loved being around Shauna. The girl had magic.

Cat swung open the kitchen door and bent to pick up a cup that had fallen on the floor and been left there, coffee spilt out onto the floor. "Shauna, you need to clean up these accidents, someone could slip and get hurt." She stood and looked right into a revolver. Dean Larry Vargas stood in her kitchen, a gun in his hand that he had pointed at her.

"You should have stayed upstairs," Larry said, his voice calm and even. "Now I have two of you I need to get rid of."

Cat froze with the coffee cup still in her left hand. "What are you doing? You're the dean for God's sake. There's no way you're going to get away with this."

As she talked, she scanned the room. Shauna was sitting wide-eyed, tied to a kitchen chair, a gag in her mouth. Linda stood next to Larry, his free hand gripping her arm. No sign of Seth.

Larry laughed. "My life was over as soon as Tom started writing that book. I always knew he killed Gloria; now he was going to frame me for his crime. There was no way I could let him get away with that."

Cat looked at Linda trying to communicate an unspoken question. The woman nodded her approval of the diversion, or maybe Linda was just shaking so hard Cat thought she'd seen a nod. Either way, she needed to dive in quick.

"Tom didn't kill Gloria. And I know you didn't either," Cat added quickly as she saw Larry's shoulders rise in protest.

"You don't know anything. You're just a silly girl who married the playboy professor and got her feelings hurt when he cheated on her." The gun waved toward the table. "Oh, yes, I know all about Michael's taste for young girls. The school has had to pay off several over the years. Covington's lucky to be rid of him. Now move over to the table so Linda can tie you to the chair."

"I won't," Linda said, but a cry of pain followed her words as Larry squeezed her arm.

He leaned toward her. "I can see we are going to have to work on your attitude. Obeying me is rule number one. Rule number two is always follow rule number one." He looked back up at Cat. "Move!"

Slowly Cat inched toward the table, not taking her eyes off Larry and Linda. "Gloria's alive. I talked to her yesterday."

"Cat, stop. I'll go with him if he promises not to hurt the two of you." Linda turned toward Larry and put her free hand on his forearm.

He shook off Linda's touch. "Impossible. I looked for her for years. Even that cow of a mother doesn't know where her precious daughter went."

"So you've been following up on her, even now?" Cat stopped walking, turning to face Larry. She might as well get the entire story, especially since she didn't think Larry would take Linda up on her deal. The guy was ready to kill. Heck, he probably killed Tom, and poor Rose was sitting in jail, paying for his crime.

"I know he killed her, but just to be sure, I call the brat's bitch every year, just to play the grieving boyfriend. It's kind of fun, I'll have to admit. I thought about going into theater as a minor during my college years." Larry's eyes were wide and un-focused. Cat knew in that instant the man was completely mad.

"Sounds like you had it all under control. Why this?" With a bravado she didn't feel, Cat swept her hand around the kitchen. "Why kidnap Linda and threaten us?" Cat avoided the word kill. Maybe she could talk him out of harming her and Shauna if they promised they wouldn't report him for a while, giving the two a chance to escape. It was a pipe dream, she knew it, but she had to hold on to some hope.

"So you want me to explain all the reasons I killed poor Tom to give your uncle time to save the day? What, is he expected for lunch?" Larry waved the gun toward the table. "Just get over there and sit down. Linda, grab the rope and tie her tight. If you don't, I'll shoot the other one."

Cat moved to the table and glanced at Shauna. Her friend seemed calm even with the situation. She nodded once, and Cat knew Shauna had some sort of plan going on in her head. Maybe Linda hadn't tied her as tightly as Larry had ordered. But even if they could break their bonds, they still had to deal with the crazy with the gun. Cat didn't think their odds were good.

"I'm sure my uncle has better things to do on a Monday afternoon than visit me." Cat sat in the chair and waited as Linda approached her. "So you admit you killed Tom, but why?"

"I told you, he was framing me for Gloria's murder. No wonder Michael pulled so many strings to get you hired at Covington. You're not very bright, are you?" Larry sneered as he watched Linda tie Cat's hands behind her back. "The ankles too. Can't have them walking outside and alerting one of the busybodies that live around here."

"I heard that, but how was he going to frame you?" Cat leaned closer to Linda as she worked on tying her ankles to the chair. Whispering, she asked, "Are you okay?"

Linda's nod was almost imperceptible, but Cat saw it.

"The book. Tom's newest was going to be based on Gloria's missing-person case. You don't really think he came to your little writing retreat to be part of the group, do you? He was here researching the case." Larry sneered. "The guy would have gotten away with killing her and made a bundle on that piece of crap that would finger me. He even said I just might lose my position at the college after the book went public."

"And that's what you fought about at the library." Cat tested the ropes that held her arms behind her. As she suspected, they gave easily. She looked at Shauna who blinked her eyes twice letting her know that Linda had tied her just as loosely. But they still had the gun issue. She needed to keep him talking until she figured something out.

"You've been doing some research of your own. Maybe you aren't just a pretty face." Larry came close and ran the gun up her face from the jawline over her cheek to the top of her head. "Too bad you won't be around much longer."

And with that, he stepped back a pace and aimed the gun. Linda tackled him and sent him flying toward the door. The gun skittered out of his hand. Cat watched as Linda scurried over to retrieve it only to have Larry grab her from behind and lift her and the gun off the floor. He held her back with one hand and wrenched the gun from her with the other.

"You really must start obeying rule number one."

He stage-whispered in Linda's ear and aimed the gun again at Cat. "Good bye, Catherine."

Cat closed her eyes bracing herself against the shot. Instead of the expected gunfire, she heard a door open and a loud crack sounded. Her eyes flew open and instead of seeing Larry with the gun, Seth stood there, helping Linda up from the floor and standing over a now unconscious Larry. A two-by-four lay on top of the man. Seth held the gun and smiled at Cat. "I can't leave you alone for a minute, now, can I?"

By the time Uncle Pete arrived to take Larry into custody, Linda had already untied Shauna and Cat and helped Seth tie Larry's hands behind his back. "This time, I'll actually tie the rope tight," Linda said as she sank into a chair next to Cat. Shauna was at the counter, making coffee, and Seth stood guard over Larry, just out of reach of the guy.

Two deputies followed Uncle Pete into the kitchen, and he nodded to the still-reclining Larry. "You two take him back to the station and lock him up. I've got some stories to hear before we can charge a Covington dean with attempted kidnapping and murder."

"Coffee or iced tea?" Shauna asked as Uncle Pete walked over to the table to sit across from Cat.

"Coffee would be great." Uncle Pete looked around the table. Seth stood next to Cat. "Go ahead and sit down, boy, this might take a while."

Shauna put a steaming cup of coffee in front of him and looked at the rest of the group. "Who else needs coffee?"

"I need a shot," Linda muttered, but when she got a look from Uncle Pete she shrugged. "Coffee's fine."

"I'll help." Cat tried to stand up but Seth gently pushed her back into the chair.

"Let me." He went to the cabinet and pulled out cups.

While the two of them worked on getting the coffee poured and delivered to the table, Uncle Pete leaned toward Cat. "Are you okay? You've had quite a welcome-home party this last week."

"You don't know the half of it, but we'll talk about that later. Larry killed Tom, but I didn't understand his reasoning. If Larry didn't kill Gloria, why would he kill Tom?"

Linda sighed. "I know why." She waited until Seth set the last coffee cup on the table and he and Shauna had pulled up chairs.

"Go on," Uncle Pete gently prodded.

"The manuscript Tom was working on was based on Gloria's story. But since Tom didn't know what had really happened, he did what all good writers do—he filled in the blanks with his own story. I guess he told Larry that he knew he had killed Gloria and after the book came out, everyone would know." Linda straightened her shoulders, facing Uncle Pete straight on. "Your experts weren't going to know what to look for in his writing. I did."

Now he did look up from his writing and considered her for a long moment. Even Cat felt the tension in the air between them. "So what did you find out?"

"Tom never was good at keeping a secret." Linda looked around the room. "I figured he'd taunted Larry, but he never expected this reaction. I think Larry is certifiable."

"You sure your husband would take a poke at a killer?"

Linda looked at him over her coffee cup. "I knew

my husband. He would want to see the reaction on Larry's face when he'd told him about the reveal."

"I meant the book, what he was writing." Uncle Pete didn't look up from his note taking, avoiding eye contact with the woman sitting across from him.

"I'm sure because I read the entire manuscript last night." Linda rubbed her eyes. "I didn't get to sleep until about five, then woke up a few hours later. I've been running on caffeine and adrenaline since then. The book is amazing, even if the main premise was wrong. I should have told Tom the truth."

Cat noticed a hesitation in Linda's voice. There was something she was still holding back. "So why didn't you tell him?"

The smile that landed on Linda's face was more sad than happy. "I knew Larry had abused Gloria. And I also knew she thought Tom was her way out of the relationship. I didn't want to lose him to her, so I helped her escape. I'm not proud of my jealousy, but you saw the picture in the yearbook. If Gloria wanted something, she got it."

Uncle Pete walked the group through the rest of the afternoon's events as Shauna stirred up a pot of potato sausage soup. Cat knew when her friend was stressed because soup always fell on the menu. Shauna said it was a way for her to relax. Today, Cat was glad her friend used cooking as a stress reliever since she craved the thick potato soup as her own comfort food. The smell of baking beer bread to go along with the soup was calming Cat's nerves as well. Sometime during the questioning, Daisy had arrived and was sitting quietly in the corner of the room, sipping a cup of tea Shauna had fixed for her.

"Does this mean Rose can come home?" Daisy's

quiet voice filled a void while Uncle Pete went over his notes. His head came up, and he found the older woman with his gaze. He studied her, then his eyes dropped down to his notes.

"I need to make a call." He rose from his chair and stepped outside. A few minutes later, he returned. Addressing Daisy, he smiled. "Your sister is on her way over. We tried to get her into a cab, but she wanted one last ride in the back of a police car to cement the experience. She says she has a brilliant idea for a new story."

Daisy chuckled. "That's Rose. Don't be surprised if she doesn't grill all of you about what happened and how it felt to be a hostage."

Shauna started setting out bowls on the table. "Well, at least no one can say we have boring conversations with our meals. The bread should be ready as soon as she walks in the door. You all may want to go get washed up for dinner."

Linda and Daisy left the kitchen for their rooms. Seth nodded to the kitchen sink. "Okay if I wash up there?"

"There's a powder room next to the living room. You and Pete can take turns there. I want to talk to my girl for a second. And don't tell me you don't have time for a proper meal, Pete Edmond. That man can just chill in his cell for a few more minutes." Shauna nodded to the door and the men shuffled out reluctantly, following her orders.

"You have my uncle wrapped around your little finger." Cat stood to grab silverware but Shauna shooed her down.

"You don't need to help. Wash up here at the sink

and tell me how you are? I can't believe you stood up to that man so long. Weren't you scared?"

"Shaking to the bone, but I've dealt with bullies before. And if Larry Vargas was one thing, he was a bully. I can't believe he killed Tom because of a book. Everyone knew Tom wrote fiction. Even if he made the killer just like Larry, no one would have believed the story. The guy was loved over at Covington."

"Maybe he just couldn't deal with the possibility anymore. He does seem to be a bit of a control freak." Shauna finished setting the table and then added a small bouquet of flowers to the table. "There we go. Now that's a proper Monday evening meal."

"Flowers are always needed after catching a killer and avoiding a kidnapping." Cat shook her head. "How do *you* stay so calm?"

"Believe me, bartending in that dive taught me a lot. This day doesn't compare to the worst day I had there. At least no one died today."

Because of Seth, Cat thought but didn't say aloud. She didn't know how she felt about being saved by the guy, but she pushed away her doubts and allowed the gratitude to take over her thoughts.

Daisy and Linda returned, chatting about the events of the day, and the men followed behind. As soon as they sat at the table, the kitchen door flew open and a rumpled but grinning Rose came into the kitchen.

"Hello, dearies. Oh good, soup. Let me take a quick shower and change out of these prison clothes, and I'll be back to hear all about the excitement." She paused to kiss her sister on the cheek. "Thanks for staying around. It meant a lot to me."

As Rose disappeared out of the kitchen to her room, Cat heard Daisy mutter, "And I'm going to remind you of that often."

A group chuckle filled the room as Shauna filled the bowls with the steaming soup. For a minute, the house and the group of friends were at peace.

Chapter 23

As Cat wandered through the house, it felt empty. Rose and Daisy had left the day after Rose got released from jail. Linda had stayed on a day longer, but even she had finally returned to her New York home and life, promising to keep in touch. Cat laughed at her own sudden loneliness. She was the one who had wanted the peace and quiet, but now she was going to miss the people she'd come to know in just over a week. Would every retreat be this bonding? Or was the fact she felt close to the people mostly because they'd gone through a trial by fire with her?

She poked her head into the kitchen. Empty. Walking to the back door, she noticed the SUV wasn't in its parking spot. Shauna must be out shopping or exploring. But in the backyard, she saw Seth loading up lumber and tools into his truck.

Opening the door, she walked out into the cold. "You done with the attic?"

He started, then his mouth quirked into a grin. "Not yet. But the weather report is calling for snow, so I need to set up a new staging area. I'm going to have this set up in my garage. It will be a pain hauling everything over here, but it's better than warping the wood."

"You could work inside." Cat ran through the rooms in her mind.

He leaned on the tailgate. "I'd either have to work in the cellar, which adds another level of stairs, or haul everything up to the attic and work around the stuff for the next three months. My plan will be better. I'll just be away from the house more."

She stood in front of him, her arms folded across her chest. "That will be okay. We should have started earlier, I guess."

He patted the tailgate next to him. "Come sit by me; you look like you're freezing."

Cat glanced back at the house. "I forgot my coat. Last week, I didn't need one." She scooted up onto the tailgate, and he slipped his own coat on her shoulders.

"Better?" He tugged the edges close and turned her head toward him. Then without waiting for an answer, he kissed her.

As they came up for air, he grinned. "I do have a question."

"Now what?" She teased. "Do you need more money for the attic project?"

Shaking his head, he stared into her eyes, and her insides went all gooey. She shook off the instinct to lean into his shoulder. The guy could make her feel safe and in danger all at the same time. Safe, because he wouldn't let anything happen to her, but in danger of losing herself to him and not wanting to ever come up for air.

"What are you doing Saturday night?"

The question had come out of nowhere. "What?"

"Simple question. What are you doing Saturday night? I'd like to take you on a real date. Nice clothes, nice restaurant, see the play that's being put on over at the college. Then I'll bring you home, steal a kiss on the front porch, and leave. But I'll call the next day." He grinned. "What do you say, Kitty Cat? Want to try some traditional dating rituals until we get to know the grown-up us better?"

She thought about the man sitting next to her. So different than the boy she'd loved. But, in a lot of ways, still the same. She felt the same draw to him as she had the first day she'd met him. Could you have two soul mates? She had been in love with Michael, she'd been sure of it. Now she was remembering how strong the connection with Seth had been before.

She realized he was waiting for an answer. And she also realized she had one.

"What time?"

He glanced at his watch. "It's about three."

She swatted his arm. "No, what time will you pick me up?"

Now his grin widened to full megawatt power. "Six thirty." He leaned into her and gave her a quick kiss. "I'll be expecting a little more heat than that on Saturday."

"We'll see." She slipped off the tailgate and handed him his coat. "I've got things to do inside where it's warm and cozy."

"Leave me all alone out here in the elements." He

took his coat and put it on. "You go on inside. You'll freeze out here, and then dinner will be a bust."

"It's always all about you, Seth Howard." She ran to the kitchen door, but stopped just inside. "Shauna has a pot of coffee on if you need to warm up later."

He waved her inside and she shut the door, wanting to peek out at him to see if this was truly real. Her heart had butterflies. "Well, look at me, I'm going on a date," she announced to the empty kitchen.

She was drawn down the hall to Michael's study. She'd put the journal on the side table next to her reading chair. She sank into the chair and thought about all the good times she'd shared with Michael in this space. She'd come home with one thought, that she wouldn't let what Michael had done ruin her future in the house. Now, she didn't know what to think.

Cat looked over at the desk and imagined her smiling husband sitting behind it, a book and a notebook open on the surface in front of him. "We're not done talking about this," she told the vision. As it faded in her mind, she wondered if she'd made the right decision saying yes to Seth. Maybe it was too early to be starting a new relationship? She shook the question off. Today she'd deal with today, not the echoes of yesterday.

After closing and locking the door to Michael's study, she headed upstairs to her own office to work on a release promotion schedule and answer emails. The bad thing about being a full-time author? The workday never stops. People think you can just do whatever you want, but there's always a book to write, or a book to edit, or a book to sell, which left little time for playing or goofing off.

The room had grown dark before she heard the sound of the car pulling into the driveway. Seth had left hours ago, stopping into her office to say good-bye and that he was locking the downstairs doors when he left.

Cat ambled down the stairs, her stomach rumbling for food. Maybe Shauna had brought home sandwiches. When she reached the kitchen, she found her friend standing at the stove, heating up a kettle for tea.

"Did you see outside?" Her face glowed with excitement.

Cat glanced over to the window. "Did you wreck the car?"

"No. Why would you ask that?" Shauna took Cat's arm and drew her to the door. When they reached it, Shauna threw it open. Large flakes floated down from the sky, starting to coat the ground in white. "It's snowing."

"Seth said it was going to. I thought it was too cold today, but it feels like it warmed up a little." Cat held her hand out to catch a snowflake.

"It's so pretty. I was talking to Kevin at the pub today, and he says he'll teach me to ski, no charge."

Cat searched her memory for the conversation about Kevin. "Oh, yeah, he's the ski instructor?"

"He's not a ski instructor. He owns the ski lodge on Little Ski Hill. I know I've told you about him before. He wants me to come be his executive chef at the lodge." Shauna reached both arms up and danced in a circle. "It's snowing."

"I guess you didn't think it would snow in Colorado?" Cat watched her friend, bemused at her joy. "You're not quitting anytime soon?"

"Bite me. I've lived in California too long. I miss the snow." She put her arm in Cat's. "I'm waiting for a better offer from the guy, like one with a ring involved? Anyway, it's time for dinner. Sandwiches and some beef stew okay?"

"Perfect. I'd like to talk to you a little bit about the next session. We only have a bit before we're hosting again." Cat shook her head. "I can't believe we have one retreat under our belts."

"Let's just hope this one is a little calmer than the last," Shauna said as they walked back into the warm kitchen to start preparing dinner.

Cat stood in the doorway and gazed out on the backyard. With the snow gently falling the view looked like one of those postcards you could buy in the travel stores. The home she'd inherited from Michael was starting to feel like hers, not theirs. They were booked for retreats for six months in the future, and she had a date on Saturday.

Life was good. She whispered the one word, "Home." She hadn't known Aspen Hills could ever feel like home again. And Cat felt more at peace than she had in years.

"Come away from the door, you'll freeze us out of here," Shauna called from the stove where she'd started the stew.

As she went to shut the door, Uncle Pete appeared in the doorway. She kissed her uncle's cheek and helped him out of his coat. "I didn't hear your car."

"I walked over from the house. I figure it's long past time to tell you what you need to know." He stomped his boots on the welcome mat before walking into the kitchen.

Cat shut the door behind him, wondering what was so important to bring her uncle out on a chilly evening. "Let's go into Michael's study and talk." She shook her head. "Someday I'm going to start calling it 'the' study."

"I'll bring by hot chocolate in a few for you both," Shauna called after them.

Today, Cat had spent some time lounging in the study's big easy chair, reading Michael's journal. Having finished the first draft of her book, Cat was letting it rest, so she'd been anxious to work on something else for a while. Yesterday she'd boxed up all the papers from what they were now calling Michael's secret lair and set the computer up in his old office.

She didn't read long each day, just enough to make notes on a few pages. The emotions that hit her as she read were unexpected and threw her back in time to when their marriage had been perfect. At least, she'd thought it had been perfect.

Uncle Pete took in the room. "Looks like you've been spending some time in here."

"Just stirring up old memories. I'm not really sure what I expected to find in all this, but the journal portrays the Michael I fell in love with, not the monster I divorced." She sighed and moved the journal so she could sit down. "What brought you over today? News about Larry?"

Uncle Pete sat on the chair facing her and leaned back. "I always loved these chairs. Your ex knew how to be comfortable."

"And you seem to know how to avoid answering a question." Cat smiled at her uncle. "Don't tell me Larry's going free?"

"That wouldn't happen even if he hadn't confessed to murdering Tom to so many witnesses. No, he's being transferred to the county lockup to prepare for trial, so expect to be called in to testify if he pleads not guilty." Uncle Pete leaned his forearms on his knees and templed his fingers together. "Actually, I think it's time we talked about Michael's death."

Cat's stomach twisted a bit, and she regretted that last cup of coffee she'd consumed a few minutes ago. "What about it? He is dead, right? You said you saw the body."

He waved his hands downward. "Calm down. I want you to know, I questioned the coroner's report. I don't think Michael died of a natural heart attack. The guy was in great health. The college makes him get a physical every year, and his doctor was shocked when I told him what had happened. There were no signs."

Cat thought about Michael's habit of running every morning. He'd even dragged her out of bed a few times to join him. "Sometimes it happens that way."

"I know, but I had the crime-scene guys come in when we first found his body in this room. They didn't find any fingerprints where his body was found." He paused letting the information settle.

"Isn't that good?" Now she was confused.

He looked around the room and Cat could see he was remembering the scene. He turned back and shook his head. "No fingerprints at all. Not his, not yours, not even from the housekeeper he hired after you moved out. The room had been wiped clean."

Cat stayed in the study for a while longer after Uncle Pete had dropped his bombshell. He hadn't come right out and said Michael had been murdered, but there had been clearly too many unanswered questions at the time for her uncle's taste. She stared at the journal, wondering what other secrets it held. The whole thing was weird. Even Michael keeping her in the will and passing on the house to her. Had she even known her husband at all?

She heard Shauna walking down the hallway to tell her dinner was ready. It was time to close the door on this mystery, at least for a while. She'd pull a Scarlett and think about it tomorrow, when the darkening sky outside the windows didn't make her shiver. Tomorrow would be soon enough to face the growing questions.

Tomorrow she would read the rest of the journal.

As much as I love having Catherine here with me, especially as she sleeps next to me, I know I've made a huge mistake. I've put her in danger. What started out as a fun project has turned into something more sinister. I can't believe what the conglomerate has been hiding all these years. I'm sure they hired me thinking I'd miss the signs of their deceit and give my approval to their financial fitness. But they hired the wrong small-college economist if they wanted just a yes man. I need to keep silent until I've discovered the evidence that will put these big shots away for life.

Keep reading for a sneak peek at

FATALITY BY FIRELIGHT

The next Cat Latimer mystery
Available March 2017
From Kensington Books

Chapter 1

The world outside still clung to the previous night, the shadows not quite releasing their hold to the breaking light over the mountain ridge outside Aspen Hills, Colorado. With the first rays of morning, the fresh snow glistened and covered the lawn all around 700 Warm Springs.

Cat Latimer, owner of the Warm Springs Writer's Retreat, sat at the kitchen table drinking a mix of hot chocolate and coffee. Cat thought Shauna's winter concoction, with a dab of freshly whipped cream, just about the most perfect drink ever invented. The group sitting around the table was drinking the "virgin" version. Retreat guests had the option of adding a shot of Baileys Irish Cream or Kahlúa to their cups. Just the smell of coffee and chocolate mixed together made her sigh in delight.

"I can't believe you're taking the group up the mountain. I thought this was supposed to be about writing. They aren't going to get many words down by spending the day skiing." Uncle Pete had become a regular at the breakfast table, when the retreat was in session and when it was just Cat and Shauna milling around the empty house.

"It's part of the Colorado experience," Cat explained, thinking about her own manuscript sitting on her computer waiting for her to make time to write. During the first retreat, she'd managed to get a few pages written—before one of her guest wound up dead in his room. This retreat she'd promised herself that she'd focus on her own work, even when they had guests. Shauna was in charge of the day-to-day activities when the retreat was in session. Cat's job was to be the resident writer. And to set a good example *as* a professional writer.

But today was about building relationships and having experiences. Writers needed both.

"Who do you have visiting this month? Anyone I need to put some eyes on?" Uncle Pete was the police chief and overprotective when it came to Cat. At least that was her experience. Cat had moved back when her ex-husband had died and left her the huge Victorian. She and Michael had bought it when their marriage was young, before he started cheating.

Now the house was hers. Karma was sweet.

"We have five guests, including the student from the college. They're writing sweet romance, paranormal suspense, speculative fiction, non-fiction, and poetry. They all seem pretty harmless." Cat had a list of the guests in front of her. "Although one's not joining in the ski trip. Bella Neighbors told me last night she has no interest in skiing or going outside in this weather."

The door blew open, and on the wind a few snowflakes entered around the tall man covered in skiwear. "Who ever said that is a smart cookie. It's c-c-c-cold out there."

Cat watched as Seth Howard stomped his feet, then shrugged out of his heavy coat and sat on the bench to take off his shoes. Seth had been her high-school sweetheart, and apparently, was now her after-divorce boyfriend. "We'll be one guest shy on the ski trip." She focused on Shauna. "You going to be okay here alone?"

Her second-in-command, Shauna Mary Clodagh, ex-bartender, amazing cook, and Cat's best friend, nodded. "We'll be good. Miss Bella can write or go wandering through town, and I'll have a fine dinner of shepherd's pie waiting for you when you get back."

"Sounds great." Seth made his way over to the table, taking the cup Shauna held out for him. He kissed Cat on her neck, then sat next to her. "Hey, Pete. How are things in Aspen Hills?"

"If we didn't have the book thief over at the college, my days would be filled with counted cross-stitch." The big man drained his cup and stood. "I'm heading back to the station. You guys be careful on the road to the ski resort. I'm getting reports of slide-offs every day."

"I put the chains on the tires just now. We should be fine." Seth sipped his coffee. "I hear that guy stole some rare books from the library. You got any suspects?"

Uncle Pete pulled his belt upward and put on his coat. "I can't comment on an open investigation, but since I have squat for evidence, I guess I still can't comment on nothing."

"See you tomorrow?" Cat called after him as he made his way to the kitchen door.

Uncle Pete didn't turn around as he waved. "Yep."

Cat watched through the window as he made his way to his police car. The black Charger looked more like a white hill, so much snow had fallen in the hour her uncle had been visiting. She looked at Shauna and Seth. "Does he look tired to you?"

"You worry too much. Your uncle looks fine." Seth took the plate of fried potatoes and ham Shauna handed him. "Thanks."

"I don't know. He didn't eat as much as usual." Shauna returned to the counter where she was finishing the buffet items for the guests. "I think the college is putting pressure on him about those missing books."

"That could be it." Cat wasn't convinced, and tomorrow she'd confront him about the last time he had a physical. She took her plate to the sink and poured herself another cup of coffee. Glancing around the kitchen, she paused. "Do you need help with anything?"

"No. I've got it handled." Shauna waved her away from the stove. "I don't need you messing in my kitchen."

Cat put up her hands. "Fine, I was just asking." She focused on Seth. "When are we leaving?"

"No later than ten. So, yeah, you have time to sneak up to your office and write. I'll come get you when we're ready to go." Seth didn't look up from his plate of food. "Just be ready to lose when we race down Mountain Top."

"Who said we were racing?" Cat smiled at the memory of winters growing up skiing at the local resort. Back then, they'd gotten their season passes as early Christmas gifts as soon as the snow arrived.

This time he did look up, and the look he gave her seared her with desire. "We always race."

She ignored his comment and left the kitchen with a filled carafe of coffee Shauna handed her word-lessly. Her office was in the third-floor turret, the same floor where she and Shauna had bedrooms. The guest rooms were all on the second floor, with the first floor open for guest use.

Except for Michael's office. She had locked that room.

She opened her office, turned on her computer, and got lost in the world of her teenage witch trying to navigate the horrors of high school.

True to his word, a knock sounded on her door exactly at ten. She saved her document, then turned off her computer. The writing was done for today. "Just a minute."

When she opened the door, Seth walked her back to the wall and kissed her. She relaxed into his kiss, feeling the desire she'd only just brushed away a few hours ago flow through her. After a few minutes, she turned her head and whispered in his ear, "I thought we had to leave."

He groaned and stepped away from her. "We do."

Everyone had already loaded into the van by the time they got downstairs, and Cat slipped into her ski jacket. Shauna handed her a bag. When she peeked inside, she saw a thermos of cocoa and what looked like a Tupperware container of sandwiches. "In case we get snowed in?"

Shauna shrugged. "I know they just ate, but some-times people need a little something to tide them over."

Her friend had been right. The sandwiches were

gone before they hit the Little Ski Hill's parking lot. As they unloaded their passengers, Cat gave everyone a card with her cell and the house number listed. "Call if you need something. We'll be meeting in the great room in the main lodge at three to head back to the house."

As the guests made their way to the rental shack, Seth took their equipment down from the rack on top of the SUV. "Do you have a season pass?"

She stared at him. His pass was laminated and hung on a chain around his neck.

"I guess you'll have to stand in line with the newbies then." He started to turn away but Cat stopped him by putting a hand on his jacket.

"Unless you mean this?" She pulled out the season pass she'd bought last month when the ski hill had been advertising a buy one, get one half-off sale for Aspen Hills residents. She and Shauna had already been up to the resort a few times.

He grinned and grabbed her skis. "Bring along the poles and we'll get going. The line for the chair lift gets busy on Saturdays."

They skied together for hours, taking the same runs they'd skied when they'd been in high school. The snow was powder, and Cat felt like she was running on feathers except for the spray of cold that sometimes snuck around her goggles and scarf. Rays of sunshine on the hillside turned the white into bright. Ending a run, Cat waved Seth over as they slid into the area around the lodge. "Let's go in and warm up."

They took off their skis and left them and the poles near the door. Stamping the snow off her boots, she stepped into the warm lodge. She pulled off her gloves and took out her phone to make sure she hadn't missed any calls. She hadn't, but she was shocked at the time. Two already. They only had another hour before they would be meeting up with the guests. Laughter echoed out of the bar area and they followed it inside.

They squeezed into the last two seats on the edge of the bar. "What can I get you?" A man in his early twenties stood in front of Cat and cleared the empty glasses and wiped the bar.

"I'll have a coffee, black." Seth looked at Cat. "Merlot for you?"

Cat pulled the knitted hat off her head. "I don't know. I guess I'll take a beer. You got a dark on draft?"

"Of course. Let me get you a sample." He walked away toward the taps.

"You see any of the guests?" She looked around the crowded bar but before she could recognize anyone, the bartender was back.

"Tell me if you like it." He pushed a small glass filled with a dark amber liquid toward Cat, then set a coffee cup in front of Seth. "You sure you don't want me to jack that coffee up a bit?"

"Black is fine. I'm the designated driver." He took a sip of the brew.

"Too bad, man. I make a mean mixed drink. You two are going to have to check out our condo rentals. They're cheapest during the week when we don't have out-of-town visitors." He turned toward Cat who had finished the mini beer. "Do you like it?"

"Most definitely." She turned to Seth as the young man walked away to get her a normal pint of the draft. "I think he's got a great idea about the condos.

Maybe next week, when the retreat's over, we should look into staying a few days."

"Ski by day and snuggle by night?" Seth raised his eyebrows. "I could be talked into playing hooky for a few days."

"You're only working for me," Cat reminded him.

A loud cheer sounded from a table across the room. A very drunk woman stood on the table and downed what looked to Cat from this distance to be a boilermaker. A man swept her off the table and into his arms on the couch where they kissed so long, Cat became uncomfortable watching them and turned back to Seth.

"Kids." She shrugged and sipped her beer.

"That's one of your writer guests." He pointed out one of the women across the room. "Don't know her name, but there's another one, Nelson something."

Cat choked on her beer. "What did they do, just ignore the slopes and come right to the bar? That girl is hammered."

"And she's kissing the wrong guy. He's engaged." Seth pointed to a third person sitting farther down on the bar watching the scene unfold on the couch. "There's another one, the poet?"

"Jeffrey," Cat answered absently. "How do you know that other guy's engaged?"

"He's Brittany's fiancé. The bartender down at Bernie's." He looked at her. "Don't you read the local papers?"

"Not really. Shauna does. I'm busy." She sipped her beer and glanced at the clock. "So we're only missing one. Maybe we should start moving everyone to the van. I can call Jennifer and have her meet us there."

"No need. She's at the same table with our party girl." Seth shook his head. "Brit's not going to like this one bit. And Bernie has connections."

"That's just a rumor." Cat finished her beer and dug in her purse for cash. Seth stilled her hand and took out his wallet, throwing some bills on the bar.

"Not a rumor I would want to test out." He looked at Cat. "I don't think that guy's going to like it if his future father-in-law finds out about his extra-curricular activities. He might just be skiing down a mountain side with some concrete boots."

Connect with Us

Visit us online at
KensingtonBooks.com
to read more from your favorite authors, see books
by series, view reading group guides, and more.

Join us on social media

for sneak peeks, chances to win books and prize packs,
and to share your thoughts with other readers.

facebook.com/kensingtonpublishing
twitter.com/kensingtonbooks

Tell us what you think!

To share your thoughts, submit a review,
or sign up for our eNewsletters, please visit:
KensingtonBooks.com/TellUs.